THAT
BUSINESS
AT
BRODY

Also By Jack Winter

Stage Plays

15 U.B.
The Evil Eye
And They'll Make Peace
Before Compiègne
The Mechanic
The Death of Woyzeck
Hey Rube!
The Golem of Venice
The Wrecked Blackship
Party Day
The Centre
Waiting
Mr. Pickwick
Letters from the Earth
Ten Lost Years
You Can't Get Here from There
Summer Seventy-six
Family Matters
Golovlovo
Ravers
Caboose to Moose Jaw
Haydon

Books

Scales
The Island
Misplaced Persons
The Ballad of Bladud
Nomad's Land
The Tallis Bag
My TWP Plays: A Collection Including "Ten Lost Years"
Tales of the Emperor
That Business at Brody
Agnes Dea (work in progress)

THAT
BUSINESS
AT
BRODY

a Novel

JACK WINTER

Winnipeg

That Business at Brody

This book is a work of fiction.
Names, characters, businesses, organizations,
places, events, and incidents either are the product
of the author's imagination or are used fictitiously.

Copyright © 2024 Jack Winter

Design and layout by
Lucas c Pauls and M. C. Joudrey.

Published by At Bay Press July 2024.

Library and Archives Canada cataloguing in publication
is available upon request.

ISBN 978-1-998779-34-5

Printed and bound in Canada.

This book is printed on acid free paper that is
100% recycled ancient forest friendly
(100% post-consumer recycled).

First Edition

10 9 8 7 6 5 4 3 2 1

atbaypress.com

MIX
Paper | Supporting
responsible forestry
FSC® C016245

For me and mine, a gift of family.

Contents

Writer's Note

The assassination of Czar Alexander II in 1881 launched a play of forces and a sequence of consequences amid European Jews that, during the next two decades, impelled the birth of Zionism and, in the opposite direction, the flood of transatlantic migrations. Simultaneously, a combination of Old World animus and New World opportunism unleashed that swarm of inhumane humanitarians and narcissistic careerists who always have gathered around easy prey and made a meal of them.

Within days of the peremptory execution of five suspected assassins, one of whom bore "an unmistakably Jewish physiognomy," the first Russian pogrom of the modern era broke out in Elizabethgrad. More than two hundred Jews were beaten to death with no arrests made or governmental intervention noted, setting a pattern for similar events throughout the Russian Empire. These "punishments" were particularly severe within the so-called Pale of Settlement, that vast geographic slum into which four million Russian Jews subsequently were confined, and where the notorious May Laws – regarding their education, occupation, taxation, identification, property rights and conscription obligations – were punitively defined and pitilessly enforced.

The consequences of such state-sponsored savagery proved inevitable. In less than a year twenty thousand Jews fled across the Russian border, the majority reaching a single small Galician frontier town the population of which they augmented by several hundred per cent. Fearing the outbreak of epidemics there and throughout the former Habsburg Empire, the Austro-Hungarian authorities threatened to deport those Jews back into Russia unless they moved on, something none had the energy or the wherewithal to do. Until they got out, or were got out, the engorged enclave of Brody was where they were, and where they would remain.

The response of western European nations to the humanitarian crisis varied from hostility to indifference to ambiguity. In Berlin, schools already were conducting courses of study in what they inventively christened "anti-Semitism," employing textbooks that proved the superiority of their "race" and the inferiority of that of the Jews, and current events in Russia duly were entered as corroboration into the Teutonic syllabus. In Paris, the government was distracted by its own "Hebraic debate"; the focus there was on one Jew not thousands, but the issues and the passions raised – are Jews alien to France? do they penetrate the highest echelons of its institutions? if so, where (beyond Captain Dreyfus) will their perfidy, sabotage and treason lead? – were as excitingly extensive. In London, the recently elected Liberal government of Gladstone despatched to Brody a Mansion House delegation authorized to distribute funds raised by public subscription as a tiny measure of charitable relief to assist a few refugees to continue their journey further south toward the cloaca of the Diaspora: Romania. Even in America some of these ideas caught on with the "Know-Nothing Party" and other splinter groups less aptly named. Meanwhile the Jews of Brody huddled in a swamp of pestilential dilapidation. Alts azoy ... ever thus.

That Business At Brody tells the story of a family of Russian Jews congregated and scattered by persecution and penury and reunited by chance, as well as the stories of some of the zealots, entrepreneurs, plutocrats, fantasists and sociopaths who manipulated the fortunes and determined the destiny of a family that happened to be mine. That any of us escaped any of them is a tale of survival against best laid plans, a parable of happenstance.

Laurence Oliphant and Alice, Shaftesbury and Gladstone, Doctor Barnardo and Father Seddon, Albert Edward the Prince of Wales and his family, the barons Edmond de Rothschild and Maurice de Hirsh and their families, Theodor Herzl and his, me and mine ... lived, though not exactly as they do in this novel. The Rabbi of Brody and his precise posterity did not, though that failure should not be held against them; they are antecedents I have awarded myself, given Hitler's comprehensive erasure of others.

The human torrent into Brody, the Mansion House mission to it, the exodic seepage of Jewish refugees into Romania, Ukraine and Canada transpired more or less as recounted. So did the various pre-Zionist attempts to found settlements in the Holy Land at Rishon LeZion, G'dera Outpost, Zikhron Ya'akov and Gilead, which I have located and populated to suit the spirit if not the letter of those pioneer endeavours.

The starry personal encounters in Sandringham House on the Sandringham estate, on the Rothschild yacht in Haifa Harbour, at the Maison De Hirsch in Paris, as well as the suffering (sufferance?) of little children in Albert Hall and the death (murder?) of a saint on a Canada-bound Allan Line steamship are matters of historical record, the details of which I have adjusted to requirements. The suicidal barge-trip down the Dniester did not happen; the homicidal steerage-passage across the Atlantic famously did.

Although the story does not quite get there, Grosse Île lives on – can you believe it! – as a tourist attraction.[1] Montréal is still, well, Montréal, the edgiest city in Canada and the most complex, and Regina remains, as I suspect it always has been, a flatland of hopes and a repository of discarded dreams.

Inadvertent colleagues like Anne Taylor,[2] Samuel J. Lee,[3] Kenneth Bagnell,[4] Andrea Barrett,[5] Louis Rosenberg[6] and Rabbi Solomon Ganzfried[7] whose work I have plundered for information would recognize my indebtedness and should be aware of my gratitude. Most of the words telling the tale and all of the imaginings are mine ... as are the political opinions.

The Stones of Brody

The moving of the stones began some time before we noticed. Even when it became too apparent to be ignored, doubt remained among us. How could stones that size be moved? Who would bother to move them and for what purpose? In the centre of Brody, in the midst of the Castle Square, in the vicinity of all the others ... as a residence for historical stones the new locations were as good as the previous. What was wrong with where these stones had lain before, lain for centuries undisturbed, lain like stones? If someone had found it necessary to move them, why not to a more advantageous position, one less of an impediment to pedestrians? After a time, it begins to occur that perhaps there's some mistake. Perhaps these stones always have been where they are right now? Perhaps our memories are at fault? Who, after all, remembers stones, even such notable stones as these? Perhaps inscriptions always have been etched into them, but for one reason or another they never were read or were forgotten once they had been? Of course, now that our attention has been drawn, we see and we read and we remember and our questions persist. Who was the first to have noticed the movement of the stones? What caused it to be noticed? Why was it noticed just then and not at any other moment during the centuries since the wall or the tower or the parapet they once were became the pile of stones we are accustomed to? Who knew G-d so well as to dare inscribe His nickname on stones? Of course we don't expect answers to such questions, especially since we fail to utter them aloud or, if we do, always indoors. Besides, to the impoverished any causes beyond nature are unnecessary *to know. Even the Rabbi has hesitated to call the moving of the stones a sign and a portent, hesitation being our rabbi's usual position in controversial matters though he prefers it to be called contemplation. As for the inscriptions, the Rabbi's best student doesn't seem to think they're anything more than rock-seams. Even less convincing, the Shamas of the Synagogue says they're the tracks of thousands of years of rain, a theory he's offered to prove for a fee. Ordinary folk remain sceptical, but of what and to what end not one of us is certain.*

Chapter One

London to Brody

At a relaxed hour in an alcove of the Egyptian Room of the Mansion House in London on the morning of Sunday the eighteenth of December 1881 something very like the following took place.

"Mr. Charles Darwin."

"Lord Beaconsfield."

That phase of the rollcall was perfunctory; it was the former who had propelled the latter into the hall moments before, so presumably they were acquainted. Those already assembled rose as the enormous contraption rumbled toward them. Wicker in body on a cast-iron frame, a kind of a hooded chaise on four wheels, it was designed to be drawn by a large dog or a small horse ... or pushed by an attendant more robust than the present one who, once his cargo was parked at the head of the conference table, dropped into the nearest chair and slumped there behind a vast sepia beard, clutching his stomach and panting.

Popularly known as a Bath-chair due to the location of its invention and its employment among invalids in that and other spa towns, this particular model was custom-built to a design inspired by the throne room at Windsor. Lined in goose-down, of royal purple encasement with an imperially embossed matching over-blanket said once to have embraced her own unimaginable knees, it was a gift of the Empress herself upon the occasion of its present occupant's electoral defeat and his immediate decline in health. It dominated any room however grand, diminished its passenger to the verge of disappearance and accounted for the assemblage's reluctance to refer to him as "Mr. Chairman."

His Lordship coughed and continued. "Mr. Matthew Arnold."

"Lord Beaconsfield."

"Mr. Robert Browning."

"I hardly know where to begin – "

"Thank you, Mr. Browning, not yet."

Browning muttered something though it might have been: "Lord Beaconsfield."

"Thank you, gentlemen, for attending."

The assemblage intoned: "Thank you, Lord – "

His Lordship coughed again. "Names, not titles, this morning, I think."

The assemblage reprised. "Thank you, Mr. Disraeli."

Disraeli coughed again, then again and again and again. Darwin rose to see if he was required but was waved off with the practised gesture of a chronic asthmatic who recognized a crisis and knew this was not one. Eventually the paroxysm abated. Wiping his mouth with a corner of his imperial over-blanket, Disraeli frowned in a mischievous manner. "Benjamin to those who know me, Dizzy to those who no longer wish to."

A titter fluttered and subsided.

Disraeli adjusted himself into as upright a position as his Bath-chair allowed, which was slightly on the rise from utterly horizontal. "Gentlemen, we have been convened by our lately re-elected Prime Minister – "

"Mr. Gladstone." The prompter, an elongated gentleman in scarlet robes seated at the foot of the table, swivelled regally, his extraordinary beaked nasal appendage scything from one side to the other.

At this naming Disraeli was racked with a single cough so convulsive Darwin had to rise and re-engage the braking mechanism. The scientist also took the opportunity to extract a limb from the interior of the carriage, to locate a protuberant vein and, with a syringe unsheathed from a purple embossed medical pouch, to inject into it some life-prolonging elixir prepared earlier.

Disraeli nodded and took what, in him, passed for a deep breath. "Thank you, Cardinal Manning, for the timely reminder. To resume, we have been convened by that newly re-arrived political gentleman as an elder committee of concern in the helpful presence of His Eminence the Cardinal to consider and to advise upon the recent unpleasantness abroad respecting certain religionists of another persuasion and, to one degree or another as prominent litterateurs of the day, to draft a resolution that may be acted upon in public forum on their behalf, though I privately suspect we have been chosen because at our age no one of us can reasonably be expected to live long enough to witness his lack of effect. That, gentlemen, is politics. I call upon the informative Cardinal Manning to address us."

He fell back among his pillows to enjoy the expanding benefits of the elixir.

The scarlet gentleman uncoiled like a basking reptile and arranged his demeanour becomingly. "Thank you, Benjamin. Gentlemen, for the last twelve months we have watched a certain ethnographic movement in Europe flourish and become predominant. I and my Church look upon it with abhorrence as tending to disintegrate the equanimity of social life, and, secondly, with fear, lest it ignite a doctrinal animosity that has taken fire on the Continent and has begun to spread and could consume us all. Now it seems our gravest trepidations are beginning to materialize. Following the assassination of Czar Alexander in March last and the unfortunate circumstance that one of the several dozen conspirators bore an unmistakably Jewish physiognomy – "

Darwin snorted.

The beak swung momentarily in his direction and sniffed.

Disraeli converted his own high Anglican giggle into a diplomatic cough. "Presently, Mr. Darwin. Pray continue, Your Eminence."

The beak resumed. "Typically, it has not been the international Jewish welfare organizations nor the predominant Jewish financial and philanthropic institutions that have been the first to take notice of the situation in Brody, but our own current British newspapers."

"And subsequently, typically, our own current British Prime Minister."

"Come to consider, Benjamin, it was that very morning I received his call!"

"Quelle," Disraeli murmured languidly, "étonnamment."

Arnold suppressed a sigh. "Indeed, the world will soon be entirely with the Pragmatists and the Philistines. And then, ennobled each morning by the magnificent roaring of the young lions of the DAILY TELEGRAPH, we shall all yawn into one another's face with the dismallest, the most unimpeachable gravity."

"Actually, Mr. Arnold, it was a featured article in THE TIMES OF LONDON of March eleventh that – "

"Yes, yes, Your Immense ," Browning barked, "we all subscribe to THE TIMES."

Darwin's beard bristled with exception. "I do not subscribe. I shall not subscribe. I have nothing to learn from THE TIMES, though perhaps something to teach it."

"Gentlemen, gentlemen," Disraeli purred, "THE TIMES is not the issue. Oh dear, I fear I've made a little joke!"

"Very little," muttered Browning.

Disraeli gazed across the top of Browning's head, the only man in the room short enough for him to do it to. "Cardinal Manning, pray resume."

"I was about to conclude that our current First Minister is determined that it must be his Liberal party that takes the lead in organizing measures for the relief of the Jews at Brody. To which end I am charged to propose that this, our distinguished ad hoc committee, forthwith undertake to deliberate and to conclude and to recommend that Her Majesty's presiding government organize, sponsor and convene a mass meeting of concerned Londoners to take place at the Lord Mayor's residence, this our historic Mansion House, the object of which will be to raise a fund of money for humanitarian relief."

"Double relief," smirked Disraeli.

"Beg pardon, Benjamin?"

"Relief for the Jews at Brody, a few of whom we assist to complete their journey south into Romania. Relief for our First Minister that their destination is not here."

"Now, now, Benjamin, I doubt that Mr. Gl – "

"Now, now, Your Eminence, I don't doubt otherwise."

Browning stood. "What matter the motive of mere moderato if good be the end of his doing? What good be the deed of the keenest castrato where issue cannot be ensuing?" Browning sat, the difference in altitude negligible.

Darwin's beard quivered. "What did he say?"

Arnold had been taking notes of Browning's interjections. "I'm not certain but I think it was obscene." He consulted his notepad. "Moderato, that probably signifies the incumbent you-know-who. But castrato?"

Cardinal Manning made a global gesture of universal calm. "Mr. Arnold, I'm sure Mr. Browning didn't mean to imply that our esteemed chairma – chairpers – that our esteemed convenor, simply because he's no longer Prime Minister – "

Browning stood. "Una quarta rima improvvisata non significa niente."

"Italian," Arnold told everyone. "Give me a minute."

Browning remained standing. "'And yet and yet and yet', quoth the Rabbi Jochanan Hakkadosh Yehudah Hannasi to those of his disciples who would relinquish a portion of their lives to extend the end of his, 'to petition the Pharaoh to wrest stasis from statist, you may gather as thieves but depart as assassins.'" Browning sat.

"No clearer in prose," Arnold asked everyone, "is he?"

Browning did not bother to stand for Yiddish. "Mayn Mame volt mikh farshtanen."

"Oh," spluttered Disraeli, "for goodness sake – "

"Is much mischief done," concluded Browning.

Arnold's notebook had had enough. "Cripes, Robert, spit it out!"

"Have the Jews at Brody asked for money?"

Browning had addressed the question to Disraeli, but it was Cardinal Manning who replied. "So far as one can know, they are beyond being heard."

"Then why demean them by offering?"

"Because they are in distress."

"Then why offer them only money?"

"What more is it in our power to – Surely you don't mean – "

A political analysis was required. It was cheerfully provided by Disraeli. "Even the Liberal Party will not go to war with Russia over twenty thousand Jews."

Browning shrugged. "Is the criterion racial or mathematic?"

The reflective silence was broken by Arnold. "On balance and surprising to me, I find myself partly in agreement with Mr. Browning. Unlike him I prefer poetry to be impersonal and remote from contemporary issues. Unlike him I confess to a congenital mistrust of impulse, to an innate awareness of race and breeding and, to my eternal cost – oh, Marguerite! – to a lifetime of pain at the unbridgeable salt estranging sea between the life of passion and that of reason. Yet, precisely like Mr. Browning, I pity every Jew at Brody. I scarcely dare imagine that privation and abandonment and I'll try not to. But, Robert, we do wrong to intrude upon a man's separateness and his loneliness, his exquisite transfiguring secret sorrow, his private, self-sufficient, isolate – Ah! my father would understand me. Beg pardon, I'll recover my coherence in a moment."

"Ah, coherence," Browning said, "the virtue of those with little to say. On balance I prefer incoherence to mania ... in Matthew's manner, the mania of moderation."

"Alliteration," Arnold managed, "isn't argument."

"It'll do, Matthew, until an argument arrives."

"Literature be damned!" bellowed the beard.

"As it often is, Mr. Darwin," Disraeli said wearily. The blessings of the elixir were beginning to wear off.

Darwin, however, was too engaged just now to administer a second dose. "Saving Jews," he boomed, "is against nature!"

Disraeli smiled wanly. "A most interesting and original attitude that I instinctively have endorsed since my conversion thence at the age of thirteen. I should be glad to hear its biological vindication." He coughed, winced with an intimate pain, slumped back among the cushions and waved for the discussion to continue in his relative absence.

"The eviction of lower races," Darwin intoned, "is natural and inevitable."

Manning took up the challenge. "Biblically perhaps, but – "

Darwin's beard parted to reveal a sneer. "Bible be damned. As I in my youth witnessed abroad, the white man is predestined to inherit every country he inhabits, dispossessing its naked aboriginals."

Manning appeared mildly interested. "And what happens to the races thus dispossessed?"

The beard cleared its throat and forced itself to remain patient or, at the least, didactic. "Extinction and natural selection go hand in hand. High New Zealanders say the Māori race is dying out as did their native rat. From the war of nature, from the struggle for existence, from famine and death, from persecution and execution, from dispossession and disposal, the most exalted object that we are capable of conceiving, namely the production of higher animals, directly follows. There's a grandeur in this view of life."

Manning's beak twitched. "And how does one know for certain which animals are the lower?"

"By the evidence of our senses, some of those of some of us. Judging from the hideous ornaments and the unspeakable music admired by savages and heathens, it's obvious that their aesthetic faculty is not so highly developed as, for instance, that of the birds. Equally no bird would be capable of admiring a beautiful landscape or a refined cantata, nor would any barbarian or uneducated person. These are examples, merely."

Manning smiled horribly. "Scientific certitude, then, is based upon artistic criteria?"

The beard confronted the beak in deepest forestation . "Intellectual rather, of which art is a by-product and religion a detritus. Of course, the variability of the mental faculties between men of distinct races is so notorious that not a word need here be said, but let us consider the more subtle position of women."

Disraeli sat up. "Let us."

"It's obvious that women are inferior intellectually."

Browning forgot to be obscure. "My late mother and my late wife can hardly be said to have been – "

Darwin ignored the poet. "The young of both sexes resemble each other. The female, however, in her innocence and her ignorance, invariable aspects of her charm, continues to resemble her young offspring throughout life."

"Ah, Marguerite!" The ejaculation had escaped Arnold involuntarily.

Darwin ignored a second poet – this was beginning to be an excellent day! – and continued. "Yet there I was, a lusty twenty-year-old on a voyage round the world with all great nature before me to collect and eviscerate" – here the beard curved fondly – "while oscillating in my hammock and wondering only: as for a wife, that most interesting specimen in the whole series of vertebrate animals, shall I ever succeed in capturing one and in being able to feed her when caught?" The beard curved downward with chagrin. "What a waste of youthful vigour and occupation!"

"Then, Mr. Darwin," Disraeli inquired, "shall women, too, quelle dommage, become extinct?"

"Not if they are protected from their innate inferiority, as they hitherto have been, by men. We do as much for our dogs and cats weakened by domestication, so naturally we perform like service for those upon whom our gestation depends. Moreover, the exercise is genetically useful because men's greater intellectual energy and courage and wit and power of invention have evolved from the very practice of battling other men for the possession of their women."

"Thrilling!" Disraeli was as erect as his conveyance and his condition permitted.

"Of course, both sexes ought to refrain from marriage if they are inferior in body – nothing personal, My Lord – or disturbed in mind or incapacitated by theology, but such hopes are utopian and will never be realized until the laws of inheritance are vigorously implemented. In the meantime, everyone does good service who aids toward this end and bad service who diverts it. To interfere with the natural processes of annihilation for no good reason is to impede them."

Arnold's eyes rounded like a child's. "And once the Jews at Brody naturally have evolved into extinction, who or what will replace them?"

"I'm aware only of the process, not of its prognosis. That's the nature of a theory."

"Then how," said Arnold mildly, "do you know a theory when you've seen one?"

"Or," added Browning, "know it was a theory you saw?"

"Or," Arnold smiled, "know it was you who saw it?"

The beard inclined ceilingward. It admitted a deep inhalation and expelled it. "Even the late Doctor Thomas Arnold, bumptious headmaster of Rugby College, bigot and braggart and bully though he was ..."

Arnold leapt to his feet, but the beard did not falter.

"... even the unlamented Elizabeth Barrett Browning, hypochondriac and hysteric, voluminous poetess of verbose romantic gush, textually insensitive to the value of rhyme sounds and the benefits of compression ..."

Browning stood shoulder to navel with Arnold, but the beard was unyielding.

" ... even they agree in print that THE ORIGIN OF SPECIES is the chief work of my life and of theirs as, more importantly, do Hooker, Wallace, Lyell, Huxley, Gray, Tennyson, Thackeray, Ruskin, Chekhov, Whitman, Twain, Lincoln, Marx, Engels and – excuse me, My Lord – Gladstone. I have all the clippings. There is also an essay in Hebrew showing that my theory is implied in the Old Testament. As for a few thousand Jews at Brody, save them, don't save them. In millennial terms, which are geology's and God's, it makes little difference."

Two scarlet slashes in the shape of a St. Andrew's Cross – the cross saltire, an emphatic deadly X – signalled to the poets to delay their ripostes, and they subsided to the edges of their seats. "Some of Mr. Darwin's theological detractors," the Cardinal hissed, "disagree."

The beard elevated belligerently. "As did you, Manning, in the October 31st issue of THE GENTLEMAN'S MAGAZINE of 1857, and the spring number of the EDINBURGH REVIEW thirteen years and five months later."

"Well, what if I did?"

"Less than nothing." The beard resumed its horizontal attitude. "I never read the critics."

Cardinal Manning rose, arranged his robes around an imagined lectern, sucked in his cheeks already cadaverous with self-denial, and pursed his lips in a liturgical manner. "Mr. Darwin, it appears, implies that the Jews of Brody be left to die in order to exemplify a hypothetical theorem of conjectural anthropology based upon problematic geology and popular pseudo-science: suicidal compliance, in his view, being the only and the invariable function of a race predisposed to natural extinction. My authority is somewhat less sales-worthy than his but infinitely less impeachable. There are no passages in scripture relating to the second coming of Christ more explicit and express than those foretelling Antichrist, and it therefore behooves the faithful to consider the matter more fully than they are wont to do.

"In the first place, Antichrist is a person: to deny the personality of Antichrist is to deny the plain testimony of Holy Scripture, and we must remember it is a law of Holy Scripture that, when persons are prophesied of, persons appear. Again, there is every reason to believe that Antichrist, when he does arrive, will turn out to be a Jew. Such was the opinion of St. Irenaeus, St. Jerome, and of the author of the work

DE CONSUMMATIONE DE MUNDI ascribed to St. Hippolytus, and of a writer of the COMMENTARY ON THE EPISTLE TO THE THESSALONIANS ascribed to St. Ambrose, and of others who add that the Antichrist will be of the tribe of Dan: as, for instance, St. Gregory the Great, Theodoret, Aretas of Caesarea, and many more such as Bellarmine who calls it certain and Lessius who affirms that the Church Fathers, with unanimous consent, teach us undoubted that Antichrist will be none other than a Jewish descendant of Dan while Ribera repeats the same opinion and cites Aretas, St. Bede, Haymo, St. Anselm, and Rupert all of whom affirm that for this very reason the tribe of Dan is not numbered among those that are sealed in the Apocalypse.

"On the solid empirical basis of this evidential testimony I think no one can consider the providential preservation of the Jews and their generous dispersion among all the nations of the world and the indestructible vitality of their race without believing that they are reserved for some future action of God's judgement and grace as is foretold again and again in the New Testament of which the Old Testament is the inadvertent porter, blind to the burden of the good news which it bears on its back like a scroll. To conserve the Jews for their nefarious role in the passion play to come is the demonstrable duty of every Christian of whichever cathedral or church or chapel, and whatever degree of devotion or conversion or lapse, among whom I number the present assemblage as predominant representative national exemplars. In a word, we must allow the Jews to live so that Christ may have cause to live again."

Manning sat, panting slightly.

Arnold stood. "As my despised bumptious father in his bigoted, bragging, bullying manner might have said: I've done with this committee; I hope it has done with me."

"But, Matthew," Disraeli remonstrated weakly as Arnold vanished from his field of view, "we appear to be all in agreement!"

Browning stood. "Hypochondriacally we are only in hysteric agreement regarding voluminous conclusions. Arnold!"

Arnold had almost reached the door. "Browning?"

Browning scuttled across the parquet. "You can't walk out on me."

"Why can't I?"

"I've always walked out on you."

Three old men watched two old men walk out on each other.

"Benjamin?"

"Your Eminence ...?" Disraeli signalled to Darwin for another medicinal ministration, which that worthy undertook.

Thus encouraged, the Cardinal resumed. "What of the Prime Minister's – What of our proposal?"

"What proposal?" A second injection so soon after a first had a pleasant disorientating effect.

"A mass meeting here for the relief of the Jews at Brody."

"Oh, moved, seconded, and carried by all means. If you don't recommend the Liberals use the Mansion House from time to time, you can be sure they'll sell it."

"And the wording of the resolution to be put forward at that meeting?"

"Outrage at iniquity, tolerance of religion, subscription to be raised on the behalf of, several nice things about Jews ... yes, yes, I'll draft something in the railway carriage home I daresay will pass muster and constrain our blushes as a people and the PM's as a party."

"And shall you be there to propose it?"

"I think not. As a lapsed Semite and a prolapsed Prime Minister my motives may appear to be mixed. I charge you, Cardinal Manning, with that bit of theatre, thereby lending it a pleasant whiff of ecumenicism. Besides, I have an invitation from Her Majesty to attend the grouse shooting at Balmoral. Rather like the goings-on at Brody, I daresay, though with greater accuracy."

"All the same, Benjamin, Mr. Gladstone should prefer it if you were there."

Disraeli stifled a cough. "Was the recent holocaust not enough for him?"

"Benjamin, Benjamin, I hardly think that a mere triumph in a general election is equivalent to ...." Manning found he was addressing the top of Disraeli's head. "Please, Ben, everyone considers that, in view of the traditional national prejudice against the church of Rome and the relative newness of the Liberal government, an established Anglican and Conservative presence – famously you represent both – would be expedient."

"Postpone." Disraeli had been consulting a pocket diary.

"Postpone?"

Disraeli pocketed the diary and pencil, and looked up. "Marked in for Wednesday the first of February. Day after the last day of the grouse. No birds left by then."

He signalled to Darwin for propulsion toward the exit.

"That business at Brody, the distress of the Jews ..." Manning persisted over the departing rumble.

"Has accumulated for millennia." Disraeli's voice diminished as his Bath-chair receded. "What's a few months more? Now, Charles, about those naked aboriginals ..."

Meanwhile in the market at Brody the price of month-old bread escalated, or it would have done had there been a stall still displaying some which there was not, although it was common knowledge that under the counter most bakers reserved a loaf – the extra that made up the fabled dozen – for a special customer: the one who could pay. Even the Rabbi's seventh wife was finding negotiations to procure such a loaf unproductive. Because she was no more than sixteen no stall-holder would take her seriously. This one just now had accused her of loitering with intent to purloin, no longer a crime in Brody so much as an inevitability to be delayed by the surveillance of one's loudest offspring or a tethered dog a week short of butchering.

The neighbouring stallholder whispered her identity. The baker touched his skullcap and bowed without for a second removing his eyes from her quick young hands.

The market area was known as the Castle Square because it occupied that vacancy in the city core where, in the dim days, either a sixteenth-century Polish overlord or a seventeenth-century Russian czar had built himself a fortification of which very little remained … an evocative mound of boulders of hewn contours … an uncanny air of menace at midnight when no one dared linger. Regardless of who founded the city and when, of which country it belonged to and for how long, of what it was called before it was Brody and why, this stone-strewn cobbled portion of what might once have been a castle courtyard was where the Rabbi's Wife stood and the baker grudgingly bowed. Even that half-gesture of respect, however, was not sufficient to yield bread. So she fainted.

"The Rabbi's wife is dead!" The cry was launched by the stallholder adjacent to the baker, the one who had whispered the initial identification and, as a coffin maker, was anxious to display his distress lest he be implicated in its cause, which could be seen as unfair trading. The report was taken up and spread among the aisles of merchandize-less merchants and the meandering clumps of futile shoppers. Within the commercial vacuum a listless crowd coalesced, willing to witness a disaster greater than its own.

"Dead shmead," the baker snorted. From under the counter he produced a loaf, knelt and held it to the stricken girl's nose.

Jack Winter

She stirred, opened her eyes, grabbed the loaf, staggered to her feet and fumbled in her purse.

"The Rabbi's wife is alive!" The cry was taken up and communicated to those on the fringe of the crowd who had not yet received the original message and were less than astonished by the report of something they already knew.

The baker clambered onto his table, elaborately waved off the girl's proffered coin and, in a voice that addressed the entire marketplace and the suburbs beyond, proclaimed: "This loaf is for the Rabbi with my best wishes for his continued good health or a speedy recovery!"

The baker's proactive generosity succeeded in removing the immediate threat to his person and his reputation. It also signalled that this baker probably had another loaf, another thirteenth, and the inner crowd instantly grew friendly, even ingratiating.

"Did you see how his loaf revived her?"

"Such a baker!"

"Such a bread!"

"And then to make of it a gift!"

"Such a – Does it mean there's another?"

"Maybe several?"

"Maybe more?"

"Maybe many?"

"Maybe many more?"

Nonchalantly the baker touched one finger after another. He was brushing crumbs from them but maybe he was counting. "Maybe," he murmured.

"So for how much a loaf?"

The baker named a figure.

"Nathan's is less."

"So buy from Nathan."

"He doesn't have any."

"And if I didn't have any, my price would be less than Nathan's."

"So that means you have some?" The question was a skilful one. If the baker confessed to a multiplicity of loaves, he could hardly continue to demand the price of the only loaf in the market. Stimulated by negotiation, the baker savoured the moment. Perhaps Brody was not such a bad business after all. There were plenty of mouths, some of which, when there was something to sell, perhaps would still be alive. And spring was due to arrive in less than half a year, and after that perhaps the wheat. And bread had the power to restore life and to preserve it, at least perhaps his own and his family's. The floury countenance beamed with optimism and condescension. "Perhaps."

"So now for how much a loaf?"

The baker named a figure twice the previous. "You think," he said, "it stands still?"

Before minds could change and things get ugly, the Rabbi's wife headed home, pausing only to retrieve a fish reserved earlier from a monger who was an uncle and, for several years, had owed a contribution to her trousseau. Hair tucked under her wig, wrapped under her kerchief, pinned under her shawl, figure indecipherable through lumpy layers of homespun, eyes downcast lest they encounter a man's and inspire lasciviousness, loaf and fish wrapped in her apron to present no temptation to thieves and to prevent hounding by beggars, down Market Street and Fortress Lane she scurried toward the Synagogue where she stopped a moment to watch the wailing against the wall as there was not time to climb to the Women's Gallery for a prayer. She continued around Ring Place, past the Old Textile Factory, its windows plastered with ants moving on top of one another that turned out to be abandoned children scrambling for a sill to lever their way in or hanging on to one having been pushed out, up New Hospital Passage where the curbside dead awaiting collection so little resembled anything human as not to be too disturbing and all along Great Lyubeshov Alley to the point near Backgate Way from which she could see her husband in his rocker on the veranda.

Even from a distance she could tell he was doing his best to concentrate on higher matters with a twin on each knee and his eldest daughter propelling his chair like a piston. All around, leaning against the pillars, draped across the balustrade, squatting on the steps, lounged the pale young students of the Synagogue watching their rabbi being rocked or, the Rabbi's Wife suspected, watching the rising and the falling hem of the maiden doing the rocking. It was that child – child! she thought, the girl is already a woman, almost my age but still a baby, pure and tender, being the daughter of a rabbi not the wife – who spotted her in the distance with a shout.

The Rabbi's Wife could not hear the shout but she could see its result. Child after child tumbled out of the house, around or under the students, down the porch steps, and up the street toward her ... even, she noticed, her own first-born who toddled at the rear, his progress impaired by the enormous diaper she had fashioned from her husband's cast-off gabardine.

She waited, smiling, till she was engulfed. Then she scooped up her eldest and straddled him on her shoulders where he plucked at her shawl and cooed in pride of place while the flock of his semi-siblings hopped along the cobbles at the skirts of their approximate mother who broke off pieces of the loaf and dropped them chunk by measured chunk into their mouths and his.

The Rabbi's eldest daughter who feared the effect of bread on her narrow hips abandoned the rocker and floated off as the clamour approached the veranda.

With undisguised relief the Rabbi relinquished the twins to his wife, freed at last to undertake an unburdened concentration on his present study: an especially fascinating point in an ancient Talmudic debate proposed by the immortal Rabbi Moshe Zentner regarding house-fire and the permitted sequence of precedence in the articles of worship and the family members and the pets to be rescued from the blaze. The students avoided the risk of seeing any part of a married woman by adjusting their gaze to the mouth of their rabbi and waiting faithfully for an accidental word or two instructively to drop.

By the time The Rabbi's Wife reached her kitchen, the entire loaf had been reduced to an apron-full of crumbs that she swept into a bowl to thicken the batter of her husband's breakfast fish.

With the twins slung in her shawl and clamped to either breast, she shrugged her eldest from her shoulders into his converted scuttle by the stove where, amid clean parchment side-walls, atop clean feathered rag-ends, he snuggled into a blissful bread-induced stupor. Tucked into the pocket ludicrously remaining in his gabardine diaper was the coin saved from the baker, reserved, his mother intended, for hard times.

In this household there was a rota of care: the elder child takes care of the younger; the students take care of themselves; the wife takes care of the husband, and so does everyone. It was a plan approved by the Rabbi, containing as it did a pleasing Talmudic circularity and a spiritual dynamic in accord with his own. The preparation of the Rabbi's breakfast was a case in point. A fish, after all, is only a fish until it is gutted, scaled, salted, scented, coated, and baked. For such a procedure knives must be sharpened, water pumped, herbs pulverized, coals gathered, ovens stoked, napkins ironed, tables laid, entrails burned or offered to the cats, each task performed by the sole mistress of the kitchen ... work enough for many hands and impossible to accomplish with only two unless the rest of the household busies itself elsewhere without intrusion into her specific domain.

The rota took care of it all, leaving The Rabbi's Wife free to sharpen, pulverize, gather, and stoke, with a demeanour as cheerful as if she had just discovered a new way to skin onions without tears or to streamline two tasks into one when timing an egg pan and estimating a stew pot, all with a balletic skill it was a shame no others were present to witness, none except her nurslings who dangled and sucked, and her firstborn who snored gently in his scuttle by the warming oven.

Eventually all was completed, and she signalled out the kitchen window to the Rabbi's second-eldest daughter – the eldest still was nowhere to be seen – to interrupt the Rabbi's contemplation and to summon him to dine. Then, using the water bucket as a looking glass, mirrors being the apparatus of courtesans and adulterers, she tidied herself for the serving-out.

"That loaf," said the Rabbi, settling at the table to receive his fish, "how did you manage such a miracle?"

"I'm," she said shyly, "after all The Rabbi's Wife."

The Rabbi understood the meaning of her reply, although perhaps not its every nuance because he took it as a compliment.

"Never mind perfection," he smiled, slipping comfortably into his breakfast benediction and the slippers and the house-coat laid out at his place. "In Jewish tradition it is just the opposite. Man's past is linked to history's sacred origins. A reflection of the Divine, the first man was more righteous, more accomplished, better suited to his surroundings, and more capable of survival than the most perfected of his descendants, even the rabbis among them, ever would become. That each generation further away from the first is less perfect than the preceding is what's to be expected. That this generation is the least perfect of all can be a surprise only to a Gentile. And so we must make do with the generation we find ourselves in and seek to bring order out of its chaos and precedence out of its order, while a few of us on behalf of the rest try to reach back a little further to see if we can manage with our rabbinical contemplation to touch the hand of Adam, the fallible firstborn, and perhaps to receive a slight scratch from the least fingernail of the smallest finger of The Perfect Parent Who Fathered All."

Here the Rabbi prepared to launch himself at his fish that by now was cool enough. "Ahhh ..."

"... men," enjoined his wife.

During the benediction, the students had arranged themselves unobtrusively against the walls of the dining room to take notes. The Rabbi's Wife had assembled her brood around the table in ascending sequence, at her feet her own eldest still asleep in his scuttle, in her shawl on either breast a twin still glued but asleep as well. Suppressing salivation, they all attended respectfully as their mentor, their husband, their father, fulfilled his canonical injunction to survive and to thrive for the good of the community. "Ahhhmen," chanted the students and, as far as was possible, the children.

The Rabbi's best student, a pale young man who read newspapers when available, nudged the Rabbi's second-best student, head bowed reverentially beside him. "What the Rabbi just said," he whispered, "that's the opposite of evolution. Has he never heard of Darwin?"

"Has Darwin," the second-best whispered back, "never heard of Jews?"

The Rabbi's mouth was full. His eyes, however, moved round the room and stopped at an obvious vacancy. "And," he mumbled to his wife, "Miriam?"

"You know she doesn't like to watch the eating."

"That girl, that girl needs a good old fashioned – "

The Rabbi's Wife nudged forward his second-eldest daughter. "Channah, however, is – "

A fishbone had intervened and required the Rabbi's full attention. After a tussle with napkin and fork it was dislodged and lay displayed upon an index finger. The Rabbi swallowed.

"Of such small things as a fishbone," he began but, to save him the embarrassment of watching him choke, his family and his students had departed.

Left alone at the breakfast table staring at the skeleton of his fish, the Rabbi thought about his absent eldest.

It was not as if, pretending to sleep while Miriam agitated his balcony rocker, he had failed to pay attention to the banter of his students with his daughter and to note her witty incisive responses. How else other than by overhearing was he to keep up to date with the idiom of the young so as to improve his instruction of them? True, when Miriam recited his favourite rabbinical tales to his students she always omitted his own citation of origins and attribution of authorities and parenthetical insights and demurrals ... typical, the Rabbi smiled inwardly, of a generation inclined to rush and to risk generalities.

Perhaps a little worryingly Miriam also was inclined to invent puns with a double meaning that a passing stranger might mistake for sensual, and to improvise dialogue that happened to emerge from her sweet mouth in a parody of his own voice ... yet, the Rabbi sighed, was it not natural for the young standing upon the shoulders of their elders occasionally to inflict some pain? But why with her inquiring mind and her open heart and an imagination that bordered on the masculine, why with the example of his knowledge of the ancient world and his affection for this one and his horror of another, why was her loving father, a rabbi and not the least among his peers, unable to convince her to eat?

Did she not realize? Could she not imagine? Did she not fear?

The Rabbi shook himself and prepared to rise and to ready his mind for the Synagogue and for a day's work of enabling his disciples to watch while he educated himself further. Perhaps there at last he would find the one answer to all his questions.

"I may be a poor teacher," said the Rabbi to himself and to G-d if He was listening, "but I'm an excellent student."

The district Miriam wandered into, when avoiding the loaf of bread, she had visited before, once only when she accompanied her father on a death-watch. At the end of Morass Lane, where several roads converged but failed to meet, in an open area that never properly had been built upon because the ground was too spongy to support a substantial structure and foundation trenches flooded as they were dug, Morass Place was an island of huts in a sea of hovels where the very poorest of Brody lived but not long. As the town filled up like a seaport from which departing ships had been cancelled, the Rabbi was summoned more and more often to the sodden precincts of Morass Place to attend the dying or to bless the dead, often accomplishing both on the same visit to the same address for the same parishioner.

Which was how Miriam met Dan.

On that first visit Miriam had not so much been invited to accompany the Rabbi as acquiesced to by her father who was so depressed at the prospect of yet another duty-call to Morass Place – and to such a house where Jew and travelling-Jew and, perhaps, unthinkable others mingled! – that he welcomed the presence of this child as an extra pocketful of rose petals held against the stench. In any case, he assured his wife who, as a wife, feared the worst, he had read somewhere that the young were more resistant to airborne contagions because of the smaller capacity of their lungs, just the sort of medical wisdom the Rabbi could retain because of its equational nature.

For her part Miriam's enthusiasm to experience Morass Place, a district she and her siblings and every one of her respectable playmates always had been forbidden, had more to do with a natural inquisitiveness than with an intuition that the visit would change her life. That occasion, like all the others, was a death like all the others. Like those, of course, it also was unique, though neither her father nor she could remember who in that family it was who lay dying, the Rabbi because had watched so many do it, Miriam because she saw Dan.

The beauty of Dan had little to do with his stature that was smaller even than Miriam's who, at that age, stood no higher than the fringe of a prayer shawl and was slighter in form than a tassel. In the eyes of Miriam, the beauty of Dan was that he hardly seemed to be there at all. Everything about him aspired to invisibility. His hair, his eyes, his skin were too profoundly dark to appear of themselves in the dimness. The attention of Miriam was drawn only when she heard a remote rustle and glimpsed the iridescence of an eye.

While her father murmured to the ear of G-d and did something to the form that lay motionless under a mound of bed sheets, Miriam lowered herself to the dirt floor and crept among the legs of the mourners. Dan was hunched, naked as a kitten, in a corner of the single room his knees drawn up under his chin, as far from the death-bed as possible while still remaining within. When Miriam reached him, there was a flash of white. He had grinned. Long after she forgot the exact location of the hovel, Miriam remembered that flash of white in a blackened space, and the fact that Dan covered his head indoors like a Jew though only with a cloth cap. So her solitary wandering this morning had not been entirely random.

In the months since her first sojourn there, the deterioration of Morass Place had deepened. Held within a moat of open sewers surrounding the district, Morass Place was further contained by the Volunteer Jewish Militia which, in the face of municipal chaos brought about by the unquenchable influx of refugees into Brody, was determined to make a stand where it was easiest. These hard-faced men took measures to ensure that, once a pauper entered Morass Place, he never left it, not until he left Brody which no pauper could afford to do alive. Admittedly, their firm proscription was porous in application because the members of the Volunteer Jewish Militia, being volunteers, frequently failed to appear for duty due to prior social or recreational engagements, and pretty much all refused to work after dark when the footing became inconvenient. Their mission, however, was rigid in intention, which energy alone was sufficient to deter limper denizens.

A kind of double ghetto, Morass Place thus had become a compaction of the worst aspects of Brody itself, a jungle of decrepitude where human traffic pulped the ground into an adhesive slime of which the least component was mud. Since there had been no other direction in which to go, architectural expansion had been upward and the profile of Morass Place was beginning to resemble a favourite resort of Miriam's wanderings ... the Hassidic cemetery where, after centuries of interment, the graves were multi-storeyed, each new incumbent a tier closer to the surface, and the memorial stones leaned against one another like eternal gossiping neighbours.

After much meandering in the slime, Miriam at last thought she had found the shambles that contained Dan and what was left of his family. She recognized it by the curtain of black shells that clacked from a lintel and constituted its doorway. By now the shack itself had become the ground floor in a pyramid of accommodations that teetered skyward and weighed upon each other in desolate strata. It was impossible to knock, so Miriam parted the shells and entered.

Since her first visit to Morass Place, Miriam had a dream that repeated itself nightly with little variation. Someone like Miriam – not precisely Miriam because a characteristic of the dream was that she remained aware that she was dreaming, and that the Miriam she dreamt of was not the Miriam she was otherwise she would not have been able to bear it and would have willed herself awake … this virtual Miriam was wandering in a dark place where there was the sound of weeping.

The Miriam of the dream had no fear of the darkness. It was a medium as unremarkable to her as the air to those who breathe or the sea to those who swim or the palpable black to the congenitally sightless of which this Miriam happened to be one. The weeping was another matter. How could the blind Miriam of the dream be certain the weeper was not she? The source of the weeping seemed to be elsewhere, and it grew louder when she turned her head this way, softer in the other direction. Yet, when she tried to follow where it led, the sound of the weeping seemed to remain always the same distance away, not far away, not quite where she stood and just beyond where she moved. When she awoke, the weeping was all Miriam could remember of the dream. She was certain there was more, but it had vanished with the dawn, though an ominous unease tended to linger till noon.

On this day, the moment the real Miriam passed through the curtain of shells she entered a semblance of the dream. The blackness was entire. It wrapped itself around her, a perfect drape, no, a cloak, no, a veil because she could breathe unhampered, though with each breath she seemed to inhale black air and to blow it back into a fabric that enclosed her and moved with her as she shuffled forward, arms outstretched. Again, there was no fear, except perhaps in the ends of her invisible fingers that flinched at what they might encounter. And there … no, there … somewhere out beyond the cone of perfect black was the gentle sound of weeping.

As her eyes began to adjust, shapes emerged in the gloom – a chair, another, a table too low to be seen before her knee crashed against it with a clatter that made her gasp – and there, where it had been before, a bed containing, as before, a sheet in the shape of a human form. This sector of the room contained the weeping, though it stopped when her knee encountered the table. It resumed now that she knew with a certainty beyond seeing what it was that lay beneath the sheet, who it was who was being mourned, and this time she knew the weeping to be her own. She was too late. That was the part of her dream her waking mind had refused to recall. A flash of white in the blackness of Morass Place was all there ever would be of him.

Steeling herself – she was months older now – she folded back the sheet over the face. Then, when she could bear to, she peeled back the rest and dropped it into the pit at her feet. He was as beautiful now as then, with no mark of what had passed on any part of him. She moved to touch his face and her fingers retracted. His cheek was wet. When she reached again and traced the moisture to its source, she knew it to be tears.

His eyes flew open. "I thought," he said, "you'd never come."

He grinned, threw aside his cap and seized her.

Without a moment's doubt she let herself be seized.

Chapter Two

Miriam's Child

Nearly a year had passed since the union at Morass Place, months absent of event and filled with incident. Miriam did not return to the home of her father. Dan did not leave his, though by one means or another, usually terminal, by now every member of his family had. Together she and he barely ventured outside and rarely beyond Morass Place and never during daylight. Their waking hours were occupied with dance ... no, not a tasteful metaphor ... dance, the instruction in it, the preparation for it, the performance of it, the recovery from it, the same and the same over and over again and again.

Miriam had danced before, once notably – she was eight – atop the dinner table at the end of the Passover service when the cautionary chronicles and the ordained grovellings petered out and the wild songs began and the sweet wine flowed without sacrament or agenda. Throughout the ritual tedium the little girl had been eyeing the ceremonial cup reserved for the magical prophet Elijah should he deign to call. He had not. So, while the adults were congratulating one another at having once more evaded deadly plagues visited upon ancient Egyptians, she had nicked his tipple and crept under the table to savour its mystery and clambered on top to celebrate its effect.

At that point the postprandial song being shouted was Miriam's favourite, a traditional ballad with an incremental chorus beginning at a goat and amassing a catalogue of barnyard animals augmented by mythical crossbreeds and trans-species freaks. The only zoological boundary was the stamina of the celebrants who did not want the song to end. While the chorus accumulated, it accelerated as did Miriam's rotating dance.

At the head of the table her father, preoccupied with protocols of tipsy hosthood and enhanced recollections of life in Mother Russia, failed to notice that with chorus after chorus his students on every side were conspiring to see how fast they could cause his little Miriam to spin and how high her skirts could be made to rise. Obligingly, helplessly, she spun and spun until at last she tumbled amid the crockery and was sick among the leftovers and lay on her back like a spitted lamb, staring at the ceiling candelabra while song-animals and the student menagerie chanting them whirled about her. It was then that her repugnance for the consumption of slaughtered flesh was born.

At the weddings of her father – the many he performed and the several performed upon him – her role was mainly vocal. There, she was required to sit bobbing rhythmically next to the accordionist and, in a fine thin voice drowned out by clashing chords and showy arpeggios, to yell lyric invocations of fecundity cloaked in botanical metaphor ... which humiliating performances contributed to her lifelong distaste for edible vegetables.

At such events even the bray of the accordion would be overwhelmed by the raucousness rising from the dance floor. Little Miriam would sit paralyzed with alarm as the groom and the bride – too often her father and her latest girl-mother – were chaired and circulated shoulder-high by a sweating stamping herd of students bawling with zeal, dizzy with sanctity. At such moments she lost her appetite for dairy products, and her desire to vanish into transparency became palpable.

Between formal festivals and domestic celebrations there was little opportunity for Miriam to dance. Her father's usual ministry contained ageless synagogue lamentations bewailing historic calamities with a gusto that made the destruction of the Temple seem as current a mischief as the wave of dysentery engulfing Brody, and the failure of Moses to enter the Promised Land an irony equivalent to the mortality rate of Morass Place.

None of it involved dance, no dance apart from the rhythmic tipping backward and forward of the entire male congregation during prayer. Interminable, mesmeric, prone to convulsive excess, the congregational sway was a motion not unlike the rocking of her father's contemplation chair, and it too excluded Miriam. Watching it in G-d's house or assisting it on the Rabbi's veranda, Miriam's role was that of a motionless attendant, females being relegated to the rear in both places and explicitly forbidden to gyrate. In either location she obediently fulfilled her engendered function while inwardly imagining what it would be like to fly, or at least to float beyond the ceiling of the synagogue and the verandas and the roofs of Brody.

Dancing to the music of Dan was quite another matter. Here intoxication was a convention, sensuality a technique, spontaneous improvisation and guileless abandon and shameless joy painstakingly rehearsed. It all had to be learned and practiced, and practiced and perfected. And there was no ceremonial occasion for it, none beyond the performance.

There was, however, a need. Months spent in a feculent shack in Morass Place made her aware of it. A need experienced both by the dancer and by those who, when she was proficient enough to invite their attendance and sufficiently emaciated to be credible among them, would gather to watch her dance. It was to fulfil that need of their fellow denizens of Morass Place that Dan made his music and guided her in the perfecting of her dance. A need to forget for a moment who one was and where one was so as to enable oneself to survive the moment to come as the same person in the same place. A need to forget, and to forget over and over again and again.

31

Naturally Miriam was unaware of any deeper significance to her dance, being too occupied in the exertion itself to concentrate on anything but the voice of Dan's violin and the instructions emanating from it. When, after a time, she came to understand his spoken language as fluently as she did her own, he explained his music to her as best he could:

"Your people are afraid of forgetting, you can hear it in their music, well, I can. With them when a keynote is needed, two are played, one behind the other with nothing in between. You have to listen hard to catch it, that nothing that's barely there, that doesn't seem to be there because the first note, the one a little further along the tune, is the right one, the one your ear expects. But always, just after, there's the note that isn't wrong just not quite right looking back to the other, the one before the next right note, remembering it, wanting to remember it, to touch it, to hold on to it, which can never happen because between the two there's this little unbridgeable nothing. You hear it there and expect the worst. For such a music of longing the dance is a circle, fast it can be and wild but always a circle with no way out.

With the music of my people as well there's a doubleness, but with us the second note, the shadow of the first, is in the direction of the next, a little step ahead on the road the tune must travel. If there's a gap, it can be slurred across. At the most it's a moment of waiting for the correct note to catch up. Whether it does or not, the tune forgets where it's been and moves on, playing happy in a sad key.

Naturally, for a music such as ours, a music of forgetting, the instruments must be portable. A tambourine, a violin, a castanet ... the most portable is the body. So we never play without a singing, we never sing without a percussion, a percussion on the body of the instrument, a percussion on the instrument of the body. And, of course, the worse things are the more we speed the tempo. Once our music has begun, we're never still. Our hands and our feet, our faces, our dress, are never at rest, never not on the move in every direction at once. And when we do the dancing, it's in a line. From a line there are two ways out.

For some, your music and ours are the same. For us, they're the opposite. Your dance is a circle. We're not the ones who are afraid of forgetting. It's the name of our music."

Miriam, it must be said, paid little attention to Dan's interesting musicology. The problem, as always, was his face. When he spoke, she was aware only of its beauty. When he spoke at length, the sensation intensified and she was impelled to interrupt him with inevitable consequence. That consequence aside, Miriam had the ability to hear without listening, or of listening to a language other than the words being used ... a habit she had acquired with her father who spoke unendingly of higher things, and only made her aware of how much she was loved and of how little he could find the vocabulary to say it.

So of Dan's music she felt much and understood nothing at all, though she knew that in Brody, for a dancing such as hers was destined to become, there was a suitable venue, a place where the ground was lumpy and broken but mireless and hard as bone, where the seating was brittle and tilted but congested and plentiful, where the dead and the near-dead hobnobbed and the militia feared to patrol.

The first music festival at Brody was little more than an outdoor training session happened upon by a family on a sultry midnight stroll in the Hassidic cemetery in search of air fresher than that of Morass Place. Attracted by distant sounds unlike the raven's pointless cough and the whistle of the moussing owl, the family's most adventurous boy wandered on ahead. Then he stopped and stood halfway down a slope. Then he turned and scampered back to the others to drag them forward to what he thought he had seen.

The whole family stood on the brow of the basin and peered through the smoke at the apparition below. In the profoundest depth of the oldest part of the cemetery where the gravestones had eroded to barely protruding stumps, burning torches embedded in the ground demarcated a strip of relatively level terrain. To one side, perched atop the stunted stone sculpture of a broken oak, the traditional memorial replica on the grave of one who died too young, Dan swayed, his cloth cap firmly anchored across his brow, a leg crossed on the thigh of the other, his eyes shut and his mouth contorted, lost to the wail and the quaver of his bow. In the centre of the illuminated area Miriam danced.

The family on the hill did not know it was Miriam who was dancing or that what she was doing was a dance. To them it seemed the music had come alive and she was the form it took, so already there was a spiritual dimension albeit a fault of perspective due to smoke. As quietly as they could, the family settled themselves on the stumps of nearby gravestones while below them Dan made a music of many voices that seemed to rise from the ground and to shriek a while and to subside and to rise and shriek again, and Miriam spun and spun in a choreography none had seen before, none other than those whose revered Hassidic dust lay beneath her feet.

The family watched for hours that seemed like minutes, an illusion attributable in part to the aromatic vapours that rose from the torches. When the slant of dawn began to unlace the curtain between them and the dancing, they crept away to protect themselves from being spotted by those they had been watching, and to tell neighbours what they told each other they thought they had seen.

Word of mouth lured other families out of Morass Place to the second midnight music festival at the Hassidic cemetery, and to the third and the many subsequent. As the reputation of the event grew, those who attended were predisposed to see what those who spread the word believed they had witnessed, and to stay longer, and to approach closer, and to risk calling attention to themselves by a participatory behaviour that enhanced their experience. Their clapping to the rhythms and their swaying to the tunes became a kind of involuntary accompaniment, almost a music and a dance in itself.

Eventually, reports of what went on hour after hour until dawn at the Hassidic cemetery on the outskirts of Brody attracted so many onlookers that every gravestone in the vicinity was occupied nightly. A few particularly good vantage points were booked ahead by the stratagem of filling each with a family member, the fattest or the fiercest, who was prepared to guard it with his life.

Informants, of course, made the militia aware of what nightly was draining the human congestion from Morass Place, though what went on after curfew was largely irrelevant due to the night watch's nearly perfect record of absenteeism. Furthermore, the fact that the festival-goers, most of the residents of Morass Place, spent many of the other hours catching up on lost sleep only made it easier for the militia to patrol there by day.

So, by any standard, the midnight music festivals at Brody were entirely successful. By public consensus the last one was the best. Certainly, it was the best remembered. It was the first time Miriam danced with a partner!

That all-night entertainment had begun in its usual inauspicious way. No matter how soon after sundown he or she set out, no truant from Morass Place ever arrived at the cemetery venue before the performers. Even the earliest trickle of spectators seeking to disarm militia spies by pretending to have chanced upon an event already in progress were aided in their deception by the fact that they had. The first few routines – a tuning of Dan's strings and a limbering of Miriam's sinews – already had transpired and, by the time the trickle became a stream and the stream a torrent and what appeared to be the entire population of Morass Place had emptied into the gruesome amphitheatre, musician and music, dancer and dance, newcomer and habitué, melded into a throbbing unity that late arrivals found it embarrassing to invade but did anyway.

The special ambiance of this final performance was due in large measure to its unprecedented format. As the music and the dance progressed, the intervals between the segments decreased in frequency and diminished in extent. Eventually there were no intervals at all and, however beyond human endurance it seemed, Miriam's became one continuous dance. And not a dance she had prepared and rehearsed. Although she could not have witnessed the dancing of the ancient Orphanics nor, probably, been aware of the existence of that tiny Hassidic extremity before its historical extinction, Miriam's miraculous performance began to follow the shape described in the imperfect text discovered among the corrupt relics of the Rabbi Moshe Zentner who, though not himself a member, was its enthusiastic chronicler:

"The formation of the dance of an Orphanic Hassid is not a circle. The formation seems a circle. For days, for months, the Orphanic traces the identical path round and round the floor of the dance hut. So it seems to those who watch only for days, for months. The Orphanic dances for decades, for generations. The Orphanic's is a lifetime of dance, and the dancer knows the dance he dances is not a circle though it appears to be one. Imagine an Orphanic dancing. Round it goes, round and round, not only round the dance hut, but round and round itself ... arms raised, fingers clenched, eyes afloat, round and round it turns as round and round the hut it goes.

The other Orphanics, are they not like the first? As like the first as like to like, and round and round they – Wait! Detach yourself from the dancers! Observe the dance! A dance hut full of dancers, a dance that fills the hut: eyes open, arms up, yet the dancers never collide? They rarely touch? Their orbits, see! their orbits differ, and their years. Those on the outskirts, those of the dance of the greatest arc, those of the greatest number of turns, those like the dancer we first imagined, those are the youngest Orphanics of all. Those within the peripheral arcs, those are the elders, their cycles smaller, their turnings fewer. Those within the arcs of their elders, those within the arcs of those, older and older the dancers are, slower and slower their dance, fewer and fewer their turns. And that Orphanic nearest the centre of the hut, it hardly dances at all, its cycles but an arm's breadth radius, its turns but one or two. And its song? Ah, there it is! a murmur only, little more than an exhalation, hardly that. Imagine again our youngest dancer, coattails flying, mouth agape, dance and dancer, song and singer, filling the hut, the hall, the air. See that same dancer years and years from now, years and years from then, how low its arms, how lax its fists, how soft its chant, how slow its dance, how much nearer to the centre. See it decades thence, a quiet stepper now. As you watch, it nears the point at which the floorboards join. It reaches the point. It stops. It is no dancer. It is no Hassid. It is nothing, not even an Orphanic. Its dance is done, not a circle but a spiral, a dance of death not life."[8]

Miriam's terminal dance at the final midnight music festival at Brody followed Rabbi Zentner's description of the Orphanic pattern with obvious discrepancies in respect to gender, age, century, theology, venue and occasion. Another divergence from tradition was that, at the same time that her dance slowed in tempo and tightened in spiral, it deepened in sensuality, a definite contrast to the historic torpidity of the average limp Orphanic.

As Miriam's body surrendered to a series of terpsichordic contractions and her limbs developed a frenzy of their own, members of her audience were mesmerized into a state of virtual participation. Tombstone after tombstone became the podium where an otherwise respectable resident swayed and twitched in intimate convulsion. Neighbour clutched neighbour in unprecedented society. Parents forgot to cover the eyes of their children, and none departed in outrage despite the manifest provocation. The erotic effect was heightened by a subtle rear-illumination that intensified until Miriam's slender form became an ecstatic silhouette flickering against a backdrop of red.

At some point Dan threw away his violin – it was unearthed amid the headstones generations later by Israeli forensic archaeologists seeking Zionist roots in Diasporic hinterlands – and he joined Miriam at the centre of the performance area and began to weave his own slow circles round and round himself and nearer and nearer to hers. Despite the withdrawal of Dan's instrumental accompaniment, the music continued, an eerie phenomenon perhaps attributable to audience participation, perhaps to another scarcely-to-be-contemplated agency. Together their dance achieved its nadir. It slowed, it stopped and, exhausted by her exertions or as a melodramatic gesture, Miriam collapsed at the feet of Dan and lay there writhing in what appeared to be the aftershocks of orgasm but in fact were the advanced stages of the pangs of childbirth. Not many of the spectators, however, were any longer paying much attention. They had been distracted by the background light-show that by now out-dazzled the stage performance. To a man and a woman and a child they wondered how, amid economic austerity, the producers of the event had managed to contrive such a convincing display of distant flames.

What happened after that is not ascertainable. The precise incident on stage was actually witnessed only by those few dozen spectators in the best seats, and every one of them was too horrified to recall the moment or to speak of it in the span of a natural lifetime nor even in a ghost-written memoir for which many Zionist publishers offered competing commissions. One or two remoter witnesses were overheard suggesting that, before a curtain of smoke obliterated the scene, they had a glimpse of Dan astride the turbulent body of his partner slowly withdrawing from the waistband of his trousers a terrible knife, presumably intending to ease the passage of a difficult birth or, as any responsible parent in Brody, to abort an infantile wretchedness before it began. For the majority of the audience, however, the aromatic smoke from the torches had blurred too much of the entire performance for a reliable critique. In fact, most maintained, it was that very smoke that made it difficult to isolate the odour of Brody burning.

It was, of course, a famous fortuity that the night of the final midnight music festival in the Hassidic cemetery coincided with the second great fire of Brody. The first, nearly two centuries earlier but still discussed, had decimated the Jewish quarter and incinerated most of its inhabitants. The latest inferno blessedly spared the hordes watching Miriam perform. Confined by the sewage trench surrounding Morass Place, this time the catastrophe consumed only that entire wretched district along with several dozen residents too dispirited to attend festivals.

In the Hassidic cemetery a burial posse hastily was assembled, though nobody at the final festival would admit to having been a member of it, fearing to be linked to a coup de théâtre that probably would be construed as a crime. A few brave citizens re-excavated an existing grave, tossed aside the ancient bones, shoved the two fresh corpses into the vacant hole and scurried off, leaving the filling-in to the last to leave ... a task that, in the universal rush to return to Morass Place to rescue what precious personal mementoes had escaped the inferno and to loot the rest, was not accomplished.

Meanwhile, back in the Castle Square of Brody another stone inscribed with the nickname of G-d had moved.

"In England where we hear the king is a Jew and therefore every Jew is a kind of – Queen? In England there's a queen? So, in England where we hear the queen is a Jew and therefore through the maternal line every king and queen of England will be also – Not the queen? The prime minister? The prime minister of England is a Jew? Was? So, in England where we hear the former prime minister is a – Was? Already what I said means was ... in England where the *former* prime minister is a – Again was? Not a prime minister? Not a former prime minister? Surely not a former – How can that be? You're a Jew or not even in England. Not in England? In England it's possible for a Jew to become not a Jew? What do you do, resign your circumcision? So, in England where we hear the former prime minister is a former Jew and – Dead? That we hadn't heard."

The Rabbi's best student absorbed this latest piece of current affairs and tried to work out how he could improvise it gracefully into his lecture of welcome addressed to the pair of Mansion House delegates he had been assigned. While he pondered, his honoured guests awaited the continuation of their celebrity tour of the Hassidic cemetery and poked idly about amid the gravestones. By the time the student was ready to resume, Laurence and Alice Oliphant had wandered away and disappeared into the maze of headstones where the smoke of Morass Place lingered. From one of the macabre alleyways there came the sound of a crack followed by the accumulating reverberation of an avalanche. "Hey!" shouted the student, plunging after his personal charges into the vapours, "you can't go breaking them like Cossacks!"

Sometime later – dawn being unable to pierce the gloom, it was difficult to judge the hour – through an accident of blind navigation, the student broke into a pocket of clarity. Recognizing the Oliphants from behind, he suppressed a whoop of relief and advanced upon them in a casual manner, coughing discreetly and wearing what he hoped was a genial but a gently disapproving smile.

Though the couple must have been aware of his approach, they remained seated on the ground, their legs dangling into a vacancy before them the depths of which seemed magnetic. The student followed their gaze. From his frozen grin there emerged the sound of a whimper ascending to a scream followed by another and another blending into a continuous wail terminating, when Laurence Oliphant reached up and slapped him across the face, in a sigh and subsidence to the edge of the pit. The puddle that the student's head encountered proved momentarily refreshing and he roused from his faint long enough to comment on the tableau at the bottom of the open grave. "It's – it's – oh G-d, tell the Rabbi!" His observation delivered, he splashed into a second stupor more profound than the first and, as far as anybody else was concerned, one he was better into than out of, certainly quieter.

The Oliphants returned their gaze to the grave and its contents, the most remarkable feature of which was dual occupancy ... one of either sex, fresh but clearly exanimate beyond resuscitation. In the hiatus of the student's intervention something else had emerged. Alice Oliphant slowly raised one arm and pointed a shaking finger forward and down, the symmetrical features of her face unbecomingly contorted and her mouth repeating "born-a-miracle born-a-miracle born-a-miracle!"

Laurence stared into the abyss and did not blink.

As they watched from above, a purple sac on the chest of the female cadaver writhed like a purblind kitten nosing for a vacant teat. A tiny fist had projected. It clutched – of all things! – a cloth cap. From the sepulchral profundity there arose the faint sound of mewing. Alice uttered a shout that contained a strangulated version of her husband's name. Laurence Oliphant smiled grimly and precipitated himself from the lip of the grave. He was captured pretty much in mid-air and dragged back by his wife who, half a head shorter, was outweighed twofold but whose fear of widowhood due to a broken neck doubled her strength.

Applying restraint by the therapeutic exigency of a knee on the thorax, she prised open the pill-case she carried in a pocket and slipped a tranquilizing lozenge under the protruding tongue of the man she had saved and was throttling. As an afterthought, she administered one to herself. When she was certain Laurence was not about to embark on a further exercise in suicidal heroism, she set about reviving the student who in any case was beginning to bubble and despatched him to summon emergency assistance.

As usual the militia arrived late, reticent to undertake an uncongenial task in inclement surroundings. Scalability was solved by lowering one another down and raising up one another and their burdens by means of a human chain. The corpses were wrapped and bound for removal to a forensic examination that would never take place, the cause of Dan's death of no interest to anyone outside his inaccessible tribe, the cause of Miriam's obvious, bloody and umbilical. The squirming bundle born-a-miracle was detached and handed to Alice Oliphant, the only embosomed bystander, where it mewed amiably, still clutching the cloth cap.

When the time came to take the tiny survivor back for delivery to the house of Miriam's family, Alice refused to let go of it. To a man the militia shrugged. Let the goyim make what deal they could with the Rabbi; the problem was theirs not the militia's. The militants among them debated arresting the Oliphants for double murder, decided against it on the grounds of jeopardizing Mansion House philanthropy, shouldered their ghastly burdens and moved on. The cloth cap, prized from the grip of the infant, was tossed back into the grave.

As commanded, the Rabbi's best student ran to the office of the militia, alerted them to their mission and described the location. Then he ran to the Synagogue where he knew the Rabbi was in mid-seminar. Along the way he rehearsed what he was going to say, accepted it as basically unutterable and decided to rely on spontaneity.

When the messenger burst into the study chamber and stood in the doorway panting and wondering how to begin, the Rabbi completed an interrupted sentence in his lecture, carried on with the subsequent several to the end of his paragraph, held up a hand to signal a pause in the argument rather than a conclusion to the session, laid aside his spectacles, settled back in his chair and waited for an explanation of this uncharacteristic disturbance.

The student found his voice and exercised it strenuously. "It's Miriam!"

"Tfoo! Tfoo! Tfoo! She's found?"

The student nodded.

"Praise G-d." The Rabbi replaced his spectacles and shuffled his references.

The student stopped nodding and took a deep breath to achieve an order of intensity commensurate with the occasion. "Dead!"

The Rabbi did not retract his praise. Instead, he located his place in his notes.

The student adjusted his resonance upward. "She's dead! Miriam is dead!"

The Rabbi paused, shrugged, shook his head and prepared to resume his lesson, the subject of which was the incineration of Morass Place. He was proud of his pedagogic technique of illuminating historical topics by the use of current events and modern instances, in the present case with an occurrence so recent its embers could still light a candle. On this occasion he was particularly eager to resume his exploration of the rumour, already a legend, that before the conflagration went beyond control a shadowy figure too dark to be identified had been seen at Morass Place running from hovel to hovel with a knife in its belt and a torch in its hand.

"Dead!" wailed the student with an apex of wail he had not intended to attain. "Dead! Dead! Dead! Did you not hear?"

"Who," said the Rabbi, "didn't?"

The student gave it up, fell into the nearest vacancy on a bench and slumped there sobbing. Adjacent students shifted a little to give him more room to do it. Several snuffled empathetically and were silenced by the Rabbi's flat stare.

The fact that, after slipping away from the veranda to avoid the bread, Miriam never returned had perplexed the Rabbi but not surprised him. A loss, in the Rabbi's lexicon of emotions, always involved one's dearest, otherwise it would not be a loss but a deprivation or an inconvenience or, in some instances, whether or not one admitted it, a blessing. During the year of his daughter's absence, through gossip in the market square ostentatiously hushed in the presence of the Rabbi's wife so that she could not fail to overhear it, whispers circulated from stall to stall that Miriam had been glimpsed in the Hassidic cemetery. And, it was alleged, not by the present whisperer who was only whispering what had been whispered to her, the girl danced nightly there or thereabouts clad only in gaudy scarves and illuminated by a perpetually burning aromatic bush and accompanied by a dusky musician of infernal origin, almost certainly a Gentile though wearing a cap.

When the Rabbi's wife duly reported these rumours to her husband, he evicted his students from the veranda and fell into a hermetic communion with his rocker. When it became clear to the mind of the Rabbi that – even discounting hysterical female exaggeration – his daughter had, if not married out, at least betrothed herself thither and that the arrangement was more than whimsical, he came in from the veranda, instructed his wife to soap the windows and any other reflecting surface and to replace the dining room chairs with stunted stools and to rend some expendable garments and to lay them out for him to don, and he entered a month-long period of formal mourning for one whose name was not be mentioned again without the prologue of three consecutive spits. As for the excreta of such unholy couplings, there was always the sacramentally ordained sanctuary for foundlings, mongrels, illegitimates and waifs buried so deep in the bowels of the Synagogue that the Rabbi himself had never visited it, its sordid custodianship consigned to the Shamas who by vocation was accustomed to feculence.

So the student's report was old news, current data for a closed file; Talmudic ruminations on the laying of cutlery were more pertinent. Thus, Miriam's death had been registered, recorded, mourned and absorbed long before she died. Nevertheless, the Rabbi did dismiss this particular seminar rather earlier than usual, and he sat alone in the Synagogue study room for a night and a day. Students peering in through the window said he seemed to be weeping, though the feeble flame of a memorial candle someone carelessly had ignited on the Rabbi's desk made it difficult to be certain.

Chapter Three

Sandringham

"As Prince of Wales for forty-one years, six months, three days, and a bit of a breeder ourselves, we confess we've been waiting to have our name on this trophy for nearly as long as ... other matters. This year, however, the entitled owner of the Ascot Gold Cup is M. Lucien De Hirsch of Berlin and Paris with his foreign gee-gee, Bucharest, a rather lucky winner by fifteen lengths over our own La Fleche, British-through-and-through. No matter, no matter. As we say round the stables when tempted by a filly with promise: not at the moment but next year perhaps. Of course, our dear mama wishes to add her congratulations to our own, or would if she had the slightest interest in the racing of horses, which she hasn't. She might have if her bloodlines and those of our late papa had more favoured the French than the German. Lucien, your nag's French, isn't she? Irish? Amounts to the same. Give him the cup." Albert Edward sat, eased his paunch over the edge of the dinner table and quaffed a compensatory claret.

Lucien De Hirsch stood and extended his glass in royal tribute. "Thank you, sire, and my greetings and those of my father le Baron and my mother la Barone to His Highness whose long long long patience in future bereavement is a model to us all." He smirked, sat, stroked his trophy and contemplated his entrée. Who but the English would risk oysters in midsummer? Tant pis, de miuex, peut-être une.

The table remained convivial through sorbet and the cheese plate. Every ceremony complete, the gentlemen then withdrew from the dining hall to the billiards room for cigars and, as Albert Edward quipped to the hilarity of his guests no matter how many times they had heard him quip it, "for any port in a storm." The ladies were left to do whatever it was they did after coffee.

The game was pocket billiards. Albert Edward did not play. He presided as matchmaker and referee. Particularly entertained by provocative couplings, it was he who determined the teams. This time the Prince's mischievous pairings were of elder and younger men with known agitation between them.

Laurence Oliphant found himself coupled with the Earl of Shaftesbury, now geriatric but so much his superior in every respect that, despite their slight acquaintance and shared Evangelism, he found it hard to overcome a paralyzing deference, which attitude, because of his deafness, the Earl mistook for mockery and loftily ignored. Lucien De Hirsch, whose fey Franco-Yiddish ebullience fitted him for the companionship of gamesters and other impetuosities, was coupled with the Right Honourable William Ewart Gladstone, four times Chancellor and twice (and present) Prime Minister, whose aggressive Christianity and tetchy judgementalism made the taking of offence endemic and the giving of it inevitable. Unlike their respective junior partners, neither elder smoked nor took port though, as renowned benefactors of chimney sweeps, lunatics and whores, they tried to tolerate such dissipations in others.

The participant who flourished in these confines was young De Hirsch. His bilingual chatter was vigorously risqué though, to the frustration of his royal host, mostly incomprehensible. At the billiards table the Frenchman was rapid, careless and accidentally brilliant, at one point potting both the red and his opponent's white along with his own white by a cannon off the red, thereby scoring the maximum possible on a single stroke, a feat unequalled at Sandringham since the reigning

British champion had given an exhibition performance at the inauguration of the room.

Bored by the incompatibility of the play and the incohesion of the conversation, the Prince took the opportunity to wander off to inform the women of De Hirsch's remarkable shot, leaving Gladstone and Shaftsbury to risk self-expulsion by sulking. Lucien nattered on while whizzing round the table in a turn that never ended, and Laurence Oliphant enjoyed his favoured position of opportunistic neutrality, content to contribute a stroke or two in his turn and to defer gracefully, leaving the balls in a position advantageous to his opponent. The royal arbitrator did not soon return to the billiards room, having discovered greater delights away. When eventually he did, something even more extraordinary had happened there.

Its elegant Jacobean precursor having been demolished and rebuilt "in the Old English manner" by an architect whose previous credential was a pair of royal mausoleums, Sandringham House combined a sprawled immensity without and a cramped inconvenience within. Forever undergoing inconsistent modernizations and uncoordinated modifications, its tiny unheated bedrooms were augmented by such modish considerations as "electrolier filament lamps" and "flushing water closets," and its claustrophobic corridors led to a vast recreational annex containing the ornate billiards room and, next to it in the same style and volume, an "American" bowling alley.

Presently Sandringham's ballroom was in the midst of acquiring a separate entrance off the forecourt so that the royal couple could avoid unplanned contact with the neighboring gentry or the tenant farmers or the estate servants, each gaggle of which deserving substratum was granted an annual Sandringham ball. As a consequence, at the time of the Oliphants' visit, even reputable guests invited to lodge at the palace had to enter over builders' rubble, during which passage Alice Oliphant lost a shoe, an incident with far-reaching consequence.

The disappointment of this weekend particularly was felt upon the distaff side. Twenty years a widower, Shaftsbury thoughtlessly contributed no wife to the occasion. Lady Gladstone, who possessed the virtue of being alive and the reputation of having "opinions," had been unable to attend, unconvincingly citing her work with orphans, paupers and fallen women. Flamboyant young De Hirsch, of course, was more likely to have brought along a stable boy, if permitted, and probably had a jockey concealed in his portmanteau. Whatever the various excuses, Princess Alexandra faced an evening in the appalling sole company of the wife of a notorious enthusiast.

Just look at her! Religious hysteria and mediocre birth with no idea of how to dress for the country. Pretty enough in a twitchy sort of way, the Princess reckoned, but no Jenny ("Saint") Jerome for spirit and conversation and a knowing discussion of Bertie's drawbacks in bed, no Daisy ("Babbling") Brook for lavishness and adorable indiscretion despite that vulgar commercial affair with Bertie's letters and her tendency to litigate, no La Bernhardt nor even a La Snédèr whose collective reputation as "les passages des princes" puts Bertie in his place. Even Miss Langtry would have been preferable despite a tendency to sing without provocation.

But this one! Surely not even Bertie .... No, nothing along those lines was certain. For jollity and style, however, one may as well be spending one's time with Eddy and Georgie on school hols or in the nursery with Maudie and Tonia or lying below the wall of St. Mary Magdalene Sandringham with dear little day-old Johnnie. Alexandra sighed, smiled and gave the appearance of attending graciously as Alice Oliphant once again described her tedious travail amid the continental Semites.

Well, if her travelling wardrobe resembled her present attire, what did she expect?

To the practised eye of Alexandra, a certain standard of dress remained essential. As Her Majesty frequently was heard to observe when she still permitted herself to be quoted: "Opulence is little. Temperance is all." Difficult to achieve, of course, if one is short and fat and confines oneself to two-toned ebony lace-ups with sturdy soles. But who among even the furthest fallen would wear a decorative opera slipper to Sandringham, regardless of the tiny shapeliness of the foot it advertised? Why, the operation to excavate this one from the snare of a loose floorboard on a temporary walkway over a builders' trench and the effort to remove the effects of its having lain overnight in an exposed sewer had employed a crucial member of the below stairs staff until noon!

Alexandra longed personally to return the frivolous footwear to its owner, accompanied by a rebuke disguised as sisterly advice on the vanity of flouting fashion. But Bertie already had pocketed it, doubtless intending as an expression of royal condescension and a demonstration of rural hospitality to return it himself to its pretty owner in her bedchamber whilst her equally tedious husband was engaged elsewhere. Alexandra sighed bravely and listened to Alice's palaver about exile, extermination, incineration, resurrection and revelation in an unfashionable resort called Brody for as long as she was able. Then, with the cosmetic excuse of a headache, she released the poor awkward thing to its adulterous destiny.

When Bertie entered the dining hall to report de Hirsh's magnificent billiards stroke, he found his wife alone at the table slumped in a familiar manner over the brandy. He pulled the bell rope to summon the usual discrete assistance, unpocketed Alice's wayward slipper and sauntered off along lubricous corridors to demonstrate that, at Sandringham, the irretrievably lost could easily be retrieved. That mission accounted for his long absence from the billiards room and his rumpled appearance when he returned to it. It made his astonishment at what he found there all the greater.

Long before he reached the games annex a second time, the Prince of Wales was aware of the voice emanating from it. Amplified by reverberations along the narrow hallway, the tone was unmistakable. He endured one just like it every Sunday thundering from the pulpit of St. Mary Magdalene fit to wake little Johnnie slumbering in the crypt. As he neared the door, the Heir Apparent began to discern words amid the thunder – "venture," "gain," "province," "protectorate," "conversion," "sanctification," "sphere of influence," "second coming," "miracle child," "throw of the dice" – and was able to identify the thunderer. Laurence Oliphant was systematically fracturing every prohibition of the room regarding the mention of politics, religion and wagers! Pleased to have his authority required after so long a recess and to be enabled to direct it at so self-justifying a target, Albert Edward burst confidently into the recreational chamber. He stood transfixed in the doorway, unable to reprimand anyone because no game was in progress.

The possessor of the stentorian voice, startled into silence, stood upon the billiards table at the centre of its fragile slate bed, grasping his cue like a conductor's baton. Two of the incandescent bulbs in the chandelier above him were fractured. Evidently Laurence Oliphant had been striding amid their debris, crunching glass into the hugely expensive green baize that marked his spoor in tatters ... and in blood, for his feet, like the rest of him, were naked.

"What the – " the Prince began.

"Hush!" Gladstone instructed. Then, recalling which house he was in, he appended a belated "sire."

De Hirsch whose monopoly of play had been ended by Oliphant's delightful bare-arsed invasion began a hurtling explanation in French which stuttered, tripped and fell because of the failure of even that hypersonic tongue to convey the precipitousness of events.

Shaftsbury's collapsible celluloid ear trumpet was of a three-sectional "tobacco pipe" design in faux tortoiseshell. A foot-and-a-half at maximum length, it admitted no responsibility for injuries to bystanders whilst swinging perilously from side to side in the attempt to separate foreground sound from background and to make sense of either. When it registered the crash of the billiards room door being flung open, it whirled in that direction and remained there. Renowned as a fluent and a persuasive master of cool Harrovian oratory, its owner said: "Oh!"

The silence was broken only by the crunch of Oliphant shifting gingerly from foot to wounded foot, and shivering.

The Prince of Wales found three pairs of eyes and an enormous implement trained upon him as if somehow he contained the answer to his own unarticulated query. So he articulated it. "What the fuck is going on?"

The question precipitated a cascade of overlapping Parliamentese, Evangelistics and French, from which the Prince was able to deduce two conclusions: his naked guest was mad; the madness was contagious. He raised his hand to arrest the torrent. "Yes, yes, all very interesting, I daresay, and illuminating, very. And what has it to do with pocket billiards?"

The Prime Minister's sigh was galactic. "Pardon, sire, we have been through all that."

"For our benefit, pray go through it again."

"All?"

"As much as is necessary for our understanding."

Gladstone, whose long experience of the Lower House

made him familiar with the filling of bottomless pits, stood and undertook the task. "Let me endeavor, very briefly, to sketch in the rudest outline what the Ottoman was and what he is. It is not a question of Mohammedanism simply, but of Mohammedanism compounded with the peculiar character of a lesser race. The Turks are not the mild Islamics of India, nor the chivalrous Saladins of Syria, nor the cultured Moors of Spain. The Turks, upon the whole, from the black day when they first sought to enter the West, are the one great anti-human specimen of humankind. Wherever they go, a broad line of blood demarcates the track behind them and, as far as their dominion reaches, civilization vanishes from view. Everywhere they represent government by force as opposed to government by law. Let the Turks now carry away their abuses in the only possible manner, namely, by carrying off themselves! Their Zaptiehs and their Mudirs, their Bimbashis and Yuzbashis, their Kaima-kams and their Ali-alis and their Omar-omars and their Pish-pash-pashas, one and all, bag and baggage, shall, I hope, clear out from this sacred Anglo-Saxon soil they have desolated and profaned!" Gladstone sat, his face an alarming shade of red.

"Ah yes, of course," the Prince smiled encouragingly, "and what have the Turks to do with it?"

Gladstone prepared to heave himself again to his feet. Concerned at his Prime Minister's mottled demeanor, Shaftesbury waved him off and considerately took up the challenge. "It is they who are in possession of the Holy Land."

The Prince turned his attention in that direction and shouted directly into the bell of the ear trumpet. "We see, we see. And what has the Holy Land to do with anything?"

Shaftesbury received the enhanced transmission with a wince. He stood, collapsed his hearing aid, stowed it to prevent further misuse and launched his own explication. "Is the government of this kingdom as tranquil, as secure as it was before?

Will discontent always be frowned down or rebellion always be checked with facility? Today the two demons in morals and politics, Socialism and Chartism, those twin conspiracies against God and good order, are stalking our land. But here comes the worst of all! Elsewhere than in this kingdom there is a Semitic residuum angry and excitable in itself and rendered still more so by oppression and neglect, a vast minority which is daily surrendered to the philosophy of infidels and democrats. I speak of the Jews! Unless they are reclaimed and freed from the forces that bedevil them, who can doubt their eventual recourse to the false gods of Socialism and Chartism? And who can doubt the effect on every nation including our own of a vile and dangerous compact and conspiracy between Socialism, Chartism and International Jewry? Let us catch at this opportunity that may never return. Let us betake ourselves with eagerness to do the first works and, while we yet have strength and dominion and wealth and power, let us break off our sins by righteousness, and our iniquities by showing mercy to the godless, if it may be a lengthening of our tranquillity. Daniel 4:27." Shaftesbury sat, glowing with benefaction. He extended his ear trumpet and inserted it.

Gladstone perspired.

Oliphant shivered.

The Prince yawned.

Clearly a peroration was required. Shaftesbury stood again and delivered. "Premillennialism is the vehicle! Anti-Semitism the fuel! Jesus Christ the conductor! Palestine the destination! Will the heir to the throne of this great domain but open his eyes and expand his heart to the spiritual crusade of the present day? If so, the world lies before him, and in time and time he shall be conveyed under a spotless banner through the length and breadth of this and all lands, not in a spirit of conquest and ambition, but as the moral sovereign of Divine power, spreading religion and happiness all around by preparing the way for the restoration and the protection of God's once loved people, the Jews, who may yet be loved again!" He sat again and glowed.

"Yes, yes, the Jews," said the Prince. "But the hour, you know, the hour. And at dawn tomorrow there's the shooting."

Lucien De Hirsch tried his hand. "The Prime Minister says it's good for the Parliament. The Earl says it's good for God. Laurence Oliphant says it's good for everyone and for the Jews. My father le Baron says: Mit der goyim solt der gornisht helfin. Laurence Oliphant wants a trip to the South, and why not? By the look of him, a little sun, a little sand, a little Arab .... Ah oui, mais premierement pour lui il faut faire la retour à la ville de Brody! Là il va retrouver un miracle de Dieu! Pour ça il besoin la petite bébée en present dans la crèche de la synagogue! Mais de qui et comment et pourquoi ...." The contribution dwindled to a shrug as eloquent as anything that had gone before.

The Prince stood, stretched, rubbed his eyes, scratched his crotch and began to wander off to bed. "Yes, yes, daresay. And what has any of that to do with any of – "

"I await ..." said Gladstone

"God awaits ..." said Shaftesbury.

"Oliphant awaits ..." said De Hirsch.

"... your royal – " they chorused.

At last Laurence Oliphant spoke or rather he quoted, muttering as if thinking aloud and addressing himself. The effect was more silencing than a shout. "How then shall they call upon Him in whom they have not believed? And how shall they believe in Him of whom they have not heard? And how shall they hear without a preacher? And who shall preach unless he be sent? As it is written: how beautiful are even the bare feet of the naked preacher who brings glad tidings of good things to come!"

The voice gained volume, its message intensified by decon-textualization and editing. "And the children of Israel stood before the Syrians like two little flocks of sheep, but the Syrians filled the country. And Israel cried out with one voice and saith, 'The Lord hath forsaken us, and the Lord hath forgotten us.' And the Lord replied: 'Can a woman forget her sucking child that she should not have compassion on the child of her womb? Therefore, I send thee a prophet of my will bearing a child of my loins to lead my chosen people again to Zion!' And there came Elijah, a man of God from another land bearing in his hands a miracle child born of God, and he spake unto the children of Israel and he said, 'Thus saith the Lord to me: because the Syrians believe the Lord is God of the hills but he is not God of the valleys, therefore will I deliver all this great multitude into the hands of the children of Israel so that they shall know they are my born-again children and I am their especial Lord.' And so it was that for six days the battle was joined: and the children of Israel slew of the Syrians an hundred thousand footmen as Elijah the prophet of the Lord had foretold and the miracle child born of the Lord had signified, and the thrust of the Lord thereupon was delivered and delivered and delivered and delivered and delivered an hundred-thousandfold! And Zion was reborn!"

There was a crash. Oliphant had raised his cue and fractured another bulb. Filaments glowing like meteors descended upon his beard.

Arrested at the door, the Prince felt an impulse to kneel. He shook it off and turned to his other guests. "And pray, gentlemen, the reason for our friend's, in a manner of speaking, unseasonal display of, not to put too fine a point upon it – "

"I await appropriate vestments."

Relieved that Oliphant's cerebral convulsion had not entirely extinguished his ability to converse, the Prince felt duty bound to reply. "Which are?"

"Whatever it is the royal pleasure to provide."

"Such as?"

"Prince's Special Envoy to revisit and to revive the Jews at Brody and to lead them thence into the Promised Land,. Which royal livery, were it to be conferred along with the diplomatic documentation of the presiding British government added to the moral authority of the international Evangelical movement and the fiscal resources of the universal sporting community already undertaken by the several colleagues here assembled, would be an appointment best kept secret from the ear of Her Majesty who, inspired by decades of affectionate friendship with – excuse me, Prime Minister – the late Disraeli, is bound to be unaware of – excuse me, My Lord – God's answer to – excuse me, Monsieur De Hirsch – The Jewish Question."

The Prince took a tentative step back into the room. "Indeed, indeed, The Jewish Question. And what is God's answer to it?"

"Gilead!" The response spurted simultaneously from the mouths of Gladstone and De Hirsch and, after a moment, from that of Shaftsbury.

The Prince took another step. "Beg pardon?"

"Gilead," repeated De Hirsch.

"Gil-e-ad," mouthed Gladstone to compensate for the Gallic.

The Prince rejected Shaftsbury's offer of a loan of the ear trumpet and returned to the remains of the billiards table. He stood at its periphery, looking up. "And where," he said, "is that?"

Oliphant lowered his gaze from beyond the chandelier and focused it upon the Prince. "Ask not, sire, where Gilead stands! Ask where you stand in Gilead! Ask not what Gilead can do for you, but what, together, we can do for Gilead, and Gilead for the Jew! Two thousand years ago the proudest boast was 'I am a son of Rome', Rome the oppressor of the Jew! Tomorrow the proudest boast shall be 'I am a son of Gilead.' Gilead the new traditional homeland of the ancient traditional Jew!"

Shaftesbury was not one to leave a nail-head unhit. "There is a balm in Gilead," he assured the Prince.

"To heal the sin-sick soul," Gladstone hear-hear'd.

De Hirsch shrugged sympathetically.

Oliphant lowered his cue and brought it to rest upon the shoulder of his host. "Albert Edward, patient son of the interminable Victoria Regina and the blessed hope of advancement for us all, to some who would question your ability ever to perform a worthwhile task, those of us who are privileged to have seen beyond the fallibility of your body and the vanity of your manhood into your bare and fragile soul, as one we join our voices in the collective reply ..."

Oliphant raised his cue and led a chorus of the others. "... yes, you can!"

He had fractured another bulb, the last. For an instant, as dimness descended, the assemblage was bathed in a radiant nimbus. In the market square at Brody, another inscribed stone moved. Somewhere in the Sinai, dunes shifted to prepare the way.

The Prince slipped out of his dinner jacket. He beckoned and, when Oliphant limped to that edge of the billiards table, he draped it over Oliphant's blueing shoulders. The tails were sufficiently pendulous to cloak if not to warm. On second thought he added his cummerbund and knotted it in front at a level slightly lower than the fashion.

Gently the heir to the throne assisted the descent of his wounded guest from what was now little more than a bloody baize mound. For some reason he found that he had developed an indigestible lump in his throat and an unfamiliar flu-like dampness behind his eyelids. "Laurence?" he whispered.

"Sire?"

"Do you never fear?"

"Fear, sire? Fear what?"

"Abasement?"

"Business is based upon abasement."

"Contempt, then?"

"Admiration can be purchased."

"And insignificance?"

"What is necessary is to have transacted at the highest level. That is the importance that is noted."

"And notation is important?"

Laurence stared at his host. At last he was speechless. Or perhaps it was the pain in his feet.

In her chamber Alice Oliphant prepared for bed. Her shoe retrieved at such cost lay before her on the dressing table, the metallic threads of its floral embroidery tarnished, its silken birds fallen. "Sanction and subsidy," she whispered to the mirror. It was a mantra she had repeated in her mind throughout her grapple with the Prince. Now she rinsed her mouth and prayed that she had delayed him long enough for Laurence to work his enchantments below.

Chapter Four

Brody to Succeava (Clara, part 1)

Dnieper, Dniester ,דניאסטאר, דניאפאר it was a natural mistake, anyone could have made it. And when you throw in the tributaries, well, between Styr and Stryi, there's a difference of one letter but the first leads you to a gentle journey on a lovely river across the bosom of Mother Russia to the nipple of Odessa on the sweet Black Sea and the other on a trip straight to Hell, it should be Styx not Stryi. That last part about bosoms and Styx I got from books but that doesn't make it not so.

Such a trip is better forgotten. So why keep a journal of such a trip? The truth is I didn't. I wrote it down later when we were settled in Succeava and I went to cheder and learned to write. And to spell. I wrote it down as a journal because the whole time was still as fresh in my mind as this morning's breakfast though breakfast didn't take up the whole of my childhood and that trip down the Dniester and what happened after did.

Everything would have been different if we had launched on the Styr. Brody is on the Styr. During flood-time the Styr is on Brody. You only had to slip in the mud and you were on the Styr, well, in it. If we had started out on the Styr, we could have carried on down the Dnieper. Of course, the Dnieper finally drops you off near the Crimea where they had a terrible war for a year not long ago, so I wouldn't exactly want to go there even now. But the rest of it ... such a famous Hassidic place, Chernobyl, that in Russian means "black grass," and also Kyiv with its beautiful ravine named after the old woman Shamas, Baba Yar, who sold it to the Dominicans ... well, I certainly would have liked to have seen those!

But no, for some reason Laurence Oliphant told us we had to walk from Brody all the way to the Stryi. Maybe he made a spelling mistake for Styr? Those who were too little or too old to walk got carried along with the livestock and the bedding. We walked all the way through the hills to Podgorodtsy where the Opir meets the Stryi at Nizhneye-Sinevidnoye and the dying blood of Oleksa Dovbusch who stole from the rich and gave to the poor stained the riverbank and made the red rocks that the adventurous traveller can see today, which I also got from books though the rocks are there all right and red. The books I got from Morris. I'll tell you about Morris later. From those bloody rocks we should have guessed what was ahead and turned around and gone back to Brody that, however bad it was, couldn't be worse. But no, we launched on the Stryi down to L'viv where it passes into the Dniester and everything bad happened that's in my journal.

This isn't my journal. This is from my journal. You wouldn't want to see my journal. There are things in my journal you wouldn't want to know. Like how you relieve yourself on a river barge with a hundred or so people watching, you wouldn't want to know that, would you, unless you would, in which case who would want to know you? And then after, in Succeava and in Bucharest, well, there are lots and lots of things like that in my journal, so I wrote them down there but left them out here.

So why write those things down in the first place? Have you noticed how, when something is so bad it's best forgotten, it helps to write it down because then you remember what you've written down and not what happened? It's not that you take something out of you and get rid of it. It's that you put something else between you and it that's easier to think about. At least I do. With special attention to the spelling. And it makes it easier for me to do if there's a you to be telling it to though I know it's only me telling it to myself but not out loud where people would notice and say something and then there'd be a fight.

I suppose I should start out by telling you about my family. It's not that simple. Is someone really your father who says that your big sister is dead to him just because she ran off with a fiddler in a cloth cap, a goy or worse, certainly darker, which means she died to her father a year before her daughter called Berthe was born! Is that really any kind of a father and a grandfather to have even if he is a rabbi? And then that baby niece of mine called Berthe gets given to a goy pretending to be a Jew and his wife who call her their daughter until they exchange her for me because I'm bigger and more likely to survive a trip down the Dniester! What kind of a family is that? So don't ask me about my family. I can't tell you much.

I suppose a lot of families are like that. On the barge nearly everyone's was, though not everyone's so-called father's name was Oliphant that sounds like a joke so I never took it on but stayed with my own until I could have a husband and take on his. And no one else's father of any name was to blame for as big a mistake as the Dniester! When I asked him about it later, he said "the voyage is as important as the arriving" which at the time I thought I understood but I didn't, and I still don't though the word 'voyage' is a good one. I think it's just something he said instead of that Dnieper/Dniester was a big mistake. Which is too bad because it's practically the only thing he ever said to me and I would like to know what he thought he meant.

He did look magnificent though, striding the main deck, well, the only deck, like he owned it. Which he did, or the one who sent him to us did and loaned it to him for the tr – the voyage down the Dniester to save us. That's what I remember, it's the first thing of any kind of thing about the voyage that I remember ... my second so-called father Laurence Oliphant striding the deck in his black coat and his black hat and his beard that in those days was black. Actually it's the beard that I remember. It wasn't till I got bigger that I saw he had a face. A good enough face, I suppose, though without the beard there wouldn't have been a hair on it, not even over the eyes and on the top and under the nose where it's supposed to be. It's as if all the growing that face had in it went into that beard. The rest of it looked like a baby's, a grown-up one of course, but a baby's face, round, you know, and smooth.

His hands were like that too. He touched me once on the cheek and told me to remember to say I was born-a-miracle even though it was my baby niece called Berthe who really was the born-a-miracle, not me, and I remember thinking it's exactly like being stroked by my own wax dolly.

My so-called mother, his wife, the whole entire voyage she never got wet. And she didn't mind relieving herself in public though no one could say he'd seen her do it because no one dared to look. And when my so-called father said something, she looked at him like she didn't mind anything at all. Only I never saw him touch her cheek, so how was she to know how it felt? She looked like a wax dolly too but of the princess kind. And her name was Alice which is like a princess too.

What Laurence Oliphant and his wife were saving me and the rest of us from was Brody. About Brody I mostly remember what I've been told. My big sister who ran off was the only one of us all who managed to get away from the porch and look around Brody even as far as the old Hassidic cemetery, but she didn't tell me much about it because I was too little to understand anything, and then she ran off with a fiddler in a cloth cap but a goy or worse certainly darker and she wasn't there any more to be heard by me or anyone. And then she and her fiddler died at the exact same moment of having their baby called Berthe in the exact same grave in the old Hassidic cemetery or got killed there or dumped there by someone maybe the Shamas trying to please the Rabbi and get paid for it which everybody says is something only a Shamas could do, and my big sister couldn't tell me or anyone anything at all ever again so nobody knows how her baby got taken out of her belly and got rescued from the grave and got nursed and fed and got to be called Berthe who was born-a-miracle. Nobody knows that so I don't.

And nobody who went down the Dniester wanted to talk about Brody, so I don't remember enough to need to write it down. I know that the old rabbi, my real father if that's what he really is, still lives in Brody though by now he's probably dead like everyone else there, even, probably, my baby niece called Berthe who was born in a grave to a twice-dead mother and stayed behind in my place, and I can't even begin to write down about that.

So I guess that's what the rest of us were being saved from ... being dead in Brody. Which means I was saved twice, doesn't it? One more time and I'm Messiah! Except Messiah's going to be a boy, isn't he? And he's not going to turn up in Succeava, is he? Not unless he makes a big mistake like my so-called father. Not unless he happens to be my so-called father. No, that's not another joke. There were plenty on the barge who said my so-called father was Messiah. He never said it himself, just didn't argue with those who did.

He had a rolled-up paper with a seal on it, a red seal with a crown, more a purple one really, a purple seal with a crown that no one got to touch only to look at and never to break. There was something written inside that rolled up paper that made people think Messiah was who he was. It was that rolled up paper that made the hundred or so gather round him when he got back to Brody where he'd been once or twice before but without the paper and the seal with a crown. It was that rolled up paper that made the old rabbi my father agree to exchange me for my baby niece called Berthe who was really the one who was born-a-miracle so that his own oldest still-alive daughter, me, could bless the family and wipe out the sin of her double-dead sister by doing what he called "making aliyah in the Holy Land" which meant getting out of Brody and making a voyage to that far-off place.

It was me and the rolled-up paper that made everyone follow Laurence Oliphant through the hills to the Stryi where the barge was waiting. It was me, his so-called born-a-miracle daughter, that made everyone go on that barge they'd never been on anything like before, and drift down the Stryi, and cling on down the Dniester, and put up with everything I wrote down in my journal to forget like the Yampol Rapids. So it was my fault as much as my so-called father's, though probably his a little bit more because I was a girl.

I suppose you're interested to know how a girl got to go to a cheder, a real cheder with benches and books and a lehrer, not a cooking class for future wives? It was the Yampol Rapids. The Yampol Rapids were to blame. Two days after that part in my journal someone found me stuck between the decking in a way that held my head out of the water and most of the rest of me too except for a foot. I don't remember much about that time, in fact almost nothing which I suppose is just as well. Only my nose grew back with a little bump on it and the foot a different shoe size which gave me a limp, so that was that for getting married. So instead I got sent to a cheder because I had nothing to lose. Which was where they nearly found out about me.

"Channah," the lehrer would say, "pay attention!" And I did, only not what he meant. There was no way to tell the lehrer what it was I was paying attention to because at the moment I was paying it I couldn't say anything at all or see or hear or feel or hardly breathe. And sometimes that moment went on for an hour or more. And one time it went on for six days and nights, and on the morning of the seventh I got up and had my breakfast and I couldn't tell anyone anything about any of it because none of it was there to me anymore.

Of course no one believed that. Well, I wouldn't, would you? Everyone thought I was sick or strange or a liar. Not the lehrer. The lehrer thought I had a secret. Being the so-called daughter of who I was and the substitute for my baby niece who was the real born-

a-miracle, he thought that I had a secret about what was written on the rolled-up paper behind the purple seal with a crown. And that sometimes it got so hard for me to keep that secret that I lost the power to speak and to see and to hear and to feel and almost to breathe. And that it served me right because I wouldn't tell what I knew no matter how many times he asked. And I did have a secret only not the one he thought.

The secret is I've been like that ever since the Yampol Rapids because it was at the Yampol Rapids that the lady came. She hadn't been there before and she wasn't there after. I looked for her after and I still do but she was gone and she's still gone. She was there only at the Yampol Rapids. She came in a light and she held my head out of the water. She held my head out of the water until they found me. For two days she did it. That I do remember. I do remember that. Better not to but I do. It was the lady I was remembering when I should have been paying attention to the lehrer and I wasn't. It was her light I was seeing when I couldn't speak or see or hear and the rest of it.

There was no way to tell anyone that secret, so I never tried to, not even in my journal, especially not in my journal because I didn't want to remember the lady wrong or not remember her at all even though I never exactly saw her face because of the light. I'm telling it here because now that everything in my life is about to change I had better try to forget the lady or at least to make her into something ordinary enough not to matter. I can't count on her anymore. From now on so to speak I have to hold my head out of the water myself. It's my last chance.

I said Bucharest, didn't I? But first I said Succeava. So I'd better tell you how I got to the one and then to the other and back again, hadn't I? Otherwise you'll be confused. I find it confusing but I don't see why you should have to. To explain it I'll have to go back to the Dniester. I don't really want to but I must. It wasn't the Dniester that took us so long. It was the stop-offs that did. But I suppose the stop-offs were the reason we were on the Dniester not the Dnieper in the first place if there was a reason and not just my so-called father's big mistake.

The Dnieper flows on and on through goyish countryside with peasant maidens in gingham aprons tending sheep and handsome farmers bronzed by the sun picking apples in it, the books say so. But the Dniester passes through town after town exactly like Brody with Jews and Jews in every one of them dying to get out, and never dreaming that the river is the way to do it until our barge arrived and my so-called father told them it was. Every new town a new clump of Jews, sometimes only a dozen, sometimes more, some of them families, some of them a part of a family, the part that didn't care about leaving the rest behind, all of them wanting to get out, it didn't matter where to but Gilead sounded as good a place as anywhere else and that's what my so-called father promised them.

After the meetings in their synagogues where he stood on tables and talked and talked and showed them me and told them I was his daughter born-a-miracle and waved the rolled-up paper with the purple seal with a crown, lots of them would pick up their babies and their babas and their bedding and join us.

Drocobych, Stry'y and Ivano-Frankins'k, Halych, Khotin and Mohyliv, Chisnau and Chernovitsi, Tighina and Tiraspol, Katovsk, Kolom'y-ya, Kam'yanets-Podil's'kyy and other towns not so easy to say, though I may have got the order wrong because some aren't big enough to find in books, we stopped at them all. Pretty soon there was such a bargeful of Jews that every time somebody new got on somebody old fell off. But that didn't stop my so-called father. At every town we drifted into, we tied up where we could and he went into the synagogue and talked and talked, and the people came and came, and the barge got fuller than full even though after the Yampol Rapids there was plenty of space. It's a wonder really because, once we started losing people over the side, that should have warned the next town downstream what kind of a *thing was heading their way and not to pay any attention when it tied up. And certainly not to get on board. But it never seemed to work out like that. I suppose they'd seen dead Jews floating down the Dniester before.*

And sometimes we had to slow down whether or not there was a town because of the ice. And once we had to stop. The books say the Dniester gets its water from the Caucasus Mountains so it starts off cold enough to change your shoe size, and it doesn't take a lot of winter to turn a part of it or all of it into ice. The all-of-it sort happens overnight midstream between here and somewhere else. When it happened to us, we just sat there till the ice let go of us weeks later maybe months. I wasn't big enough to know dates. How did we live during that time? I don't know. My journal is blank. But after a while there was no more livestock left and even pets, and there were fewer of us and less. And by the end of it my so-called father's beard was white, which I thought was the winter but in the spring I saw it wasn't.

We knew it was his plan to drift us all the way down the Dniester to the sweet Black Sea to end us up in Odessa where everything is good after the pogrom, and where the big boats tie up that carry you on to make aliyah in the Holy Land where he planned to do his Gilead. That's not the way his plan worked out. Maybe if he'd taken us down the Dnieper it would have.

The Dnieper is wide and gentle and in the middle of the countryside, not narrow and twisty down along the side of the Caucasus Mountains. So the Dnieper just goes on and on with no ice in the winter and no floods in the spring. But the Dniester freezes. Every winter. And the Dniester floods. Every spring. And when it floods with the melt-offs from the Caucasus Mountains, the Dniester just gets higher and higher. Twenty feet higher, Morris always says. I'll tell you about Morris later.

And after the stop-offs we made so that my so-called father could stand on a table and talk in the synagogues, and after the time we spent in the ice, it got to be spring. And we just drifted off sideways on the floods and into other rivers that got smaller and smaller and had nothing to do with the Dniester and out of them again into nowhere. There was nothing we could do about it even if we had the strength to try which no one did.

And when at last the floods shrunk back to the beds of the rivers or into the roots of the ground or wherever it is floods go when they shrink, there we were in the mud. And so we got off. It could as easily have been miles and miles upstream or down, or on the other bank that's Bessarabia unless it's Romania and not on the one that's Romania unless it's Moldova, or somewhere else along the current down to the sweet Black Sea. But it wasn't. It was where the floods dropped us off in the mud and that was Succeava. Bucharest came later. But first I have to tell you about Succeava.

It was at Succeava I had my last chance. His name is Morris. He spells well and has lots of books. Morris came down the Dniester on the barge with us, not all the way down from Brody but down the rest of the way from somewhere else along the way. His wife and his three babies went over the side at the Yampol Rapids and never were seen again, not even washed up on the shore downstream. "So," as Morris always says, "at least some of us got to the sweet Black Sea." He laughs when he says it though in a Dniester kind of a way because his wife and his babies didn't get saved from the Yampol Rapids but his books and his carpentry tools did which was exactly the sort of joke the Dniester made.

Of course, Succeava was there before we got to it. And it wasn't really Succeava that we got to. What we got to was the mud near enough to somewhere near enough to Succeava. And that's where we stayed. We gave it a name, a big name so it would get noticed, Grodno-Gubernya-Succ'va-Dn'ster, which someone must have found the first part of in a book about somewhere else.

My so-called father said it didn't matter what we called it as long as it wasn't Gilead, which he had reserved for elsewhere. But then almost right away he and my so-called mother went off to Bucharest, that definitely is Romania, to make arrangements for the rest of us to go to Odessa to get on a big boat to the Holy Land. So after they were gone, we could have called it anything and he wouldn't have known. Morris said it may as well be called Gilead because this probably was as far as he was going to get which is why he built a cheder there and got to be lehrer. I said it didn't matter what it was called because it still was only mud though I never said it out loud.

Life in Grodno-Gubernya-Succ'va-Dn'ster was good. No one drowned. We knew about floods by then, so every year everyone moved everything into Succeava for a while and then, when the water had shrunk back to its bed or down to its roots, we moved everything back to Grodno-Gubernya-Succ'va-Dn'ster to see what was left in the mud. Which was why my summer holiday from the cheder always happened in the spring.

When we got back to Grodno-Gubernya-Succ'va-Dn'ster every summer, I got to go back to the cheder when there was a cheder to go back to which was when Morris, who in real life was a furrier and a radicalist with a little carpentry on the side, built the same cheder again and got to be lehrer. And I learned to spell. And my body got bigger except for my foot that got bigger slower and never did catch up. And there were all those other changes that were no worse in me than in another girl so why write them down? But before all that I got to go on a voyage to Bucharest where there were plenty of reasons for a journal.

Chapter Five

Succeava to Bucharest (Clara, part 2)

My voyage from Succeava to Bucharest wasn't like my voyage from Brody to Succeava. For one thing it wasn't by barge. It was by steam train. For another thing it was in the First Class, which means on a bench inside a carriage. The ticket my so-called parents sent me paid for that and for my meals that were served to me on a bench inside. So I got to throw away the bag of food I brought with me, well, give it away, well, drop it out the window so that someone on a bench on the open flatbed platform carriage behind the First Class that was the Second Class could catch it. I knew that's where it would land because that's where everything else did, the smoke and the cinders and every so often a burning coal, you could tell by the scream. In the Second Class you don't get your meals served to you in a special carriage or anywhere, so I knew my bag of food wouldn't go to waste unless the wind blew it past which wasn't likely considering how many screams. And even if it missed the Second Class, it was sure to land in the open flatbed platform carriage at the end of the train that was the Third Class because that one didn't have benches and was just behind the open flatbed platform carriage carrying the horses and what they dropped never missed.

Another difference from the voyage down the Dniester was how soon the voyage from Succeava to Bucharest was over. The whole distance which is three hundred miles which takes twenty hours as fast as a steam train can voyage without stopping off took us only three days including stop-offs for coal and water for the engine and sleep for the engineer. Three days. A horse took longer.

And three and a half nights because at the end everyone had to get off in Bucharest at the Gara de Nord in the dark, and I had to finish my sleep on my suitcase until the sun came up. I did it against one of the middle six pillars at the front of the station so I was sure to get found.

A small lady whose name I never knew was sent to find me by my so-called mother who, the lady told me, I was to call Mother Alice not so-called anything now that I was grown. So I called her Mother Alice when I was with her because she liked it so much and Lady Alice to myself and to you the rest of the time.

The small lady took me from the station to where lady Alice Oliphant and father Laurence Oliphant lived. No matter how hard I tried now that I was grown I couldn't call him anything else but Father Laurence even to myself. I don't know why. Perhaps it was the white beard. Perhaps it was because calling him that made him seem only one of my fathers and not the real one whoever that was, the old rabbi in Brody who swapped me for my born-a-miracle niece I suppose. And the small lady gave me my breakfast and told me I was muddy but now that I was living at the Consulate she would soon see to that, and she gave me a warm bath not like the Dniester that was cold. The place she took me to and we got to live in was called "The Consulate." Every day people came to The Consulate to meet people. But no one except me and my so-called family got to live there day and night along with the lady who was sent to find me who cleaned me up and was small enough to live in the attic.

During that time I didn't see Father Laurence except at dinner and not really then because his face and his beard were always behind the papers he brought upstairs from the office. I didn't see him at all during the day when he was downstairs in the office meeting the people who wrote the papers or the people about whom the papers were written except every once in a while when I got called into the office to get shown off to those people or others and there he was.

Lady Alice was always in the office when I got shown off and she was always there most of the rest of the time too though sometimes I saw her go off with other ladies who looked like her which she called shopping. Otherwise I saw Lady Alice at breakfast which was when she had her hair made up in the next room and got put into her day dress in another next room and had her perfume rubbed on in a next room near enough to tell me what I was going to do that day so I wouldn't interfere with plans.

After breakfast I had the small lady whose name I never knew who was something like a lehrer though she wasn't that, of course, being a lady. She looked like Lady Alice and the ladies who looked like one another, but smaller. She showed me about making up my hair and getting me put into my day dress and rubbing on my perfume so that if anything bad happened to her I could do it to myself. Then, if there were no plans to call me into the office that day, I was let go to go off shopping. When I asked Lady A – Mother Alice herself, she told me that of course shopping isn't the same as buying so I didn't need to carry money in the pocket of my day dress only my lunch.

Bucharest wasn't like Grodno-Gubernya-Succ'va-Dn'ster. It wasn't like Brody or like Succeava. Maybe there was mud but I never went into any because everything was paving stones and wooden decking. I never stepped off, not even when a Cossack passed and a Jew needs to clear the path. In my day dress I looked like anyone and it was the Cossack who stepped off and touched his high fleece cap. Sometimes I would walk above the mud in the Lipscani district between Calea Victoriei and Bratianu Boulevard and Regina Elisabeta Avenue and the Dambovita River, and I would look at the buildings some goyim get to live in. Sometimes I would walk slowly past the shops along Calea Victoriei where even to stop to look in the windows not only a Jew needs permission. Sometimes I would actually walk into a furrier's on Blanari because I'd promised to tell Morris about furriers in Bucharest, or

into a blacksmith's on Covaci or a knifemaker's on Gabroveni or a
glassmaker's on Curtea Sticlarilor or a jewellery-maker's on Hanul
cu Tei or a shoemaker's on Cavafii Vechii because I could. No one
knew that what I had in my pocket was only my lunch. By noon I
always made sure I ended up at the Cismigiu Public Gardens that,
after Romania got to be a kingdom last year, anyone could go into
even a Jew and sit on practically any bench and have her lunch.

One day standing at the gate to the Cismigiu Public Gardens
there was a man younger than Morris handing out papers to
whoever would take one. He was muddy and he wore a headscarf
as if the sun was out. His name was Abraham (אברהם ah-bro-hem)
that means Father Of A Multitude though at first, of course, I didn't
know that or even his name. He winked at me and gave me one of
his papers that he said was in colours. I slipped it into the bodice
of my day dress which made him wink again. I read it later in my
bedroom. It was very exciting except black on white so I guess he
meant word-colours that even I can do though seldom so they
stand out like lightening in a dark sky. So here it is without the
colours.

"TO OUR BROTHERS AND SISTERS IN EXILE, GREETINGS!
"IF I DO NOT HELP MYSELF, WHO WILL HELP ME?" Nearly two
thousand years have passed since, in an evil hour after heroic
struggles, the glory of our Temple vanished in fire, and our kings
and chieftains exchanged their crowns and diadems for the chains
of The Exile. We lost our country where our beloved ancestors had
lived. Into The Exile we took with us, of all our glories, only a spark
of the fire by which our Temple, the abode of The Great One, was
engulfed and reduced to a Holy Wall, and this little spark that we
re-ignited on the eve of every Sabbath kept our hope alive until
the towers of our enemies would crumble into dust, and in our
minds and in our hearts this little spark leapt into a celestial flame
and re-illuminated the ancient heroes of our race like the martyrs
at Masada and Morass Place, and inspired us to endure the horrors

of the dance of death and the tortures of the auto-da-fé. And today this little spark has kindled a pillar of fire going before us on the road to Zion, while behind is a pillar of smoke that threatens to engulf us should we hesitate along the way. O, our nation, what have you been doing until 1882? Have you been asleep? Dreaming the false dream of assimilation? Now, thank G-d, at last you have awakened. The pogroms have awakened you. The Pale of Settlement has awakened you. The May Laws have awakened you even as they have put to sleep forever your unfortunate brethren enslaved by them in Mother Russia. Now that your ears are open to recognize delusive hopes, how can you continue to listen in silence to the taunts and the threats of your enemies and be wooed by their enticements? Where is your ancient pride, your old spirit? Remember that you are a nation possessing a wise religion, a law, a constitution and a celestial Temple the remaining Holy Wall of which is still a witness to the glories of your past. Your situation in the West even outside Mother Russia is hopeless. The star of your future is gleaming in the East, it's really the South-East. Deeply conscious of all of the foregoing and of the true teaching of our great master Hillel whose words "If I do not help myself, who will help me?" still inspire us:

WE PROPOSE ... 1. to promote our national ends by the formation of a Society guided by an elite whose members will be called upon to make sacrifices in their private lives including abstaining from marriage in order to achieve their exalted purpose ... 2. to name our Society "BILU" according to the first letters of the Hebrew motto, based on Isaiah chapter two, verse five (בית יעקב לכו ונלכה Beit Ya'akov Lekhu Ve-nelkha) that means "Let the house of Jacob go!" or better yet "House of Jacob, come let us go!" with a U instead of a V so you can say it ... 3. to divide the Society of BILU into local branches according to the number of its members, all the branches to be administered by a Committee, and the seat of the Committee to be in Jerusalem when we get there ...

4. to accept unfixed donations and unlimited contributions from any of our brethren and sympathizers everywhere in the whole entire world over even if they happen not to be Jews.

WE WANT ... 1. in the Holy Land once again a homeland as our own free and independent country that was promised to us by the mercy of G-d and is ours as is registered in the archive of biblical history ... 2. in Constantinople to ask of the Sultan himself our ancient entitlement and, if it be impossible to obtain it from him or even to get an interview, to beg it of his representatives that we may at least possess a state within his larger state with an internal administration of our own where we may have our civil and our political rights and be expected to act with the Turkish Empire so as to help the Sultan and his representatives only in their times of need and their foreign affairs such as their wars.

WE HOPE ... 1. that the interests of our glorious nation will rouse the national spirit in rich and powerful men from the whole entire world over ... 2. that everyone else, poor or poorer, will give his best labours and sincere respect to our blessed cause.

שְׁמַע יִשְׂרָאֵל יְהֹוָה אֱלֹהֵינוּ יְהֹוָה אֶחָד Shema Yisrael Adonai Eloheinu Adonai Echad, that means "Hear, O Israel, the Lord our G-d, the Lord is one, and His land of Zion promised to us is our only hope."

GREETINGS BROTHERS AND SISTERS IN EXILE! G-D BE WITH US AND WITH ALL OF YOU! Yours very truly, the fourteen pioneers of BILU.

Of course it might be more exciting with the colourful words. But that noontime in the Cismigiu Public Gardens I hadn't read it yet so I didn't know how exciting it was without them. Abraham followed me in through the gate and he took off his headscarf and he sat on my bench, and that was exciting too. After a while we stopped sitting on the bench and we sat on the ground with our backs against the bench and our legs straight out. It wasn't very *comfortable but that didn't seem to matter. Which was when he told about me his name and how to spell it and what it means. And he told me about my name, Channah (חַנָּה cha-no-ah,) which means Favour or Grace unless it's really Chaniya (חַנִיָּה cha-nee-ah) which means Encampment or Resting Place unless it's really Sarah (שָׂרָה shoh-ray) which means Noble Lady or Princess and that's the name G-d gave to the wife of Abraham. And Abraham happened to be his name too, but he didn't much like it and was thinking of changing it to something shorter and more up to date like maybe Brahm. I told him I would rather be Clara and he said in that case he would be Billy. I asked him what about the name Berthe, my lost baby sister who was born-a-miracle, and he said he didn't know anything about it but he would try to find out.*

We talked about other things too like how different Bucharest was from Brody where I and my people were from and Kharkov where he and his people – he called them his comrades – were from, though mostly I forget what other things. We shared my lunch because he didn't have any, and some of the time we didn't talk at all which was the best part. When he looked at me over his half a sandwich, there shone out of his face a light I saw only once before and it may have been a dream. But his face I could see. And this time when I didn't say anything it wasn't because I couldn't but because I didn't want to, and with all my words and spelling and his there was nothing that was needed to get said. We didn't even say to one another that we would be on the same bench at the same lunchtime every day that I wasn't called into the office or that he had no papers to give out somewhere else, because we knew that we would be. So I went back to The Consulate, and that was my best shopping day ever.

Of course shopping in Bucharest wasn't the reason I got sent for from Grodno-Gubernya-Succ'va-Dn'ster. The reason I got sent for was to live in The Consulate and get shown off to someone or other every once in a while for as long as it took. The lehrer lady showed me what to wear and how to behave when I got shown off. Mainly it was day-dresses and being quiet. Mainly I got shown off in Father Laurence's office to a roomful of men who looked like him or to a roomful of ladies who looked like Lady Alice. I stood in the middle of the pattern on the carpet and they talked about me and other things. I got called born-a-miracle and daughter-of-G-d though I think they meant the so-called daughter of my so-called father the so-called Messiah. Then I still had to stand there in the pattern while they talked about other things. I was told not to listen to the other things but how can you do that when you can hear?

Some of the other things I heard I thought about later until I understood them. About the ones I didn't understand even after thinking I asked the lehrer lady. And sometimes she explained them to me. And sometimes she didn't because she didn't understand them either like the May Laws and what is a radicalist. In the whole of The Consulate there were no books like Morris's to look such things up, only papers about other papers. Father Laurence and Lady Alice must have understood everything without books because mostly it was they who got to talk about what got talked about. But I couldn't ask either of them about anything because I wasn't supposed to have listened to what I heard.

Mostly what got talked about in the office was what Father Laurence and Lady Alice called The Strategy. Mostly The Strategy had to do with The Eastern Question that wasn't a question but an answer, and with The Jewish Problem that wasn't a problem but a solution. Sometimes they talked about Constantinople and Damascus that were places, and about Turkey and Syria that were other places but bigger. And quite often they talked about Sultan Abdul Hamid who lived in Constantinople and Turkey and couldn't be seen because he was the Sultan, and about Governor Ahmet Pasha who lived in Damascus and Syria who could be because he wasn't. And it was what to say to them or to those of them who could be seen that The Strategy was mostly about.

What also got talked about was where we are which is Bucharest and where that is which is Romania. The lehrer lady could tell me about those because she'd always been right here in both. She told me about them while she was making up my hair and putting me into my day-dress and rubbing on my perfume. She said that, if Bucharest and Romania are a part of The Strategy, it must not be a good part. And when she said that she seemed to get even smaller.

You see, the lehrer lady explained, in the olden days before my so-called family and the rest of us arrived, Bucharest and Romania used to be owned by the Sultan of Constantinople and Turkey. Then he had a war with the Czar of Moscow and Mother Russia and he lost. And the Sultan got very poor and sad and angry, and had to move out of lots of places that he owned, and one or two of those places were Bucharest and Romania. And everyone in Bucharest and Romania got very poor and sad and angry when the Sultan moved out because the Czar didn't move in.

In the olden days the lehrer lady used to live in a building of her own in the Lipscani district with other goyim between Calea Victoriei and Bratianu Boulevard and Regina Elisabeta Avenue and the Dambovita River. When she lived there, she herself got herself done up every morning by ladies whose job it was to do her up. But when she got poor along with Bucharest and Romania, she had to move out of her building to live in the attic of The Consulate along with Jews, and do the job of doing up me. And, she said to me but mostly to herself, while all of us Jews were enjoying ourselves voyaging down the Dniester, Romania got to be a kingdom but couldn't afford to have a king or, if it had one, nobody knew his name. Which is why nowadays even Jews even from Moscow and Mother Russia are allowed to stay here, and not even the lehrer lady knew who it is who's supposed to tell us to get out.

Which made her sad and angry. The lehrer lady helped me to understand all that. But when I told her that getting Jews out of Bucharest and Romania is what The Strategy is all about, she said she didn't understand why Jews lucky enough to be ignored would ever want to leave the place that ignored them. And then when I told her about all of us getting to go to Gilead, she said she didn't understand why living in The Consulate and looking like anyone and going off shopping wasn't good enough especially for Jews. So I had to think about those things by myself.

What helped me in my thinking was one time getting shown off to a lehrer called Moses (no, really!) Gaster and his students from a cheder called University Of Bucharest. They called themselves Națională Comitet Bucuresti because they were all from Bucharest which definitely is here in Romania, which was where they went to their cheder, excuse me, university. I knew they were all from Bucharest and Romania because, except for Moses Gaster, Lady Alice couldn't pronounce their names and Father Laurence couldn't spell them. They looked more like an army than a committee but they couldn't have got into The Consulate if they'd called themselves that.

What also helped me in my thinking was The Loophole. The Loophole was a part of The Strategy, the most important part. Father Laurence had thought it up all by himself except for Lady Alice, so that made it even more important. What helped me in my thinking was listening to Father Laurence and Moses Gaster talk about The Loophole. Or, really, listening with Moses Gaster and Lady Alice while Father Laurence talked about it.

You see, in the olden days before his war with Moscow and Mother Russia that he lost, the Sultan of Constantinople and Turkey didn't actually live in Bucharest and Romania because he couldn't be expected to live everywhere he owned just because he owned it. And after the war it was only Constantinople and Turkey that he didn't have to move out of because he still owned those, along with Damascus and Syria which was where the Holy Land was and where Gilead was going to be, all of which were too far away for him to move into which was why Governor Ahmet Pasha had to do it for him.

But before the war, Father Laurence explained, the Sultan did own Bucharest and Romania, and he could have lived here if he'd wanted. Likewise anyone who lived in Bucharest and Romania could have lived in Constantinople and Turkey or anywhere else the Sultan owned because that was what owning something meant – whether it was a building on the paving stones in the Lipscani district or a cheder in the mud in Grodno-Gubernya-Succ'va-Dn'ster – that you could live there and nobody could tell you to move out.

And after the war the new king of Bucharest and Romania – So there was a king! Which news made the lehrer lady cry though not in a sad way when I told her, and his name was Carlos so that everyone could say it and spell it. That new king made up a new word that explained it all. Romanian! It meant born in Romania. And that included Bucharest so you didn't have to say it all the time.

Lots of kings were making it up at the same time that King Carlos was. The Czar made up that people born in Mother Russia were Russian. The Kaiser made up that people born in Germany were German. The Emperor made up that people born in Austria or Hungary – or Moravia or Bohemia or Galicia or Silesia which are fun to say – were Austro-Hungarian. Only – and this was the most important part of The Loophole – not one of any of those kings ever made up that Jews, no matter where they were born, were anything other than Jewish! Which made the lehrer lady cry again in the same way when I told her because, although she was still poor and sad and angry and small, she was Romanian and I wasn't.

Which meant – and this was The Loophole itself – because after the war the Jews in Romania weren't allowed to be Romanian, they must still be what such Jews were before the war which is Turkish! Or Jewish-Turkish which must have meant the same back then though it was too long to say every time. And that meant those Jews were still allowed to voyage to Syria and to Damascus and to the Holy Land and to Gilead when there got to be a Gilead, and nobody could tell them not to go or tell them to move out once they were there! Now, wasn't that a part of The Strategy worth waiting for?

When Father Laurence explained The Loophole to Naţională Comitet Bucuresti, his whole beard smiled. And Lady Alice looked at him and cried in the same way that the lehrer lady had but prettier, which made the students cry a little too. Only Moses Gaster didn't smile and he didn't cry. What he did was he said he wanted a volunteer to go to Constantinople to find out whether The Loophole really worked. All the students wiped their eyes and put up their hands, so Moses Gaster had to choose. The one he chose was probably the best student because, as soon as he was chosen, he asked who was going to pay for his ticket. And Moses Gaster said Laurence Oliphant would pay because The Loophole was his idea and, if it really worked, the whole Naţională Comitet Bucuresti would get to be called Naţională Comitet Elephant.

And Father Laurence said he would be honoured, and he put his hand into his pocket. And Lady Alice sniffed a little and tried to smile. And the students cheered. And Moses Gaster said they would all meet again when the volunteer got back, and he and his students took Father Laurence's money and marched out. Then Father Laurence explained to Lady Alice to consider it an investment not an expense, because the Sultan did whatever the Governor said to do, and he knew Governor Ahmet Pasha very well or had met him once, and in any case the rolled-up paper with the purple seal with a crown along with the miraculous presence of the so-called born-a-miracle daughter-of-G-d surely meant – Which was when Lady Alice noticed I was still there not listening but hearing, and she told me to go shopping. It was the first time I heard her yell.

At Cismigiu Public Gardens when I told Billy about it all, he laughed and laughed and nearly choked on his half a sandwich. And that made me laugh too. And it was another best day. Then the very next morning I got up and had my breakfast and had my hair made up and got put into my day dress and had my perfume rubbed on and got sent for and went downstairs to the office. This time there was a roomful of fourteen young men who looked more like a gang than an army. They were muddy and wore headscarves. And one of them didn't look like the rest. And it was Billy. And he was crying.

The reason Billy was crying was that during the night Father Laurence had got a telegraph message from the volunteer in Constantinople that said the Sultan had told somebody to tell the volunteer to tell the Consulate that, whoever Laurence Oliphant was, he was right (stop) and Jews born in Romania before the war were Turkish and could go to the Holy Land (stop) and no one could tell them to go back or to move out (stop) and Naţională Comitet Bucuresti could now be called Naţională Comitet Elephant (stop stop).

What the telegraph message didn't say but what it meant was that Jews born anywhere else other than Romania like Mother Russia weren't Turkish and couldn't go to The Holy Land and couldn't stay there. And that was The Sultan's Loophole. And Father Laurence hadn't known about it until last night when he got the telegraph message, and he hadn't slept much since then. That loophole in The Loophole was what Father Laurence had just explained to the fourteen comrades from Kharkov which was why some of them had their heads hanging down and their headscarves trailing on the floor. And the rest of them were telling Billy they were going to keep on trying to get permission and maybe go anyway without it and so should he, but he was crying into his *headscarf and I knew he wouldn't try for long.*

Lady Alice, who didn't much like to watch others crying, said in a loud voice that someone had to go back and tell the hundred or so who had come on the barge down the Dniester that Grodno-Gubernya-Succ'va-Dn'ster was the end of their voyage, and to forget about the Holy Land and Gilead, and that Laurence Oliphant sent them his blessing and wished them continued good luck. And now that there was no use for me in Gilead because I too couldn't go to the Holy Land, it was me who got chosen go back to deliver the message.

Billy had stopped crying and was listening and hearing. When he and his comrades were on their way out because it was time for Naţionaḷă Comitet Elephant to come in and hear their good news, he passed me his wet headscarf. It had a note wrapped in it saying to meet him in the Cismigiu Public Garden at lunchtime tomorrow to say goodbye forever or to make a plan.

And none of it mattered because the next morning after breakfast both the Oliphants, my so-called mother and father who were British from Britain and could go anywhere and stay as long as they liked and anyway weren't Jews, already had left for Gilead along with the Naţionaḷă Comitet Elephant, and I already was at the station with the lehrer lady waiting for the steam train that would take me back to Grodno-Gubernya-Succ'va-Dn'ster to deliver my bad news. She told me not to worry because I could get married now that my face was grown so the bump on my nose isn't so big, and with a day-dress down to the ground no one can see my different shoe sizes. And she gave me my food in a bag.

So this time I get to voyage in the Third Class where you don't drop anything out the window because there isn't a window, and there's nothing to distract you from writing everything down in your journal except for the horses, and most of that can be wiped off. And this time I have lots of things like Billy at the Cismigiu Public Gardens not to tell anyone before I tell Morris that we're

getting married. And all those things need to get written down in
my journal so I can forget them now that everything in my life is
about to change. And that's what I've done.

Chapter Six

Odessa to G'dera Outpost (Billy, part 1)

You never turned up so that made it easier. I'd been wavering I admit it. But after that heartbreak you gave me at the Cismigiu Public Gardens I never did waver again not once just went straight off and joined up with the comrades and got bound for the Holy Land and for doing what it took to get us there and to keep us there with or without permission for those of us as stayed. I expect it was my crying made you not show up so I'm sorry about it. I've never cried since not even when there was just as good a reason or better. Well maybe once. But I'll tell you about Yankel Zentner later. As for the business of names Billy is close enough to BILU so that after a bit the comrades took to it and Billy is what I got called for as long as I stayed.

That's the one thing that heartbreak you gave me at the Cismigiu Public Gardens did for me I never expected ... made a man of me who does what he wants to do for as long as he wants to do it and not what he gets told to do by someone official or by others especially a girl. I even started speaking up at meetings every night which was something I'd never done before on account of losing my breath when I tried and not having so much to say as the other comrades who could say it better especially Yankel Zentner.

Also I started voting which we did a lot at every meeting. Mostly I voted on the side of the others and mostly so did everyone except maybe Yankel. We voted on everything from what to do right now to what we should have done back then to what we're going to do another time to what we ought to vote on next. I know *that sounds silly to you who never got to vote on the Yampol Rapids or who to have for a so-called father or such. But that's what we did every meeting ... voted even though as Yankel always said not one of was yet a worker of the world or a Son of Zion neither an ox nor a Holy Ox so we were bound to get it wrong.*

Of course some of the comrades were all for going to Constantinople to read out our paper at the Sultan and to show it to him in colour. Yankel Zentner was all for that because he'd helped to write it out and colour it in. Really he'd done most of it himself with cribs from THE TALMUD he'd picked up at cheder and still recalled. The book of holy magic called THE KABALLAH came later and I'll tell you about that when it's time. Yankel read out our paper at us at the start of every meeting and he just couldn't see how words like those wouldn't convince anyone even a sultan. Especially a sultan who got paid to listen better than anyone who wasn't him or else why was he The Sultan and the other only a Turk?

Some of the comrades said we shouldn't have let ourselves get stopped in Romania by a goyish businessman who knows everyone and says a lot and doesn't do anything and when he does do something it's wrong. Yankel Zentner said instead of The Sultan maybe now we should go right up to the very top which is to the one who wrote out the famous rolled-up paper and sealed the famous seal with a crown but he's in England and how in G-d's name to get there even Yankel had to admit he didn't know without a Baedeker that we couldn't afford. So instead we had a meeting and we voted and we went to Odessa. Everyone knew how to get to Odessa without a Baedeker though not how to get out of it.

Odessa is very pretty. You'd love Odessa. I did as much as I could love any place after the Cismigiu Public Gardens. For one thing there hasn't been a pogrom in Odessa since the last one last year and that one was ten years after the one before it and just as many years plus a couple after the one before that one. And the

*first was so big it took three times as long to get round to the next.
And the last was even bigger so things are likely to stay just as they
are for as long as it takes to build up enough of us to make it
worthwhile to have another. Which is why no one who comes to
Odessa stays too long. Jews I mean. In the meantime, it's very
pretty.*

*First off there's the steps. I don't mean the steps that are
everywhere all over any town. Those are just steps and Bucharest
has them too to keep you out of the mud. I mean the ones they call
The Odessa Steps because you can't see steps like that anywhere
else except Odessa and only one set there. You never did see so
many steps all in a row up and down a hill for as far as you can
look and further still with a statue of a Frenchman on top. I don't
know where they go to those steps or where they come from but
when you're on them it seems you're always just in the middle and
there's always someone just behind you going up or going down
though when you turn around to see who it is it's not who you were
expecting. I kept thinking it was you but it never was. So I got off.*

*Of course like in any other place like Kharkov or probably
Brody or even Bucharest there are parts of Odessa that are older
than you need to bother with. The part you're mostly seeing was
drawn up by the Frenchman of the statue at the top of the steps.
He was someone official who ran off from France to save his head
and talked the first Alexander of Mother Russia into giving him
the job of drawing up Odessa just as he'd done back home at Paris
and Versailles for The Sixteenth Louis Of France.*

*He drew up all those French streets with a pencil and a ruler
and then they got built up like that and the houses and the palaces
too. If there was one of any one of those on one side of the street
you could be sure there was another just like it only backwards on
the other side. It made it easy enough to find your way around
from street to street in the dark but hard to remember what house
you lived in on which side if you'd lost count. And because some of*

those places that were the same only backwards were so big they were miles apart such as palaces or squares or parks or boulevards it was only the Eye of G-d that could see the sense in it all and of course the eye of the Frenchman. In Odessa a lot of it got improved by the war that blew it up.

Then there's the beach and the girls wearing not so very much which seems even less when it gets wet. I tried to imagine you were there among them, but I couldn't because of your day-dress.

Then there's the sea. For all that talk of it being sweet it's not nor black. It's just the sea only I suppose not so bitter as some though I've only tasted that one. It's blue when the sky is and grey the rest of the time. From the shore you can't see the end of it. And then later when you're on it and you can't see the shore and there's no end anywhere and you really are in the middle only this time not seeming to move and nowhere to get off and not glad and not sad just there ... well I surely do hope that where you are is a better place.

And then there's the part of the shore that's just big boats which is where we spent most of our time in Odessa trying to get on one to get out. Finding a big boat to the Holy Land was hard mainly because we had to find fourteen. That was the strategy ... to go to the Holy Land one by one so nobody official would notice you were going or you were there. And even if somebody official did notice and stopped you and sent you back or worse what were the odds of that happening fourteen times? So some of us were bound to get to the Holy Land and we would wait there and the ones who got stopped would try again. After all it took Moses forty years to get there and he never did so why not us? It was Yankel Zentner who said that though I couldn't see the point.

Yankel was the shortest of us but a reader and a writer who knew a little about a lot. And he could talk enough for all of us and did. It was Yankel who was our most tragic case and I have to tell you all about him so that you'll be able to understand all about *the rest of us including me should you ever happen to receive this which you probably won't because I don't know where to post it to except Grodno-Gubernya-Succ'va-Dn'ster and that sounds made up. Be that as it may.*

Yankel was the son of the sons of rabbis. He said he was descended from Rabbi Moshe Zentner though why he wanted to mention it is one more mystery about him or just another thing he said that might or might not have been so and even he wasn't sure. A nice enough fellow though religious and political. Everyone liked Yankel but no one could stand him which didn't matter all that much because while he was talking he didn't notice and he never noticed because he was always talking sometimes to someone real sometimes to G-d or Karl Marx.

The trouble wasn't what Yankel said because you couldn't remember a thing though you'd heard it. The trouble was the way that he said it ... not so much to you as at you in a voice that wasn't high and wasn't low but always in the middle exactly in the middle never moving from the middle and on and on and on and on and on not for as long as you thought but longer than you could stand unless you were maybe G-d or Karl Marx. Which made you think he was right about his long line of rabbis especially Moshe Zentner.

Yankel was the last of us to get to the Holy Land because he said it was important for him to read out our paper at every captain of every big boat at Odessa to show that captain how important it was to take a comrade on board. And mostly Yankel managed to get to do the reading-out part. But one time or another one of us or another would get him busy doing one thing or another like explaining THE TALMUD or Karl Marx or estimating the Odessa Steps. And then he'd forget to read out at the captain of one big boat or another. And those were boats that took us. When he finally found a captain deaf enough to take him he must have spent the whole entire time of that whole entire trip, I mean voyage, reading out at the sailors because as soon as they dropped their anchor at Jaffa they threw him into the harbour and he had to float to the pier. The moment we saw the splash we all said that's Yankel and we were glad that at last every one of us was in the Holy Land and we didn't have to wait at the dock every morning anymore. So we went to the end of the pier and fished him in and pulled him out.

"Hot" he said when we pumped most of the water out of him "isn't it?"

The Holy Land is hot. Not just when the sun is up but in between times too. Flies like it. And just when you think it can't get any hotter it does. Flies like that better. And in between the winds that can tear out your hair the dust just hangs there waiting to get breathed in like the flies. So it's not only your head you have to keep covered with your headscarf but your mouth too which is hard for someone like Yankel who talks and talks and spits a lot of dust and swallows a lot of flies. So I bought him a headscarf because when he arrived his had sunk.

When I got to the Holy Land I had to go to the Arab market and buy a new headscarf for myself because you have my old one don't you, though I expect by now you've thrown it out like me. I felt sad buying myself that new headscarf so when Yankel got on shore without a headscarf I threw mine away and I went back to the Arab market and I bought two and gave him one. Doing it that way meant that headscarves aren't so important are they because I could just as well have kept the other one couldn't I and where you're concerned I have to keep on playing such tricks. Besides a lovely bit of chequered cloth and hand stitching ... those market Arabs know how to make a headscarf you have to give them that. So from time to time I bought a few more in case another comrade lost his or just to keep and to look at. By now I've got lots of headscarves so you're welcome to yours.

Another thing about the Holy Land ... it's full. I didn't so much notice at Jaffa because it's a city so of course it's full though mostly with Arabs. But in the Holy Land even the countryside is full in an empty kind of a way like an old old family bed that's been lain in for so long by so many it's as if they're all still in there lying on top of one another doing who knows what to who knows who and there's no space left for you and me. And who'd want to lie there anyway and be just another of them which is dead? The countryside of the Holy Land is full like that. Especially with Arabs. It makes it hard to breathe.

And it's full of names as well. There isn't a place that hasn't got a name to it. It doesn't have to be a city. It can be a mountain like David ran up to get an olive or a cave like Simon Bar Kokhba hid in from the Romans or a temple like Goliath used as a footstool or a cesspit like Solomon's with two limestone shitholes ... someone sometime has given it a name usually his own or a hero's or G-d's. And mostly that name hasn't changed. Or if it has like Battir from Battar or Indur from Endor or Jib from Gibeon or Nablas from Neapolis or Yalo from Yalu or Yazur from Azura or Jerusalem from Yerushalayim or Hierosolyma or Salem or any one of the sixty-seven others making up the seventy different Jerusalem-names in all ... then you can work out what it was from what it is and you can use your BIBLE like a BAEDEKER.

Even in the desert, of which there's a lot, there's no place you can stand that's not been stood on before though it's always just looked like sand. And even that no-place has a name like Onan's Oasis or Cain's Quarry or Lot's Saltlick or Jacob's Well But Esau's Knot which is a BIBLE- joke. The Holy Land's full in that kind of a way. There may be nothing there but it chokes you.

There's nowhere as full as the Holy Land. Everywhere you turn there's some place else. Everywhere. Just everywhere. Worse than the flies or the winds or the dust it's that kind of full as makes it hard for you to breath. It's like drowning without water. I couldn't tell the other comrades that or they would tell me to quit. And no one tells me what to do. Not after the Cismigiu Public Gardens they don't. Since then I have to tell myself. All those people in all those places with all those names and hearing them all together when any one of them gets said ... well it makes it hard for you to breathe doesn't it though I couldn't tell even Yankel that because he wouldn't understand any more than anyone else would except for maybe you. Besides Yankel liked that kind of full. He liked it a lot. He couldn't get enough of it though there was enough of it to get. Way too much of it for me.

It was Yankel who told me about the names. Not just me. He told all the other comrades he could get to listen to him or would pretend to or were just too slow to escape. He told us about the names because knowing one name or another was what the book of holy magic called THE KABBALAH is all about. Naming names and twisting them around is THE KABBALAH-way of how you make new things out of old things such as a garden out of a desert and something out of nothing such as a golem out of mud and big things out of little and good things out of bad and other such holy tricks that are explained in THE KABBALAH though you need someone like Yankel to explain the explanation.

Knowing about names also is a way to meet girls though I never saw Yankel with any because he was short. Maybe I shouldn't be telling you that because it makes me at the Cismigiu Public Gardens seem insincere. Though you're never going to read any of this anyway so why not say it? Which I just did because that's the kind of man you and that heartbreak made of me. And while I'm saying what's what instead of only saying what does you good when you write it down like you do I may as well tell you there's been other girls since you. Well one girl which probably is worse. And since I've gone this far I may as well tell you she's an Arab. There. Now you know something only the comrades do. And she sold headscarves in the Arab market so meeting her was also because of you.

Also it happened because we were lucky enough to rescue

Yankel on the exact same day as Karl Netter's funeral. Lucky for us though not I suppose for Karl Netter. The way things turned out maybe it wasn't so much good luck as a bad sign. It turns out that Karl Netter was a young businessman who got old too soon and it was his time in The Holy Land that did that to him. So his funeral should have been a warning to young men full of hope such as BILU that maybe we should have stayed in Odessa. But when Yankel, who was still full of seawater, heard what the commotion at the dockside was all about and where the crowd carrying pictures of Karl Netter was marching to he lifted his head out of his puddle and he said, "Follow that funeral!" It was the next thing he said after "Hot isn't it?"

From the way Yankel looked it could have been the last thing he'd ever get to say so of course we did what he said and picked him up and followed the crowd and he threw up and dried off along the way. Which is when I noticed that his headscarf had sunk and I decided to go to the Arab market to buy him a new one which is where I met – but I already told you about that. What I haven't told you about is Karl Netter.

As funerals go his was a good one with lots of honey cake and wine and enough speeches for the rest of us to find out what Yankel mostly already knew ... about the charity business Karl Netter made in Paris to help defend Jews against Arabs in the Holy Land ... about the business deals Karl Netter made with The Emperor in Constantinople to be able to buy some places in the countryside of The Holy Land for Jews to pick oranges in ... about the cheder Karl Netter made in Jaffa out of his own pocket to teach Jews the business of how to be Holy Land farmers before he tried living in The Holy Land himself and ruined his health and went back to Paris where he lived except for visits like the last one to The Holy Land that killed him. The last part of which even Yankel only found out about at the speeches at Karl Netter's funeral when he had thrown up enough sea water to pay attention.

By the end of the speeches Yankel was up and dry and eating honey cake and talking at everyone official about the Constantinople deals and the Paris charities and finding out how to get BILU invited into Karl Netter's cheder at Jaffa to learn to frighten off Arabs and to pick oranges and writing down the address.

When the rest of us tried to express our condolences that, although Karl Netter was only a little better than what THE BIBLE says is middle-aged, he was dead. Yankel who had been putting wine where there had been seawater expressed them for us. "Out with the old in with the new!" he yelled which everyone official agreed was exactly in the spirit of Karl Netter to say nothing of G-d and Karl Marx.

So that's how I and Yankel and the comrades got enrolled in the Mikveh Israel Cheder of the Alliance Israélite Universelle on Karl Netter Boulevard in Jaffa City Palestine Syria Ottoman Empire across the street from the Arab market where Ghufran sold headscarves.

Her name was Ghufran.

At the Mikveh Israel Cheder you wore a hat instead of a headscarf. A hat the size of a straw umbrella with a hump on top. And pyjamas. Loose linen pyjamas two sizes too big being hardly enough. You looked like a bag with legs and sleeves under an upside-down basket and exactly like everyone else except taller or shorter or shorter still like Yankel because even the pyjamas couldn't hide that. Together we looked like an army of scarecrows out to pick oranges and to frighten off Arabs by making them laugh.

Ghufran laughed when she saw me. Which made me laugh. I laughed so hard I snapped the cord on my pyjama bottoms and had to use my hat with the hump for cover. Which was when Ghufran stopped laughing. Then she showed me to go into the shadows behind her market stall to re-tie my cord. Then she came *behind to help me to re-tie it. If you take my meaning. There. Now you know something even the comrades don't.*

I wasn't the only comrade at the Mikveh Israel Cheder who spent most of his time across the street in the shadows behind the Arab market. Lots of us except Yankel did. Well all of us did except Yankel. Instead of classes we went across the street into the shadows one by one so no one official would notice. No one official did. Not even Yankel who was learning a lot at classes especially words some of them Arab. I suppose you could say every one of us was learning a lot but different things not all of them at classes not all of them words.

With Ghufran and me our names were the only words we knew how to say to one another. So she said mine though it sounded more like Belly when she said it and I said hers that I suppose I said wrong too. It was Ghufran (غفران g-f-r-n) which I later found out from Yankel means Forgiveness or Pardon though maybe it only means Beg Pardon. Anything else she and I said we said with our hands or our faces or we gave it up and didn't say anything at all which was better.

It got to be a bit tiring standing up in the shadows behind the market. I couldn't invite Ghufran to my place that was a barracks so she invited me to hers that was a tent.

Her mother fed us radishes and potatoes at a low table with the other children. Her father spoke Syrian and Turkish and English and French. And Latin and Greek and Assyrian and Babylonian. And BIBLE-Hebrew just in case. He said we could use the double hammock instead of the single cot if we didn't bounce too much and disturb the goats. But first he would have to give us a M'uta marriage that can be for one night only and doesn't need a divorce. Or else in the morning he would have to give me a hundred lashes which punishment is called Hudud and would be less if it was rape that could be paid for by retaliation that's called Qias and would be none if it was murder that could be paid for by blood-money that's called Diya. So as well as passing a pleasant night and a lot more after that I learned some Arab words even Yankel didn't know. And by now if you and I were ever to meet up again and get married you'd have to be my second wife or if you want to count the M'utas every time my one my hundred and thirty-seventh.

As for the Mikveh Israel Cheder we only went for a few months because Yankel who also had learned a lot outside his classes got the Alliance Israélite Universelle to give us another invitation this time to be pioneers on a farm of our own. And besides that now we were at the Holy Land, instead of waiting to get in Yankel stopped reading out our paper at us at the beginning of every meeting every night and took to reading out Karl Marx instead. And that's where it said to unite and to get to work out in the world that was where you went to when you didn't have chains which even Yankel had to agree in our case probably meant classes. So we quit the Mikveh Israel Cheder before any of us knew everything there was to know about oranges and how to frighten Arabs. And we went to be pioneers on a farm of our own at Rishon LeZion.

All the comrades except Yankel took along someone from the Arab market. So I took along Ghufran and she took along her father who besides giving out lots of M'uta marriages to all of us had lots to talk about with Yankel in lots of languages no one else talked except in THE BIBLE. Ghufran's mother and brothers and sisters got left behind with the goats.

Rishon LeZion was hard. The ground was stones which is what the desert is before it gets to be sand. We cleared away some of those stones and what was under them were bigger stones. Well actually, Ghufran's father cleared the stones and we looked under them but we never found the ground at all not the sort you could use to make oranges which Yankel had learned the beginning of how to do at Mikveh Israel Cheder but he never got the chance at Rishon LeZion.

Of course the stones that were cleared away could be used to make walls. Which is what we did. Well actually Ghufran's father did ... one stone on top of another round and round until they joined up in a square with a hole in the middle to get in and to get out that sometimes collapsed. We would have got him to put branches across the top from side to side to make a roof to keep out the rain but there were no trees. Or rain.

So we lived inside the square without oranges and it never rained. The walls kept out some of the wind and the dust and our hats kept out some of the sun. Nothing kept out the flies. I gave out dozens of headscarves but still we swallowed lots. Big stones were smoother than small ones for sleeping, though sand would have been softer, and in a few thousand years all the stones would be that. Another thing we learned at Rishon LeZion was you don't have to frighten anyone away from what no one else wants.

The one thing we had at Rishon LeZion was grapes. Not a lot but some. And if you followed where they led out into the countryside not some a lot. The grapes had vines and the vines had roots and those roots were long enough and strong enough and wanted enough to live that they pushed their way down through the cracks between the stones and somewhere far away they found something like the ground and in that bit of ground they found something to eat and to drink. Grapes after all can't live on grapes like we did.

Now I look back we should have done like the roots ... dug down instead of piling up. At one meeting Yankel read out the part of Karl Marx that talks about deadwood at Moselle which we should have known in our case meant stones at Rishon LeZion and we should have voted for the living things over the dead because a bit of ground would have been better than a lot of walls. At least we would have got some oranges to go with the grapes. But no. We voted to pile up stones to keep out wind and dust and we got what we deserved ... a little private property and a lot of collective pain.

Do you know what eating grapes does to you? Not grapes for dessert only but grapes for starters and main course and afters? Grapes for breakfast and lunch and dinner for seven months? Do you know what that does to you? Don't ask. Anyway it did that to every one of us many times a day and that includes the nights. No one can say we didn't leave our mark on Rishon LeZion.

And what with the grapes every day and the square every night with every couple there trying to bounce on stones ... well Ghufran and I didn't get much sleep or anything else much if you take my meaning.

Not all of it was the fault of the voting. Rishon LeZion means First To Zion. BILU got there second. Before us in the same place were Hovevei Zion Des Juifs Mondiaux that means Lovers Of Zion For Jews From The Whole Entire World Over. This branch had only been in Zion a few months. And only ten of them. But just our luck from Poland!

Of course no one at Rishon LeZion was there because Rishon LeZion was where he was from. Everyone there was there from somewhere else. There were us fourteen BILU who, like everyone we knew and anyone we'd ever known, were all from Mother Russia. There were those that got brought along with us like Ghufran and her father who were Arabs and didn't count as anything to do with Zion except they belonged there. And then there were – But Poland. They may as well have been from Beyond The Pale like Grodno Gubernya.

To tell you the truth nobody belonged at Rishon LeZion for long. Not the comrades like us who wanted to find a new place to love as much as the old one that got taken away from them and hoped that this was it. Not certain other Jews I could name who no one knew what they wanted because they didn't love the place they were from almost as much as they didn't love anyplace else they got to especially the place they were in.

Those Hovevei Zion Des Juifs Mondiaux! They blamed the whole entire Mother Russia for kicking out the French and making Poland such a terrible place for Jews than which any other place was better. And they blamed the whole entire BIBLE and all the Jews in it for getting kicked out of Egypt and making such a terrible place as the Holy Land to be the chosen people of. And they blamed every one of one another for being a Jew from Poland stuck in Rishon LeZion when there was no one else around unlucky enough for them to blame such as any Jew from Mother Russia.

So when we got there they blamed BILU for the whole entire lot of it. And like Yankel always said did I defeat Napoleon? Did I burn Warsaw? Did I hang Romuald Traugutt? Did I invent the Czars? Did I? Well did I? And he said he knew what he meant when he said it. What he must have meant was it wasn't like he was a Turk. And that was what he wrote in his letter of complaint to Alliance Israélite Universelle. Why are Jews from Poland like that ... so bitter not even an orange can sweeten? I don't know do you? Until you told me different I thought maybe Brody might be in Poland and I feared the worst. But then at the Cismigiu Public Gardens I found out different didn't I? Oh Clara!

So anyway Alliance Israélite Universelle who'd given Rishon LeZion to Hovevei Zion Des Juifs Mondiaux told them to give a part of it to BILU so we could make a farm of our own. So they gave us the part without the well. We didn't see them again until we tried to borrow some water and they and their well had gone. They loved Zion but they didn't love Rishon LeZion or us. Why they also took away their well we never did find out. Yankel said it was to save the water in case they came back but wouldn't putting a cover with a lock on it have been as good as filling it in with stones?

So that's how the dead things won out over the living ones at Rishon LeZion. For shelter we were left with walls. For water we were left with stones. And grapes. A hard place. Until the Messiah came.

It wasn't really the Messiah just your so-called father the goyish businessman from Bucharest called Laurence Oliphant and his wife who had been sent to us by the Alliance Israélite Universelle because of Yankel's letter of complaint. In his bright white suit under his bright white helmet with his bright white sun-blisters at first we didn't recognize him. But he was carrying the famous rolled-up paper so we did. His wife was rolled up in a blanket under a parasol so we never got to see much of her. Still rolled up she got down from her camel that was white and we could see that her slippers were of the sort that flatten at the front and she walked on her toes in a kind of a dance that hardly touched the stones. She and the Messiah called Oliphant took a look around and nodded at one another and smiled like they'd been told what to expect. Then they went through the hole into the square and chose the smoothest stones and sat down and told us what to do and got up and left. Which is why we moved to G'dera Outpost which was the opposite of what they said.

Out of the fourteen comrades there were ten of us remaining. Out of the four who weren't remaining there were two dead of grapes. Nobody said a word about the ones who weren't there but weren't dead or even counted them or asked ... not even their own Arabs who waited a day or two to see if their Jews had maybe got lost picking grapes. Then those Arabs deserted back to the Jaffa market.

The comrades who weren't there but weren't dead weren't to blame for what they did. And if they were we weren't the ones to blame them. It was just exactly like Yankel always said Karl Marx always said ... rightness or wrongness such as sticking with the ones you're with or quitting is all tied up with what you work at or don't and what you produce or don't and what you consume or don't. And when you're working but you're not producing such as us with the stones and the walls and when you're not producing but you're consuming such as us with the grapes no one has the right to call *anyone right and no one has the right to call anyone wrong. Only G-d and Karl Marx. Or something. So we never said a word good or bad about those comrades who had quit. We just never mentioned them again which was bad enough. We looked forward instead. And that kept us hoping for the best. Like G'dera Outpost.*

Of course it was Yankel who found out about G'dera Outpost. Even before we left Jaffa to go to Rishon LeZion he'd found out about it from Alliance Israélite Universelle just in case. But it wasn't until fourteen BILU became ten that he mentioned it to us at a meeting. Yankel said that where Rishon LeZion was hard G'dera Outpost was soft because there was grass. Only it was a long voyage to get there. Right to the edge of the Negev, that's a desert. And of course there was only one camel. Did I mention the camel? Odessa the steps ... Jaffa the market ... Rishon LeZion the stones ... no, I don't believe I did. There was a camel. We didn't find it. It found us.

One day going out into the countryside to pick grapes we saw the camel coming in out of the countryside picking grape leaves. It limped past us. When we'd got our fill of grapes and come on back it was lying half-outside the square under a pile of stones licking its feet. It had tried to get in but its hump had made the hole in the middle of the wall collapse. We knew before we arrived that a camel was there. But we didn't smell so good either so we dug it out. It stayed on hoping for the best. We called it Karl.

Ghufran's father said maybe it should be Carlotta because unlike with goats with camels everything faces in the wrong direction and is difficult to see without getting bitten. After a while everyone with a vote agreed to Carlotta except Yankel who said such a matter of science should be unanimous with no abstentions and he couldn't have an objective opinion because he'd already been bitten twice trying to look. But by the time they'd finished discussing him Karl knew his name and it was too late. Karl knew other things too. Like the way to G'dera Outpost.

A camel hates stones. Its feet are big and flat and soft and get cut by stones. The only reason Karl limped into Rishon LeZion was because he loved grape leaves more than he hated stones. But as soon as he'd got his fill he wanted to quit Rishon LeZion and get to somewhere soft. And so did we. And so we packed him up with my spare headscarves and such and we let him lead us to it.

The voyage to G'dera Outpost on the edge of the Negev took us forty days and forty nights. Yankel said that was a bit ironic considering that these Jews were wandering through the Holy Land looking for a desert. And following a camel who was following us. Mostly lady camels lead the way. Mostly men camels follow so they know it's safe. Karl would only follow so probably he was not really a Carlotta. So Yankel said that maybe Ghufran's father didn't know everything about the Holy Land because a goat is only a goat but some things even an Arab has to find out as he goes along like a Jew about a camel.

Besides hating stones and loving grape leaves ... in fact any leaves even the desert ones with spikes on because he's got padded lips and chews with his mouth open ... a camel makes a dung that makes a smoking fire when it gets cold at night. And he walks through wind and flies and dust by using his double eyelashes and closing his nose. And he drinks enough for a week in ten minutes which is before a farmer knows you're using his well. And he growls when he's happy and barks when he's not and throws up when he's really not or just excited. And a camel won't go anywhere with anyone even with another camel unless it seems like he's in a caravan. So on our voyage to G'dera Outpost every one of us went single file in a straight line and Karl went last growling when we were on the right track and barking or throwing up when we weren't like a general leading from the rear.

Also a camel can count. The Holy Land has three deserts. In different directions. We visited them all. The Negev was the third. It covers more than half the Holy Land so why we didn't go there *first and how we missed it twice you'll have to ask Karl. Maybe because the Negev has stones? And some of them are mountains?*

Of course the Negev also has sand though you have to walk between the stones to find it and up across the mountains and down along the dried-up dents where there are rivers once or twice a year because the ground is baked too hard to swallow the rain that runs along the dents into craters that seem as deep as the mountains are high and the rain lies there and stinks and makes a home for the flies. Or you can stand still and wait till the sand finds you which is when the wind turns it into dust. So if we hadn't gone to the Negev I suppose in time the Negev would have come to us.

The Negev isn't what you and I and those books you like and a BAEDEKER would call a proper desert. The Negev is a desert as big as a country that can only be crossed by a camel with hard feet. So once he'd found the Negev for us Karl voted to stay with us on the edge of it at G'dera Outpost though I think he would have preferred there also to have been another camel of whichever sex he wasn't because camels can tell the difference.

When we finally arrived at what Karl decided was G'dera Outpost there were goats. They were black. Like the grass. The goats liked G'dera Outpost because that was where they were. They liked Ghufran's father who liked them because they were goats though black. In a vote they would have chosen him as their goatherd though Arab. It was just as well the goats were there. They gave Ghufran's father something to do. After forty days of walking single file collecting camel dung and forty nights of sitting in smoke burning it and bearing in mind that black grass soup has the same effect as grapes of keeping you alive wishing you were dead he didn't have a lot of M'uta marriages to perform. And none at all for Ghufran and me.

Also Yankel wasn't available to talk BIBLE-languages with Ghufran's father because he'd taken to spending most of his time

*reading the magic holy names in the book of holy magic called
THE KABBALAH, twisting them this way and that to try and
figure out exactly where we were and whether this really was
G'dera (גְּדֵרָה ga-da-roh) or whether Karl had made a mistake and
we were really somewhere in Canaan (כנען kna-an) on the ruins
of the city of Ekron (עֶקְרוֹן eq-run) that worshipped Baal and was
destroyed by the second Nebuchadnezzar of Babylon in THE BOOK
OF DANIEL and deserved it. In which case where we really ought
to be was further south and further east in Shephelah (הַשְּׁפֵלָה
ha-sha-fa-lo) near the ruins of the fenced cities blessed by G-D in
the same book on the slopes of the Judean mountains that are
green and fertile and look so good from a distance instead of where
we were which was on the edge of the stones of the Negev that no
camel can cross without hard feet and certainly not Karl who slept
with his back to it.*

*So for occupation Ghufran's father was glad of the goats. In
his spare time he made black-grass goats-milk cheeses that he
stored nearby in the craters in the sand of the Negev where they
ripened and stank. To make room for the cheeses he cleared out
the driftwood that had got washed to the bottom of the craters and
from it he built us a wooden tent big enough for everyone that
sometimes collapsed.*

*Of course Ghufran's father did try to look for the ground
under the sand because at least it had made what might have been
real grass before turning black. But all he found was a patch of
something like somebody's old garden, thick sand with radishes
and potatoes already in it that we should have kept for seed but
didn't. When those ran out it was back to black grass soup and
what it did to us and to the stinking cheeses Ghufran's father
loaned to BILU until we could afford to pay him for them.*

*At one meeting when we were still having meetings Yankel
read out the part of Karl Marx that talks about Political Naturalism
that says that the way a man produces his food depends on the*

food he finds in nature and reproduces and that the food he reproduces and consumes makes him the kind of a man he is. At G'dera Outpost we were the kind of men only Karl and the goats didn't mind the smell of.

It must have been the smell that attracted the Bedouin who were always in the market for something recently dead. They rode into G'dera Outpost out of the dust of the Negev on their Bedouin camels that didn't have hard feet but got eaten when they began to limp which encouraged them not to. "They have violated our boundaries and dispossessed us of whole tracts of our land and we are helpless" is what Yankel wrote in a letter of complaint to the Alliance Israélite Universelle asking for help against the Bedouin. Which everyone at the meeting agreed was good for a letter though it wasn't exactly true.

When The Bedouin first arrived they parked their camels in our radish and potato patch to browse on the stumps of what to them was camel food. And they made a circle outside our wooden tent. And they took out their long, curved knives so they could squat comfortably around their king. And they signalled to us to squat in a circle outside their circle and to wait for the king to speak.

The king of The Bedouin took out his knife that was longer and curvier than anybody's and he pointed it at Ghufran's father who was trying to hide behind Ghufran. And he smiled. So Ghufran's father came forward and squatted at the side of the king. Then the king pointed his knife at us and he smiled. So we stayed squatted in our circle and waited.

Then the king explained to his brothers who explained to their cousins until they found a distant cousin who could explain to Ghufran's father to explain to us that the king and his Tent – he called them his Tent instead of his Tribe the way he called himself their king instead of their sheik or their emperor – came to deliver a hospitality that it's dangerous to refuse and to accept a baksheesh of one-tenth of our wealth that it's not advisable to withhold. For the hospitality-part the king of the Bedouin showed us a chunk of dried-up camel meat that he and his brothers and his cousins planned to offer us as a gift so we could make him a Bedouin feast of welcome. For the baksheesh-part he wanted his payment in advance.

Then he stopped speaking. Then he stopped smiling. Then for the first time he looked around and sniffed. Then he looked at his brothers and his cousins who looked at each other and shrugged because they'd been looking around for a while and sniffing. At last even the king of the Bedouin began to understand that even ten-tenths of nothing was going to be nothing. So he took back the gift he'd offered which was the chunk of dried-up camel meat that now he said was an acceptable baksheesh for us to pay to him though a little less than he was owed. So he added on a piece of G'dera Outpost to make up the difference which he said actually made G'dera Outpost bigger by joining it to the Negev such was the magic of G-d.

Then the king of the Bedouin said this black shithole is a pretty place to breed holy white doves in and the brothers and the cousins of his Tent rattled their curved knives in agreement. Ghufran's father whispered to us that in the Bedouin language Bey means White and Douim means Dove which adds up to be Bey-Douim or Bedouin which is the name of G-d's people who are so holy that we'd better not protest. None of us was intending to protest and Yankel liked the naming of the names in that last part so much that he decided not to send another letter of complaint to the Alliance Israélite Universelle but a letter of contentment.

Then the king of the Bedouin stood up and put away his knife and mounted his camel and galloped back into the dust. And so did his Tent. They all returned to G'dera Outpost every so often to count their doves and to recite poems at each other and to add on another piece of us to the Negev or the Negev to us for another good reason.

Although G'dera Outpost may have got bigger every time a piece of it got taken it did get smaller in another way. Oftener and oftener there were more and more of us not to blame for quitting. Every month it got harder and harder not to count those who weren't dead but weren't there. The comrades who remained kept on trying to encourage Ghufran's father to find us some patch of ground to improve our Political Naturalism but by now what was left of G'dera Outpost was so full of holy white doves that as soon as the leaves of a baby plant got above the sand they ate it before Karl could. It was easy to see that the longer we stayed at G'dera Outpost the more of the Negev part of it and the less of BILU there was going to be.

Which was when the Messiah came a second time. The Alliance Israélite Universelle had read Yankel's letter and had told your so-called father the goyish businessman from Bucharest called Laurence Oliphant and his wife to make a meeting with us and to have a word. By now those of us who remained on what remained of the real G'dera Outpost, if that's what it was, were ready to listen not just to hear.

This time the camels of the Messiah called Oliphant and his wife weren't white. They were donkeys and grey. His donkey was too short for the Messiah's legs so the bottom of his bright white suit wasn't white but the colour of every bit of the Holy Land between here and where he'd come from. So was his beard. He didn't get down although from a donkey like that it would have been up. The other donkey dragged a litter where the Messiah's wife lay rolled in more blankets than before. What colour her blankets used to be was impossible to guess. Perhaps she was wearing no slippers of any shape of toe because this time she never got out of the litter to do her little dance. So the meeting was where we stood which was our vegetable garden that was dead.

The word of the Messiah called Oliphant didn't take long because he needed to get his wife back to where he said there was *civilization. His word was this. The Alliance Israélite Universelle wanted us to go to up to Zammarin. Just us. Not our Arabs because the rules of the Alliance Israélite Universelle said that a few Arabs are enough which there were already. Their Jews in Zammarin were in trouble and only their Jews in worse trouble somewhere else could help. Yankel's letter had been like an application for the job. The Messiah said the Alliance Israélite Universelle said their Jews of BILU at G'dera Outpost should have a meeting and discuss it and vote to go to Zammarin. Then he hit the donkeys and left.*

In fact it was at G'dera Outpost that we'd stopped voting. When fourteen become ten and ten become five plus a camel what's the point? Also what's to discuss? Everyone knows what everyone else wants to do or doesn't and that's what gets done or doesn't no matter who gets left behind. So we had a meeting where we stood. We looked at one another. And we left our Arabs where they were and we went up to Zammarin that later got called Zikhron Ya'akov which is another story.

Chapter Seven

Zammarin to Gilead (Billy, part 2)

Zikhron Ya'akov wasn't like G'dera Outpost. Not even like G'dera Outpost without the black grass and the Bedouin. Zikhron Ya'akov wasn't like Rishon LeZion that, even without the stones, wasn't like any place except maybe Poland. Zikhron Ya'akov wasn't even like Zikhron Ya'akov because when Yankel and me and the others of BILU got there its name was still Zammarin and not even Yankel knew what that meant though it should have been Heaven.

So here's the story of how Zammarin got its new name of Zikhron Ya'akov. You need to know the story because I told you in the Cismigiu Public Gardens that the meaning of names is important and so is the naming of them. As Yankel always said that the book of holy magic called THE KABBALAH always says – But I'll tell you about THE KABBALAH later. First things, as Karl Marx always says, first.

You have to pass through the hills of the forest of the Carmel mountains to go up to Zammarin which is hard to do. Not hard to go up. Hard to want to pass through. For Karl, who was only a camel, it was such a feast at every step that we had to remind him to keep on with the climbing.

It's so dark under the trees. Yes trees. It's as if you're wearing a hat of leaves instead of straw. And if you look up here and there through the brim you see tchotchkes of sunlight like sequins or stars. And if you look down there are flowers. Flowers in a forest. Not like in a blanket. More like in a headscarf. A chequered headscarf except every square is a different shade that when you get up close is flowers. Forest flowers each the size of a nothing. A *dot of dye. A stitch of coloured thread that when you add on a thousand and then a thousand more is a swatch and is a strip and is a bolt of silk flat-folded in a rainbow at your feet. Then from on top of the Carmel mountains it's the end of trees. And you look down on the other side. And far far down there's the sand. And then there's the sea and a bright white little boat and then the sea again and still the sea. The sea so blue. So blue and green. So green and grey and something like – Exactly like your eyes. Excuse me Clara I should get so personal.*

The forest of the hills of the Carmel mountains on the way up to Zammarin is like that. Even a fire in such a forest couldn't hurt and it came and it went before we arrived and twice again before we left. And after every fire there were more trees and more flowers than before and once again the air so clear so sweet so moist you could take it for tea without the sugar. And that was the trouble. From the hills comes the forest and from the forest comes the air and from the air comes the malaria that I've not heard they have in Heaven.

When the malaria came to Zammarin there were a hundred there from Romania. When it left there were half. What was worse it took the children. Those it didn't kill it made into idiots. Then it killed them. Then it took the women especially the pregnant so once again you could say it took the children. It even took the birds from the air and the chickens from the fields and the rats from the barns and killed them too. Then it started to take the men even the men of BILU. Which was when those who hadn't yet been taken decided to quit. But to quit they had to pass down through the forest of the hills of the Carmel mountains that was full of what it was that made them quit ... the malaria. So even to quit was denied them.

Then G-d sent a wind and after it some sun and some dust and some fire in the forest and the malaria was gone. So when we built stone walls at Rishon LeZion to hold out the wind and when we wore straw hats at G'dera to keep off the sun and when we wrapped ourselves around everywhere so we shouldn't breathe in the dust ... that was the opposite of what you should do for the malaria. And until G-d sent a bigger one a smoking fire of camel dung also would have helped. Who knew?

When we arrived at Zammarin most of the Jews there were what was left of the army of students from Bucharest who along with the Messiah and his wife had stolen our permission to come. Permission .... no permission ... so? So by now half of them already were gone from the Holy Land or from the world along with more than half of us plus the wives they'd picked up on the way and their children plus our Arabs that we had to leave behind. In such a devastation how could five BILU from Mother Russia plus a camel make a difference? So why were we there? We were there to beg for money.

The students from Romania needed the money to build up Zammarin after the malaria. They needed Jews from Mother Russia to show that the money would go for helping Jews from more than Romania. If Jews from here and Jews from there and Jews from the top and Jews from the bottom were building up Zammarin it would look like the money was helping Jews from the whole entire Europe or maybe the world. Such a thinking was important to the man who would give the money. Such a man was floating below us in his bright white little boat waiting to be begged. His name was de Rothschild. The delegation that got sent to beg from him was two from the students who were the best one and another one not so good. And two from BILU who were Yankel and me. Plus your so-called parents the Messiah called Oliphant and his wife who had been told by the Alliance Israélite Universelle to go along with us to visit de Rothschild to make sure we got listened to. Which the Messiah did but his wife was already dead.

The first thing you noticed about the bright white little boat was it was only little from the top of the forest of the hills of the

Carmel mountains on the way up to Zammarin. It was bigger from the beach and got bigger still when the sailor with a cap written "Aliyha" on the brim took you out to it in a rowboat written "Aliyha" on the front. By the time you arrived where it floated it was a great white cliff that moved against the sky with "ALIYHA" written on the side. There was a ladder hanging down you got pushed up from behind. It was the sailor in the rowboat who pushed saying sorry all the time. What did he have to be sorry about? Yankel was sorry. Sorry he came. He had to be pushed up from behind and pulled up from in front. When he finally got to the top he looked back down and said "oh" and threw up like a camel. So then everyone else was sorry who was on the ladder down below Yankel.

The next thing you noticed when you were on the top and being washed off by other sailors with "Aliyha" written here and there even on their skin was how not one of them spoke not even to one another not even to say sorry. And when they made a sign to tell you where to follow and what to hold on to when you tried to walk on a wet metal floor that moved up and down they never looked at you in the face only just above your head or into the middle of your chest. It was like you were there but they weren't which wasn't perfectly true because everyone was there but some definitely were there more than others and on ALIYHA the one who was there the most was de Rothschild who was somewhere down below. So when the sailors took you down below and vanished as though they'd never been there at all that was perfectly true but not exactly.

Down below the first thing you noticed was that the room they put you into was an office and it had a mezuzah outside on the doorpost but no chairs inside except for one behind a desk that was as big as a camel. Yankel said the first thing he noticed was that every door we passed along the way had a mezuzah on the outside though as far as he was concerned on any boat the only room that deserved a mezuzah-blessing was the one with the motor inside that took you home. The best student agreed but included the bedroom for the sailors who were goyim and needed a blessing because who knew what they got up to? The next best student sat on the floor of the office and held his stomach and whimpered and added on a blessing for the room somewhere that held the toilet. The Messiah called Oliphant said everyone shouldn't say another word because there was someone behind the desk. Which was when the desk said, "how much?"

No one could see who said it except the student on the floor who whispered that under the desk there were two small feet dangling. So the Messiah read out from a paper he'd written and given to each of us a copy so we shouldn't let him make any mistakes. He read out the part about the great honour it was to meet the Baron Edmond James de Rothschild of Château Rothschild d'Armainvilliers and Château Rothschild Boulogne-Billancourt who is the son of his honoured father the Baron Jacob Meyer de Rothschild of Château de Ferrières and Château Lafite Rothschild who was the son of Meyer Rothschild who was the son of Amshel Rothschild who were loan-bankers of Jew Alley in Frankfurt. Though how you could meet someone you couldn't see the Messiah's paper didn't say.

"No names," said the desk. After which no one made a sound except the student on the floor who crawled away and threw up in a corner and crawled back.

"No names," said the desk again in case the student on the floor hadn't heard.

"Let me assure you honoured sir," said the Messiah "that throughout the Diaspora and even beyond to the courts of St. Peter and St. James the name of Baron Edmond de Rothschild is synonymous with selfless generosity and pious – "

"Names or money. Choose."

"But Baron what are we to call you if not – "

"That."

"What?"

"Baron."

"Ah."

"And *you* are?"

"In the Holy Land I have the honour to represent the independent settlement of Gilead."

"And *you* are?"

"Laurence Oliphant."

"The *goy* Oliphant?"

"In Europe and the Holy Land I have the honour to represent His Royal Highness Albert Edward the Prince of – "

"The *goy* Oliphant who says Jesus will come again as if once wasn't enough?"

"The Earl of Shaftesbury and all premillennial evangelists actually maintain that – "

"The *goy* Oliphant who says that when Jesus comes again foreskins will grow back?"

"Mmph."

After that no more got said. Then sailors came in and started to take the Messiah out. When he said, "No. Why? What's happening?" more came in and he was gone.

"How much?" said the desk.

"For what?" said the best student.

"For where *you* live."

"Zammarin," said the best student "isn't for sa – " Then he leaned down to rub his ankle where the next best student accidentally had kicked him.

"Not to own as it is. To make it into a farm."

"Zammarin is already a fa – " The best student's other ankle also began to trouble him.

"A farm that makes more than malaria. And around it a town with a winery and a synagogue with a marble altar and a tower with *a copper water vessel on the top and pigeons and hanging gardens for fancy built in straight lines by a Frenchman. How much?"*

The best student wasn't satisfied. If Zammarin was going to become another kind of a farm he wanted to know what about the first sabbatical year. Nobody, not even the desk or the Messiah knew what he was talking about so the student read out from his own paper of which he hadn't made a copy because he couldn't afford it. He read out the part in THE TALMUD about letting the fields rest every seventh year that doesn't mention what you eat that year. And then he read out other parts with rabbinical opinions about five kinds of grain with a different prayer for each before it will grow and about what to do when you slice more bread than you wish to eat or serve more fruit than is needed and about who of the poor deserve to get which part of what remains after a feast and about –

"How," said the desk "much?"

Setting aside such important Talmudic matters as the proper benedictions to be said at the fragrance of flowers and the beautiful sights of nature the student said he also had prepared some arithmetic in advance. And although he was no accountant he thought it added up to a number of one or two thousand or three though that part of the paper had got wet in the rowboat on the way out and maybe it could have been as much as –

"Four hundred thousand," said the desk.

The best student started to say no the smudge wasn't big enough to have been that much when he got kicked further up both legs by the second-best student and he stopped.

"If," said the desk.

"If?" said everyone together.

"If the name is changed from Zammarin to Zikhron Ya'akov."

Everyone waited for all the rest of the ifs and after a while Yankel spoke up for the first time. "Jacob's Memorial. So who's Jacob?"

"Our father Ya'akev de Rothschild," said the desk. "Alev ha-shalom."

"Amen," said Yankel.

"I thought," said the best student, "no names?" and got kicked by Yankel.

"And the synagogue and the winery," said the desk.

"Also Ya'akov?" said Yankel.

"But not the water tower."

"Which is?"

"Brichat Binyamin."

"Benjamin's Well. So who's Benjamin?"

"Our uncle alev ha-shalom because he wasn't so well. Hah."

"Amen," said Yankel.

The rest of us said "Hah."

"But not the hanging gardens."

"Which are to be called?"

"Ramat HaNadiv."

"Benefactor's Height," said Yankel. "For four hundred thousand a benefactor certainly. But are you sure you don't want to get mentioned by –"

"Done?" said the desk.

"Done," said everyone even Yankel. And we were.

On our way out the best student whispered to Yankel, "I thought he said no names."

"No living names," Yankel whispered back. "By Turks it's not permitted."

"By Turks dead names are permitted?"

"For Jews."

The Messiah was outside leaning against the doorpost under the mezuzah muttering about saving the name of Laurence Oliphant from the stain of being attached to the name of Edmond de Rothschild who only helped colonies at the price of petty tyranny and the next time we should go to the English Rothschilds who didn't need a "de". Without the doorpost he couldn't stand especially on one side. So we helped him up the steps and down the ladder into the rowboat and we held him so he shouldn't fall out.

Then we voted and it was decided the Messiah needed to be taken home instead of left lying on the beach. Because I hadn't said anything at the meeting I was the one who got voted to do it and the rest of us got to go back to Zammarin. So it was me who got to put the Messiah on the hump of Karl who had been rolling in the sand and growling with pleasure and it was me who got to take the Messiah to his home that was named Gilead. Thank G-d it wasn't the Gilead in the Bible that was days away in another part of the Holy Land that wasn't so holy. The Messiah's Gilead turned out to be a so-called farm near the Carmel mountains not far from but lower down than what used to be Zammarin and was now going to be Zikhron Ya'akov.

So Clara I told you I would tell the story of you how Zammarin's name got changed and now I have. So now maybe you'll also be interested to hear what happened to your so-called father The Messiah after I put him on the hump of Karl. So I'll tell you that too.

All the way to Gilead he bumped and swayed and muttered about being let down. At first I thought he meant he wanted to get off the hump of Karl of which there are plenty of places more comfortable but he only was talking about what had happened to him since he came to the Holy Land.

Considering the famous rolled-up paper it was a big surprise to me how many famous people had let him down. First off there was the Sultan Abdul Hamid who told someone to tell Laurence Oliphant that THE HOLY KORAN told everyone who bothered to read it that the end of the world would come when Jews were returned to the Holy Land and having just got through a war with Mother Russia no one was in a hurry for that to happen. Then there was Laurence Oliphant's good friend Governor Ahmet Pasha who was supposed to tell the Sultan not to be so stupid but instead got himself arrested and executed in the palace garden before he could tell anyone anything. Then there were the rabbis throughout Europe who praised Laurence Oliphant for his speeches and his letters and his books about returning Jews to the Holy Land and called him The Messiah and then blamed him for the rush to make aliyha that had emptied their synagogues. Then there was everyone from Count Bismarck to The New York Sun who didn't succeed or even try to raise by public subscription the baksheesh Laurence Oliphant needed to buy himself a concession to build a railway through the Holy Land over some property he already held shares in which would have been a blessing to all such was the magic of G-d. And now that bloody bedamned de Rothschild who wants to own everything without some partners or even some – But of that exact let-down his muttering went on so fast I can't tell you what he said. Through it all Karl growled and barked as if he agreed. And when the Messiah got excited about de Rothschild he threw up.

Gilead is very pretty. You'd love Gilead. No you wouldn't. I didn't. Gilead is empty. Empty like the Holy Land is full of those no longer there. At Gilead the Messiah's late wife alev ha-shalom had left her mark on every part of the place ... beside a fountain with no water a fallen easel with dried up bottles of paint ... in a millpond full of mud a broken statue of a lady with little breasts or a man with none ... hanging from a tree a swing on ropes with no cushion for a seat ... on the veranda a hammock of silk. You could see there'd been a donkey or two and a pig and a dog and a rabbit or several because their kennels still stood but the doors were gone. There remained chickens because Karl stepped on one and sat on another.

At first the Messiah didn't want to get off Karl's hump so I helped him to do it. Then he didn't want to go into the house so I helped him to do that but he would only go in as far as the veranda. Then Karl and I tried to leave which was when I noticed that except for the Messiah and me there was no one at home not even an Arab. And the Messiah was still bumping and swaying and could hardly stand especially on one side. So to help him out Karl and I stayed on a couple of days. Which became months.

There was a sort of a garden planted with flowers not from the forest of the Carmel mountains but from England. Anything else in the garden the chickens ate except what they couldn't reach like the grapes that were from California in America and weren't supposed to do to you what the others did but I couldn't make myself want to try. By accident there were also some radishes and potatoes so I lived on those and so did Karl. The Messiah lived on the soup I boiled from the chickens Karl sat on and eggs from the ones still living. I no longer like radishes and potatoes. And crushed chicken with camel hairs I can take or leave. And eggs I'm sick of. I tell you so you'll know just in case.

Even when I got him off the veranda for a walk the Messiah wouldn't go into the bedroom. So I slept in there on one of the two narrow beds with a high bookcase between them. I slept in the first that had a mattress instead of in the second that had a board. The Messiah slept on the veranda in the hammock of silk with his arms spread out like on a cross to keep from rolling off.

The bedroom inside must have been theirs because it was the only one. Except for the second narrow bed there wasn't any sign that it had been his too. I suppose it was a lady's room though not a lady you and I would know. The walls were painted red. Dark red almost black like blood that's been there too long. There was a rail all around the walls from which hung pretty paintings of the fountain at a time when it wasn't dried-up and the millpond when it wasn't mud and the statue when it wasn't broken and the swing this time with a cushion and the hammock of silk. And in the painting of the hammock was someone with a pretty foot in a *slipper with a flat toe hanging over the side. There were other paintings of a donkey and a pig and some rabbits though I think one of them was a dog. All the paintings were like the paintings handed out for free at the cheder, THE BIBLE ones of the Garden of Eden everyone knows aren't supposed to be real. The curtains were red almost black and through the window you could see the real Mount Carmel like another painting. A good one.*

Everywhere else there were crosses some of them with a Jesus hanging some without. And on every shelf there was a statue of Jesus always naked as a boy always covered with blood always smiling like he didn't mind being dead. When I looked closer I could see that even the Jesus-statues were a kind of a painting because the blood had been put on later probably by the same person who had done the walls in the exact same color. The cupboards were full of dresses and the dresses were full of moths and the moths were full of dresses. When I asked should I burn the dresses as is the custom for the dead the Messiah said, "Why do that? The moths are eating better than we are."

The rest of the house was full of KABBALAH. Not full of THE KABBALAH itself that is only a book though large. Full of everything to do with THE KABBALAH, like chalk circles on the floor instead of carpets and letters on the walls instead of pictures and numbers on the ceilings like stars and so many candles everywhere that if they all were burning at the same time the walls and the ceilings would too.

What else I found in the bedroom was a surprise. I was expecting only more KABBALAH-things to frighten babies but what I found there would frighten even Yankel. It would frighten even you. Maybe especially you and any lady who wasn't crazy like the Messiah's late wife alev ha-shalom. I found it under the mattress of the narrow bed that must have been hers. It was a book with a dead flower to mark the place. But it wasn't only a book. Across the front was written in red The Book Of All Formations

From The Kabbalah. And then in black The Words Of Our Father Abraham.

When I climbed into the bed with the mattress and settled down to read a little before going to sleep I saw that on the inside of the book there were no words. Only letters and numbers. Always in a circle. There was no place to begin and no place to end. There was no place to start again or to stop. Reading the book was like building the wall at Rishon LeZion stone on stone side to side until it joined up in a square with a hole in the middle only this time it was a circle and I was on the inside and just when I finished building the wall the hole collapsed and there was no way out. It was dark inside, almost black. I couldn't see the wall I'd built or the stones beneath my feet. Above there was a roof of stars like stones in the sky that gave a little light but even the light was dark and between the stars more black and behind them only black. I didn't dare to move except to tremble. I barely breathed and from the sound I think I whimpered like a kitten.

And then between the stones from the outside there came a light. Not so much a light. A piece of light like a flame. It moved from crack to crack like a wind along the forest floor tree to tree like a fire. And then a stone was gone because some of the light came in. And then another stone and more light and then another stone. And when the hole was big enough the lady came in. In one hand she held a torch in the other a stone. She was red in the torchlight naked as a girl. She whispered across the circle. I heard some of her words not all. Something to do with waiting for a Jew to find her or finding a Jew who is waiting and taking a Jew to fulfill herself or filling herself full with the taking of a Jew and a union of counterparts or some parts in a union and flesh and spirit and base and divine and man and ghost and mother and son and so on.

Then like a dancer who never touched the ground the lady came to where I stood trembling. And she raised her stone above her head and brought it down on mine. There was no pain only a wave that passed through me like a sea and then another and another and on and on until they touched the shore. I couldn't breathe. I didn't want to breathe. At first I thought she was your lady of the Yampol Rapids because I couldn't see her face. And then I thought it was you because I wanted it to be. And then I knew it was the Messiah's late wife alev ha-shalom. I don't know how I knew. I knew. And then because there was no roof it began to rain which was Karl through the window licking my face so I would give him his breakfast.

Every night at Gilead I dreamt like that sleeping with her book on my belly. Every morning I woke like that ... wet with Karl and I'm ashamed to say it except to you wet with myself like a boy trying to become a man. I tried not to look at her book every night and finally I burnt it up to boil the soup but in the bed with the mattress which must have been hers the dream was always the same. I tried changing to the bed with the board but then I didn't sleep at all. I would have slept in the garden with her flowers but I was more afraid of the malaria than of the dream. So I only went into the bedroom and into her bed when I had to sleep for as long as it took and not a minute more. Into the rest of the house I hardly went at all except when I was boiling in what was supposed to be the kitchen though by now it was where the chickens lived to get away from Karl. I spent most of my time lying in her garden under her flowers forgetting about her book that wasn't only a book and thinking about real things and you.

The Messiah spent most of his time sitting up in the hammock on the veranda reading the magic holy book of The Kabbalah and muttering Kabbalah-words and writing out something like a Kabbalah of his own. His was a book about breathing that he'd been writing with his wife while she was still doing it but not very well because of the dust in the Holy Land that was what gave them the idea of writing a book about breathing in the first place.

And also they'd been writing their book because the Messiah's messiah taught the Messiah and his wife that they never had to make love and shouldn't because breathing together which is called Holy Breathing is better than making love though I can hardly believe anyone could believe that but not everyone has met you has he? Also the Messiah said Holy Breathing gives strength and resistance to disease and to impure thoughts and the length of life of ten though in her case anything more than half of one life would have been a bonus though I never said that.

Little by little the Messiah stopped bumping and swaying so much and was able to stand on both sides and to walk to the toilet in the garden. And his face got back a little color that wasn't white. At last he moved into the bedroom with the bookshelf in the middle and slept on the bed with a mattress and I got to sleep on the porch in the hammock of silk. And instead of only his own book he began to write out letters that Karl and I took into Haifa to post and to pick up the letters he began to receive that I couldn't help noticing were all from England and all in the same pretty penmanship. And the envelopes of them smelt like garden flowers.

Then I woke one morning and the Messiah was sitting on my hammock with his hand on my thigh and he said he would teach me how to holy breathe. Which was the first time in a long time I had the feeling of drowning without water. So I got out of the hammock and off the veranda and I said that it was time for Karl and me to go back up to Zammarin now called Zikhron Ya'akov because the comrades up there would come down here to get us if we didn't go back and maybe they already were on their way. The Messiah shrugged on both sides equally and said in that case he wanted to give me something he didn't have any use for any more to remember him by. So he gave me the famous rolled-up paper with the seal with a crown. On the way back to Zikhron Ya'akov when he ran out of trees Karl mistook it for a radish with a purple leaf and ate it.

I'm very sorry to report that I don't know for certain what happened to your so-called father Laurence Oliphant the so-called Messiah after that although later I heard in a gossip from the best student who heard it from the other who heard it from someone else that The Messiah quit Gilead for an English lady of his own kind called Rosamond who was his late wife's sister or her maid and who took him to England where they got married and he died the next week. Which probably means that the spirit of his first wife who danced on her toes came back to get him because you'd do that for me wouldn't you in similar circumstances?

While I was enjoying myself in Gilead the Baron Edmond de Rothschild's Frenchman or someone like him with a pencil and a ruler had been busy. By the time I got back there Zikhron Ya'akov already had got bigger by a winery and a water tower with a copper water vessel on the top and pigeons and hanging gardens for fancy and a synagogue with a bright white marble altar.

Yankel also had been busy and BILU had got smaller. He'd called a meeting to read out to the few remaining others what Karl Marx had to say about men like de Rothschild even though there probably was no one else like him. And also to explain that the exchange-value plus the surplus-value of a place like Zammarin was bigger than its price at any price because of the work everyone had put into it including dying of malaria. And also to show that the selling out of Zammarin as Zikhron Ya'akov at even four hundred thousand was giving away a surplus-value to an exploiter who even if he doesn't want to do it must worsen the condition of those he's exploiting which is us. Yankel must have read out very well because the moment the other remaining comrades understood that Karl Marx meant that at Zikhron Ya'akov things were going to get even worse than at Zammarin they all quit both names and the Holy Land as well.

Which was when BILU stopped having meetings because what's the point? When there's only two left every time you're together is a meeting. And when there's only one what's a meeting? I suppose that's what Yankel thought while he and the few remaining Arabs were waiting for me to finish enjoying myself at Gilead. I know it's what I thought when I got back to Zammarin that is now called Zikhron Ya'akov.

While I was away and he was without his BILU comrades Yankel also had been thinking about other things. I know he was thinking about them because he'd taken four of my best headscarves and sewn them together and written on them this message to me from him and Karl Marx.

1. Communism is the positive abolition of private property and thus of human self-alienation and therefore the real re-appropriation of the human essence by and for man conserving all the riches of previous development for man himself as a social i.e. human being. Which is just exactly like you and your headscarves that you never sell only give them away so who would bother to pay for any when they only had to come to you to ask for one and they got it or even sometimes two?

2. Religious suffering is the expression of real suffering and a protest against real suffering and the sigh of the oppressed creature and the heart of a heartless world and the soul of soul-less conditions. Which is just exactly like you with your Clara of whom I wish you the best of luck though I doubt it and the only benefit you'll ever get from her is the heartbreak you already got and when it gets too bad you should try a little Zikhron Ya'akov wine like I do.

3. All men distinguish themselves from the animals as soon as they begin to produce their own means of subsistence because by producing their means of subsistence men are indirectly producing their actual material life. Which is just exactly like you and me with BILU of which there are no more left so likewise there's no more actual material life. So goodbye.

4. The Romanian students told me Karl Marx died last month. In England. So why not in Poland?

Then Yankel climbed to the top of de Rothschild's new water tower and stood there waving his wine bottle and yelling in Kaballah-language at G-d and Karl Marx to come down and tell him what holy trick was next until he tripped on a hanging vine or slipped on the copper or got pushed by a pigeon and fell in. I think he tripped. Mostly the Arabs who watched from below said he tripped. What they couldn't say because they didn't know was that if he tripped or even slipped or got pushed why didn't he float? I knew he could float because in Jaffa harbour I'd seen him do it. But this time he sank like a headscarf. When the Arabs climbed up and fished him in and pulled him out and pumped him dry it was too late.

So Yankel was the first to get laid out in de Rothschild's new synagogue on de Rothschild's bright white marble altar which was a kind of an honour but not for Yankel. The Arabs gave me his headscarf to remember him by which I do lots of times a day especially at night. No one could stand Yankel but everyone liked him. We liked him a lot. He was our most tragic case and without you understanding all about him you wouldn't have been able to understand all about the rest of us including me. After Yankel I stopped with the farm work and I went into my tent to think and to count headscarves.

It wasn't the farm work. An ox can do farm work and so can I. In Kharkov there was no call for it because the May Laws said a Jew couldn't own land in Mother Russia so why would there be a Jewish farmer in Kharkov or even anywhere? But here in the Holy Land there couldn't be anything else than farmers could there? And all it takes is hands and a strong back. And I've got hands. In time I could have been an ox. Maybe Yankel was right. Maybe that's what G-d and Karl Marx wanted from me ... to be an ox ... a Holy Ox. So why couldn't they make me want to be one? Lots of times

in my tent counting headscarves I thought about that. And I never
did find an answer. I bet you could.

I suppose it was Yankel who finished it for me. He didn't get
saved by G-d or Karl Marx did he? So what was the point in staying
in the Holy Land or in coming in the first place? Maybe you have
an answer for that one too but I didn't. Which was when I decided
to quit BILU and get free to get married even though there wasn't
any BILU left to quit or anyone left to get married to.

I didn't do well in the Holy Land and I'm not proud of it. But
what with Yankel and not being able to breathe I just wasn't suited.
So I packed up Karl and we took a voyage back to find what was
left of G'dera Outpost to say a sad goodbye to loved ones. By then
G'dera Outpost was twice as big as when Karl and I left it because
of the Negev that had got added on. And it was covered with holy
white doves and what they leave behind which also is white. And
it was full of Bedouin getting paid off in stinking cheese to let
Ghufran's father keep his goats for them. Ghufran wasn't in when
I called but off in the Negev in the tent of the Tent of the Bedouin
king who she'd married more or less. So that's what I told her father
to tell his daughter the next time he saw her. That I just wasn't
suited and that's why she couldn't have me.

By now lots of camels from the Negev were parked all over
G'dera Outpost every day licking their feet. There were so many
some of them had to be lady camels. Karl could have his pick and
maybe even choose one with an extra hump. So I unpacked him
and watched him limp off. And I packed up myself with my
headscarves and quit the Holy Land to look for you. Something
else I couldn't have.

Chapter Eight

Maison De Hirsch

Herzl had waited in some of the most distinguished vestibules in Europe and the Middle East … the icy atrium of the War Ministry in Berlin where, before dismissing his petitioner with a finger-snap, Kaiser Wilhelm II took the opportunity to deliver himself of several Jewish jokes in what he thought was a Semitic accent … the seedy anteroom of the Colonial Office in London where Uganda urbanely was proposed as an alternative Jewish homeland … the internal tent at Topkapi Palace in Istanbul where the Sultan confided: "If one day the Islamic state falls apart, then you can have your Zion for free, but as long as I'm alive I'd rather have my flesh minced than cut out one morsel of Palestine from the Muslim land."

Whether for next year (Jerusalem!) or for some year (the Messiah!), waiting for someplace or someone, Herzl decided, is the natural state of the Jew. It makes it difficult for him to have a good time in the present. It makes him nervous. No wonder he cannot stand still even in prayer. Not that Herzl prayed. He never prayed. Not that he did not believe. He believed. He supposed he believed. Or did he believe, he supposed? No, he knew he supposed – everything about Zion was supposition since he had never been there – but did he truly believe or did he only believe what he supposed others supposed he was supposed to? "Theodor," his mother would say, "you think too much." "He talks too much," his father would say. "He talks because he thinks," his mother would explain. "He talks," his father would insist, "instead of thinking." "I talk," he would reply to both of them were they living, "so as to think." "See!" they would say.

Still, his mother would have been impressed by this vestibule ... tier after tier of Murano chandelier cascading from the upper reaches of a spiral mahogany staircase the banister rail of which he had no reason to suppose was gold only in hue, on the wall opposite an immense Louis XV Breche Violette chimneypiece with a central shell cartouche and scrolled fluted jambs beneath a serpentine shelf bearing a silver Star of David set in lapis lazuli, beneath his feet a dizzying field of marble parquet swirling to a central banquette that he dared not occupy because he was certain it was upholstered in Kanchipuram silk. And his father would have been impressed by his mother's being impressed.

And it was talking had got him here! As well, of course, a personal charisma remarked upon by others that Herzl preferred to attribute less to symmetrical features, slim figure, brooding attire and apostrophic beard as exemplified in the popular portrait of him leaning reflectively over a parapet of the Rhine Bridge, and more to the irresistible intensity of his gaze inspired by the glowing sincerity of his cause.

And dreaming, of course dreaming, what would life be without dreams however much they envenom the life of the dreamer? Take Socialism. It's not a matter of Socialism's being a "utopian dream," the fashionable Marxist disparagement. (Herzl snorted, then hoped he had not been overheard doing it.) Just what is so un-dreamlike, so "scientific," about utter Communism other than Marx's assertion that it is?

And what, pray tell, is so dreamlike, so utopian, about one's own more subtle Mutualism? (Now there is a word!) Why is the Herzelian mixed economic model not perceived to be what it is: the path between Socialism and Communism embracing both and leading further ... simply put, a "Third Way." (My G-d, he was cooking today!) A palace of peace erected in Jerusalem to replace the lost Temple where national and international disputes would be arbitrated! A Jewish culture superior to the vulgar primitivism borne like typhus by the refugees from the Czar, a modern Jewish culture containing the best of European heritage especially one's own beloved German! A developed welfare program! Voting rights for women and, eventually, perhaps for Arabs (some Arabs)! A universal respect for non-fanatic religions! Many languages spoken with Hebrew replacing Yiddish, that peasant babble of the shtetl and The Pale, Hebrew, modern Hebrew, sophisticated and exquisite, but only one of myriads of euphonic tongues happily sung amid a harmonious polyglot of assimilated cosmopolitan – Herzl paused to mop his brow and to allow his heartbeat to slow.

He had not meant to go on like this even in thought, and certainly he would not do it in the presence of his host. Perhaps it was the stimulating anticipation of that interview? Perhaps it was the intimidating influence of this vestibule, the irresistible lure of the unattainable banquette? Zion itself, of course, is a dream, and all the more tantalizing for being just that. Herzl sometimes wondered what life would be like for Jews were the dream finally to be realized. After five thousand six hundred fifty-four years with nothing left to wait for, what then? It wouldn't happen in 1896, he sighed, nor next year nor the next nor in the remainder of this dwindling century. Nor, probably, within his lifetime even were he feeling better at the moment. No, dammit, that was not narcissism nor hypochondria! It was no affectation of any sort. Herzl was convinced he was destined for an early grave. It complemented the Mosaic reputation he hoped to leave behind. But, he had to admit, to others it could appear to be cowardice. Certainly, that is what his wife perceived it to be. "Theodor," she would say and frequently did, "fearing doesn't make it happen. Who fears the best?"

Yes, he had to admit, as in so many obvious things with the exception of the saintliness of his lamented parents which continued to evade her, the relentless Julie Naschauer-Herzl was unpleasantly perceptive. He indeed was afraid of death. But only of it happening before his work was done, before the last Jew from the last hellhole of the Diaspora at last had attained the prospect of the blessed Z –

No, to be honest and why not be honest alone in a vestibule, it was death itself he dreaded and, more than death, oblivion in the world he would relinquish. What is worse to a writer than erasure, even to – as Julie is so fond of pointing out – a mere feuilletonier? Yet, over the years of their persistent union, was it not those very feuilletons that had bought her the best of Viennese salon life, including far too much sachertorte along with the acres of velvet required to drape what dear mama referred to as "the manner of a ballerina with the backside of a whale"? How they had chuckled over that one, he and papa! And he had immortalized it in the next day's feuilleton, attributing it to the Empress Elisabeth as she observed the once-slender Katharina Schratt at a Schönbrunn Palace ball.

And who is to say today's talk of the town is not tomorrow's oral history and next week's legend? Did this Dreyfus business not begin as freelance tittle-tattle and back-page innuendo in as base a venue as one's own NEUE FREIE PRESSE without one's endless feuilletons about the little French ramrod with the pince-nez who probably is guilty as hell though it is one's collegial duty to defend him against the anti-Semites, would a mere Austro-Hungarian hack such as oneself have become sufficiently à la mode to attain this very vestibule of the Maison De Hirsch on the rue de l'Elysée? And be scheduled for a personal interview with the Baron himself, he who has kept presidents and potentates – editors even! – awaiting his pleasure, though perhaps some of them dared the banquette?

Let the malevolent Julie digest those consideration along with her daily cup of bile! "Myn mama," he assured himself under his breath, "volt mikh farshtanen."

When it came, the encounter took less than ten minutes and went roughly as follows.

DE HIRSCH: How much?

HERZL: What?

DE HIRSCH: How much?

HERZL: How much what?

DE HIRSCH: It's you, Mr. Herzl, who sought this interview. You should have come prepared with figures.

HERZL: I wrote to you, Monsieur, asking for –

CLARICE: Le Baron.

HERZL: Beg pardon?

CLARICE: Monsieur le Baron.

CERZL: I wrote to you, Monsieur le Baron –

CLARICE: De Hirsch.

CERZL: I wrote to you, Monsieur le Baron De Hirsch, asking for a conversation beneficial to Jews. It's not a question of an interview, still less a direct or an indirect money matter merely. I want to discuss with you certain plans, the effects of which will extend to the day you and I are no longer here.

CLARICE: We have no such plans, Maurice and me.

HERZL: Maurice?

CLARICE: Him.

HERZL: Ah.

DE HIRSCH: Paris is our home, my wife's home and mine.

HERZL: Paris?

DE HIRSCH: It's true that, since the death of our son, London equally has become –

CLARICE: Did you know our Lucien was thirty-five when he died?

HERZL: Thirty-five, was he?

CLARICE: A minute, in the course of centuries hardly a second. One day he was taking oysters with the Prince of Wales, the next he was in bed looking like death warmed over. Three weeks he was sick. Three weeks, then ffft!

HERZL: Only three weeks.

CLARICE: Ffft!

DE HIRSCH: Our Clarice has never got over the loss. She still wears black.

HERZL: Black ....

CLARICE: From that day to this, black, only black, nothing but black, eleven years, black.

HERZL: Black ....

CLARICE: Except on social occasions.

DE HIRSCH: ... which is why we take sooty old Bath House on the Piccadilly for the season.

CLARICE: This isn't the season.

DE HIRSCH: So we're here.

CLARICE: In Paris.

DE HIRSCH: You can count on it.

CLARICE: And when are you leaving?

HERZL: I? Leaving? So soon?

CLARICE: Mr. Herzl, when is the day you are planning no longer to be here?

HERZL: Ah, you misunderstood!

DE HIRSCH: Probably.

HERZL: I referred to a project, to a cause, to a mission, that will outlive us all. I have prepared papers, twenty-two pages of papers. If you would care to look them over?

DE HIRSCH: Perhaps a précis? Sixty words or less.

HERZL: Anti-Semitism is an immutable factor in human society that assimilation does not solve. The essence of the Jewish problem is not individual, but national. The Jews can gain acceptance in the world only if they cease being a national anomaly. The Jews are one people, and their plight can be transformed into a positive force by the establishment of a Jewish state with the consent of the great powers.

DE HIRSCH: Sixty-nine, but why mention? Ah, politics!

HERZL: Of course politics. Without a political solution, there's only –

DE HIRSCH: Monsieur Herzl, moving out of sugar and copper into steam, we outbid Brussels by floating Turkish bonds on the Paris Bourse and the London Exchange to finance our Balkans rail line from the Hapsburg border, with a view to extending our internal rail networks between Athens and Piraeus, Bucharest and Guirgui, Constantinople and Vienna, despite the various contretemps between Romania and Russia and Russia and Germany and Germany and Romania in the 1880s and Austro-Hungary and Serbia in the current decade along with the eternal petulance of Greece throughout, to say nothing of honouring our compassionate imperative to compensate regional industrialists and handicraft producers driven out of business by the increased penetration of European manufactured goods as well as our commercial responsibility to satisfy national administrations with corrupt financial practices. So you'll understand why, as builder and proprietor of the principle railway concessions in Middle Europe, we prefer philanthropy to political activity which, though momentarily gratifying, would disturb existing interlocking international accommodations and remove our wherewithal to perform them. Did you enjoy the vestibule?

HERZL: The vestibule? What has the vestibule to do with –

DE HIRSCH: Perhaps you were too preoccupied with politics to take note of architecture and geography? The chandelier, for example, was a gift of the Port of Venice to dissuade us from expanding into Italy and diverting marine traffic to rail. The banister was a similar disincentive to facilitate, after four centuries, the remigration of exiled Jews into Spain. The chimneypiece – charming, isn't it? – was a gratuity from our own Gallic administration for steering troop and armament convoys into the Balkans and bypassing France.

CLARICE: Don't forget the banquette from the British Raj in thanks for transporting gypsies, their "Black Jews" they call them, into Romania. A little vulgar, perhaps, but effective.

DE HIRSCH: The vestibule you occupied is an amalgamated tribute to inter-continental enterprise and national disinterest. A great family such as ours, were there such another, lives off the tribulations of the body politic, its internal squabbles, its internecine conflicts, its military requirements and its need to get in and out of trouble by rail. Our status is premised on our being above dynastic and great-power politics precisely because we are the ally of all the dynasties and of all the powers when considerations of profit justify it. There are other great families – well, there is one – with a branch in London, whose aims by now are beyond profit and who don't appear to require personal neutrality. Those people might not be averse to a political project for the benefit of the Jews. You'd do well to converse with them.

HERZL: The English Rothschilds refused to see me. Their interest is in proprietorship of the Jewish nation, not its independence.

DE HIRSCH: Quite, quite.

CLARICE: You've not missed much. The finest great houses are on the north side of Piccadilly ... the Clarendon, the Berkeley, the Denham, the Cambridge and our own dear dirty Bath House. Several members of that peculiar family keep mansions at the south-western end in the part commonly referred to as "Rothschild Row." All grandly furnished, of course, but as the result of purchase. We've not been invited in nor sought to be. And, of course, there are the races.

HERZL: The races?

CLARICE: We also take Bath House for the races. We began to take it when we still had our Lucien. He so loved the English races. And we so loved our ... so loved our... our ....

DE HIRSCH: We have lost our son but not our heir. Humanity is our heir.

HERZL: Precisely! And when I read that those were your very words over the coffin of your boy –

CLARICE: Lucien.

HERZL: When I read that those were your very words

over the coffin of Lucien ... De Hirsch ... and that thence-
forth that you and Mrs. De Hirsch –

CLARICE: Madame le Baron.

DE HIRSCH: Clarice.

CLARICE: Madame le Baron Clarice De Hirsch.

HERZL: When I heard that all of you had resolved to
withdraw from your business enterprises and to devote
the remainder of your lives to philanthropic programs of
great magnitude designed to improve the situation of all
Jews everywhere, that was the moment I knew –

DE HIRSCH: Russia, mainly.

HERZL: Beg pardon?

DE HIRSCH: Not all Jews everywhere. Russia, mainly.

CLARICE: And Romania.

HERZL: Romania?

CLARICE: I have an uncle in Romania.

HERZL: Ah.

CLARICE: And he, of course, was Russian.

HERZL: Ah?

CLARICE: When it was Russian.

HERZL: It?

CLARICE: Romania. Then he was Austrian, then Hungar-
ian, then Austro-Hungarian, then again Romanian ... all
of those, one uncle!

DE HIRSCH: Clarice, Clarice, politics, politics.

CLARICE: And then, of course, there's the memory of
Bucharest.

HERZL: In Romania.

CLARICE: Perhaps.

HERZL: Perhaps?

CLARICE: We never knew what happened to her after she was sold.

HERZL: You sold Bucharest?

CLARICE: Lucien sold Bucharest.

DE HIRSCH: All those purses, all those trophies ... she was properly clapped out before her time. So Lucien sold her as a brood mare.

CLARICE: I couldn't have done it. I have a fondness for old things.

DE HIRSCH: Lucky for me.

CLARICE: In black or out, my heart, I'm afraid, is Jewish.

HERZL: Precisely! And when I heard that you and your husband had determined to devote your considerable fortune to the gigantic task of removing millions of Jews out of persecution and poverty –

CLARICE: Lucien's.

HERZL: What?

CLARICE: It's Lucien's fortune that we have devoted.

DE HIRSCH: Besides the sale of his stables for tens of thousands above the estimates, we still profit from his covers in the stud along with several droppings we continue to run to give us the opportunity to visit London to get Clarice out of the black. More fortune than enough to save our Jews, with a little left over for our English hospitals that always did such good work.

CLARICE: Though not, unfortunately, for our Lucien.

DE HIRSCH: Our hearts, nevertheless, are with our Jews, though I would wager not many of them know their salvation depends upon a horse race.

HERZL: And when I read the report of your selfless zeal and your determination to liberate and to transport –

DE HIRSCH: By rail.

HERZL: When even my own little organ recorded your public vow philanthropically to expend every centime from whatever source before you die, that was the moment I knew who it was G-d had sent to carry our folk to Zion! A modern Moses leading his co-religionists unto that new, fresh land where there are no ancient prejudices, no current persecutions, and Jews at last can become the artisans and the skilled workmen and the elegant soldiers G-d has always intended them to –

CLARICE: Zion?

DE HIRSCH: Palestine.

CLARICE: Oh, that Zion.

HERZL: The only Zion.

CLARICE: There's another in Bath, Zion Hill, admirably located for the provincial races, almost as fashionable as Essen Spa where the architecture is less fine but the waters more alleviating of the constipation, don't you know.

DE HIRSCH: Yes, yes, "Jewish Relief." Long ago we investigated the possibility of resettling Jews in Palestine, an area of the world for which they seem to have a particular affection and –

HERZL: Let's call it Zion.

DE HIRSCH: The possibility of resettling Jews in that particular Zion of yours on a large scale. You've read the Veneziani Agricultural Report of 1891?

HERZL: I consider it anti-Zionist.

DE HIRSCH: And upon a firm scientific basis. It was the opinion of the Veneziani Commission that Palestine isn't suited for agricultural settlement by European Jews, and that no further consideration should be given to establishing agricultural colonies there.

HERZL: Agriculture isn't the only culture.

DE HIRSCH: Argentina was preferred.

HERZL: What Moses beheld from the peak of Sinai was not, I believe, Argentina.

DE HIRSCH: Agreed it's a matter of topsoil and national character, and both must be considered if we're to make farmers of Jews. You're familiar with the on-site inspection report of Mr. Arnold White?

HERZL: I consider him anti-Semitic.

DE HIRSCH: We selected him because, as well as being a man of philanthropic sentiment, Mr. White is anti-Semitic in his temperament, so we could count on a report of the character, the condition and the capacity of Russian Jews that wouldn't be distorted by too much prejudice in their favour. He found the Palestine project to be problematic in the extreme. For one thing, the place is full of Arabs.

HERZL: Hardly full.

CLARICE: But Arabs!

HERZL: If not Russians to Zion –

CLARICE: And Romanians.

HERZL: Which Jews do you propose to transport, and where?

DE HIRSCH: Russians to Canada.

CLARICE: Romanians to Argentina.

DE HIRSCH: Pole position and far outside, let the adjacent starters try to keep pace.

HERZL: (sighing) So why not the other way round?

DE HIRSCH: Beg pardon?

HERZL: Russians to Argentina, Romanians –

DE HIRSCH: To Canada?

CLARICE: Maurice –

HERZL: Why not?

CLARICE: Maurice, darling –

DE HIRSCH: Canada it is!

CLARICE: Uncle will be vexed. He had his heart set on a hacienda. Now he'll have to settle for a tepee. Or perhaps he'll choose to get off along the way at Liverpool or Montréal or the Rocky Mountains or someplace else that needs Jewish farmers ....

DE HIRSCH: Clarice, Clarice, can we not make exceptions for particular deserving Jews who are both Russian and Romanian and so on and the reverse? Who's to say no to us? So glad, Theodor, that we've reached a non-political consensus. As for a prophetic vision or, as those of your generation would say, "a wider perspective" – We may call you Theodor, may we not?

HERZL: Monsieur le Baron.

DE HIRSCH: Just so, just so. You are, Theodor, if you'll forgive my observing, a young man. In due course you'll find that the law of husbandry and the law of the track are one law, and it's the law of Providence as well. In a word: "diversification." Scatter the seed to the wind and some will take root, no matter how stony the soil. It's impossible to kill Zion while it's a taste in the mouth, a feeling in the heart, a hope, a dream, a poem. Put it on the map and with one pogrom the handicap is weighted, the advantage is lost. Diversify, diversify, diversify. Disperse your breeding stock, expand your pasturage, magnify your herd, multiply your entrants and the odds favour the stable over the punter no matter the condition of the track. As you can see, the Baroness and I are ready to run our nags on any surface and in all – Herzl? Herzl? Where's he gone?

CLARICE: To Zion?

Chapter Nine

The Albert Hall

That very same evening of June 24,1896, Doctor Thomas John Barnardo, the Evangelist star of the Plymouth Brethren, the renowned saviour of hard-core urchins and street-Arabs, the designer and builder and proprietor of a nationwide franchise of children's homes bearing his name and now on the verge of expansion abroad, staged his emigration fund-raiser in London at the Royal Albert Hall.

Amid the capacity audience of eight thousand were Albert Edward, the Prince of Wales (widened in girth, narrowed in dissipation, by now a mere five years from reign), with the Princess Alexandra (upright, but asleep) at his side, the Right Honourable William Ewart Gladstone (after an unprecedented fourth term as Prime Minister, two years into a disgraced retirement having abandoned General Gordon to his death at Khartoum), and Anthony Ashley Cooper, the Seventh Earl of Shaftesbury (alas, in evangelistic spirit only, being ten years dead).

For those who never had seen him in the flesh, the show began with something of a disappointment. A stage the size of this one would have diminished a man of any stature. Doctor Barnardo was barely five feet tall. He compensated by means of a towering stovepipe top-hat that he rarely removed, a brisk darting manner that made it difficult to assess his dimensions, a barking voice that, given the notorious echo in the Albert Hall, everyone experienced twice, and on this and on most occasions by surrounding himself with children, the shorter the better.

His opening remarks, however, were ventured at the lip of the stage where he risked appearing to be a missed stitch in the fabric of the fire curtain.

His words were abrupt and brief, albeit informative. Addressing the imperial box with a shout intended to be overheard by the attendant throng, he welcomed his royal visitors (assuring them of his persistent friendship) and reminded them of the occasion of their visit (the anniversary of his humanitarian crusade), and of its contingent obligation (their fiscal support of his current transatlantic enterprise). Then he vanished through an aperture in the asbestos wall that rose to uncover the stage curtains that parted to reveal the opening pageant: a swarm of a hundred boys noisily employed at a variety of tasks with Doctor Barnardo at their centre towering benignly over them.

These little lads clad in potters' smocks, chippies' aprons and the accoutrements appropriate to brickies, tinkers and smiths, were busily employed, he informed his audience, at the fourteen separate trades in which they received instruction at every one of his children's homes. "I should like to reassure my royal patrons," he reassured everyone, "that these corner-lads and drifts and street-loafers and toughs and paupers and criminals such as they were but weeks ago, shall never again drain the exchequer with the need to police and to punish them, but eventually will make a contribution to the welfare of the realm in accord with the instruction in a noble trade appropriate to their class which they presently are receiving at the Barnardo House of Destitute Youth."

A bellow from the royal box of "Can't hear you!" produced sideward scowls from the Doctor that reduced his juveniles to a silent pantomime of their various occupations.

Barnardo resumed. "But what of their distaff counterparts in orphandom and misery, the fortunate few thousand in the

Barnardo Village for Endangered Girls?" Whereupon a hundred girls in groups of ten entered, singing occupational ballads, performing callisthenic drills, ironing and hanging-out clothes, sewing dresses and making pastry. Toying with her winsome curls, Barnardo beamed down upon the tiniest. "These neat-handed young misses – so distant from the hoydens of the hovels they once were and the unthinkable objects they were destined to become – might very well someday be employed as domestics in your own home and mine, a status they would never have aspired to without the training our various Barnardos provide them in a blameless occupation appropriate to their immaculate gender."

At one corner of the stage those least defiled girls destined for childcare had set up a nursery of cribs, cots, rocking horses and playpens complete with a babble of toddlers, some less than a year old, extracted for the evening from the haven for abandoned infants known as the Barnardos Babies' Castle. Barnardo crossed to them. After a moment's reflection upon "these tender mites of squalor and wretchedness," he pointed to a panel at the other extremity of the stage. "According to the Barnardo precept of the ever-open door," he intoned, crossing again, "none is turned away. The lame, the halt, the blind, the deaf, the dumb, the incurable are alike welcome and are equally received.

"Suffer," he stage-whispered, wiping away a tear visible to the front rows, "the little children." A panel was withdrawn to reveal a group of eight-to-ten-year-olds hobbling about on crutches – in one case, legless upon a wheeled platform – perilously attempting a game of cricket. Barnardo maintained a prudent distance but managed a courageous smile. "Indeed," he barked, "once within the open doors of the Barnardo Palace Of Pain, there's not a merrier fellow in Christendom than one of my cripples!"

The volcanic eruption of audience applause covered a quick change of scene. The stage darkened. There was a roll of thunder and a child burst upward through the floor bearing a placard that read: "CARDINAL MANNING, ANTICHRIST". The adolescent impersonator had been outfitted with a blood-red robe, once capacious but outgrown during rehearsal, and he bore a prosthetic nose of monumental proportions, historically apt and, in the circumstances, satanic. His materialization was by means of an under-stage spring-mounted platform that projected him several feet into the air thus permitting a star-trap to close beneath his feet before he landed. It was accompanied by a puff of smoke and a sizzle manufactured in the pit below upon the skillet of a juvenile stagehand who was permitted to consume the sausage after the show.

When he was certain the boards were secure beneath him, this necessary enemy stepped forward, pointed at the chest-placard that proclaimed him "CARDINAL MANNING, ANTICHRIST" and, in the high clear voice that had determined his casting, delivered a risible parody of a pro-Catholic sermon, marred only by an inability to pronounce Rs that rendered "Christ" piquant and "Resurrection" unattainable. His malevolent melodramatic monologue was frequently interrupted by enthusiastic hisses from children bearing placards reading "First Anglican," "Second Anglican" and so on. At its conclusion, the "Twenty-Seventh Anglican" shouted "bollocks!" ... an improvisation perhaps, but an effective climax to the anti-Rome jollity. The satirical interlude concluded amid renewed applause, including that of Doctor Barnardo who orchestrated it from the wings. Overcome with diabolic exhilaration, CARDINAL MANNING, ANTICHRIST bowed many times in several directions and waved his placard above his head, inadvertently elevating his hem to reveal unmistakable evidence that this appointment had preceded female ordination by more than a century and in the wrong church.

Pausing to permit the sympathetic murmurs of the Anglicans in his audience of Anglicans to subside, Barnardo signalled for a change of scene. While his little actors cleared the stage of its paraphernalia of properties and of themselves, he positioned himself in the centre to deliver his major address of the evening. "Honoured guests," he began, doffing his hat and bowing in the direction of the royal box.

"Can't see you!" bellowed its principal occupant.

Barnardo frowned, flushed and revisited the lip of the stage.

"Better," acknowledged the Prince. "But wear the topper just in case."

Barnardo obliged, cleared his throat and resumed his pitch with a brief history of "The Barnardo Crusade" over the last three decades, elongated by illustrative anecdotes. One tale featured the legendary Jim Jarvis, the Doctor's first mud-lark saved from the gutters of London's East End, nourished, trained, Anglicanized and triumphantly shipped off to Canada where he vanished even from the immigration records of that meticulous dominion, casting doubt upon his arrival or, indeed, his existence.

Another legend recounted Barnardo's prestigious face-to-face with Shaftesbury when that icon of philanthropic Evangelism was astonished to be informed of the existing degradations in Stepney and Whitechapel, was won over to the Barnardian methodology of "Social Reclamation" and was moved to conclude: "All London must know of this! God bless you and lead you, young man! Continue with your good work!"

Had he lived to attend this evening in the Albert Hall, the late Lord Shaftsbury doubtless would have explained to his fellow occupants of the royal box that, during his lifetime, he needed no tuition on human hardship in dilapidated London precincts he knew intimately, and that he recalled nothing of his reported encounter with Barnardo except that he had been out of the country when it was supposed to have taken place. Perhaps he would have appended that it was precisely such instances of Barnardo's self-serving lies that persuaded him to make room in his crowded schedule to become one of the main accusers in the character assassinations that blighted the little Doctor's subsequent career.

His chronology thus reviewed and revised, his credentials asserted and embellished, his enemies demonized, his allies amplified, Barnardo passed on with equal candour to the luminous present and the shimmering future. If one agrees not only with him, he suggested, but with every informed expert such as he who is without prior prejudice or vested interest or Roman Catholic encumbrance that such children should be removed from the wretched situation that spawned them, it follows that the further they are sent from it the better. Since overcrowding of British inner cities is the primary cause of such wretchedness, it further follows that a rural environment in an underpopulated country is to be preferred. A newspaper cutting appeared in Barnardo's hand. "Since joblessness, indolence, poverty and dissipation are endemic to the great cities of Great Britain," he read aloud, "the cure to the malaise of the motherland's destitute is their healthy occupation in a clean empty land such as Canada that needs them as much as they need it."

Under his hat and over his reading glasses, the Doctor peered significantly at his audience. "Not my words, honoured guests. Those of the universally admired father of that blessed new dominion who was but recently the lamented fatal victim of double pneumonia and – "

"Alcohol poisoning," interjected the Prince of Wales.

His wife stirred at his side, opened an eye as if she had

been summoned, closed it again and, with a discrete snore, resumed her repose.

Deciding that the remainder of his speech could be utilised at a less awkward moment during some other fundraiser, Doctor Barnardo returned the newspaper clipping to the pocket of his vest and, behind his back, delivered a hand-cue. At the rear of the stage a curtain rose to display a vast backcloth painted to resemble green fields of yellow wheat under a cloudless sky of the usual hue. The landscape portrayed was illogically populated by buffaloes, cows, mountain lions and (of equal dimensions) robins and butterflies benignly co-existing amid such rarely adjacent features as tepees, igloos, grain silos and Niagara Falls. The tableau was presided over by the immense figure of a cowboy on a bucking bronco playfully lassoing a gargantuan lady in gingham with a mixing bowl in her hand and a gaggle of huge healthy children romping at her skirts. All, despite their several occupations, were managing to produce galactic smiles of universal welcome. A banner was slowly lowered from the flies until it rested on the amazon's bosom. It read: "ONTARIO!"

The sound of a bugle reverberated through the hall. Then it reverberated through the hall. In permanent crescendo down the central aisle marched a brass-and-drum contingent borrowed for the evening from the Eighty-third London Company of The Boys' Brigade "dedicated to the advancement of Christ's Kingdom among boys, and the promotion of habits of obedience, reverence, discipline, self-respect and all that tends towards a true Christian manliness."

As band and banner progressed toward the stage with military enthusiasm and intermittent musicality, a phalanx of Barnardo boys, each dressed in a hardy suit of bristling tweed and bearing a small kit bag on his shoulder, began to enter from stage right. At the same moment from stage left the tiny lass with the winsome curls led on an impassive snow-white goat. She and it were followed by a squadron of Barnardo girls, each shapeless in a thick, unpatterned travelling overcoat with a wicker market-basket over her arm.

The three files converged in the centre of the stage where several youths laboured to raise a larger banner proclaiming: "BARNARDO'S BABES CANADA BOUND!"

Once the playing surface was filled to repletion and in danger of spillage into the pit, the incursions ceased. The cacophony petered out, and the children and the goat milled picturesquely.

Doctor Barnardo stepped forward to address his audience for the last time. He reminded them that these brave voyagers required their prayers and their donations, buckets having been provided at every exit to receive the latter. "So great is my faith in the rectitude of this endeavour," he concluded, "that I myself shall accompany the first single-gender contingent bound for their new world!"

Then he turned his back and addressed the children. To compensate for his altered stance, he was obliged to raise his voice to its ultimate volume. "May God and the Queen guide and protect you, my beloved unfortunates!" he howled. "May the charity of those here assembled transport you to the land of promise that awaits you!"

As the audience rose to deliver an apotheosis of acclaim, the brasses and the drums struck up an approximation of the single national anthem of both domains. The parade of boys and girls regrouped, wheeled smartly in their tracks and briskly set off upstage into the tableau of rural Canada that parted slightly to admit them. A sign had been affixed to the hind quarters of the goat. It read: "TA-TA!"

Doctor Barnardo brought up the rear. As the others vanished into the backcloth, he turned and bowed. Unfortunately he once again had doffed his hat, and was noticed by few against the immense rump of the bucking bronco. The applause grew hesitant. Then, like the music, it dissipated. After a while it became apparent that Doctor Bernardo had left the building. Perhaps imagining that he and his charges were already mid-Atlantic, the audience did too. Eventually they would be correct. Meanwhile, the evening was at an end.

Chapter Ten

Liverpool to Grosse Île

All this happens to her before she goes mute. She is not mute on the SS Laurentian of the Allan Line, just someone with not a lot to say. So, as for going mute, she has that to look forward to, which she does with a clarity beyond nature. It is just one more thing she knows as if it already has happened. There are other things and she would speak about them were there someone there to listen to her, but the situation never presents itself and she may as well already be mute.

They claim, if you lose strength in one of your senses, you gain it in another. That is not her experience. Her experience is you gain another, and not one of the five you are supposed to have. The nuns confirm the theory, but they think she is mute already and they only say it to cheer her up. If they really believed it, they would have too many saints to be accounted for by The Mysteries of The Rosary. But it turns out to be so. In her experience.

She thinks this time maybe it is the ship fever bringing it on. No one else thinks it is the ship fever because at sea they dare not. So no one notices anything wrong with her. One in a group of forty and the smallest, no one notices her at all, not even the sainted Father Seddon who is supposed to notice everything although he is too old a saint to notice much. When even he does notice because no more than two days out she is having a convulsion right here right now at the table during breakfast and it takes three of his nuns to hold her down, he sends for the doctor. And here it comes, Father Seddon's personal novice, an adenoidal little bum-wipe with a leaking sinus. The nuns turn around to make a screen so no one not even they can watch, and behind their backs they hold her down. The doctor, who is not much older than she and was not a doctor before the ship sailed, sniffs and swallows and says, "What seems to be the trouble?"

One of the nuns says, "Maybe the ship fever?" and the doctor says, "Pish and tosh. Tell her to lie back and be brave."

After a while he seems to think it has to do with between her legs where he is spending a lot of time pushing with his fingers and getting redder and redder on the back of his neck because it is so hard to do and it even hurts her a little. Then his face explodes and collapses, and he gives it up and hurries away which makes her feel a little better. So she guesses he is some kind of a doctor after all. The nuns let go and turn around. She gets off the table so they can mop up before lunch. Father Seddon, who has been watching, smiles that gentle smile and takes a brandy bottle from the medicine chest and wanders off.

She is sleeping now. She has been sleeping for the two days since the last convulsion, leaving eight more for the passage give or take a favourable wind and no floating ice. She is not afraid of floating ice or contrary gales or high high seas, and it is the nuns who have to name those horrors and pray for courage. Right now she is not afraid of anything. She is asleep.

The dreaming is much the same as before ... crowds of people pushing around her and against her and, when it gets especially bad, right through her. They are on their way to someplace else and they never make a sound, just push on past in one direction with staring eyes with terror in them. They are afraid but she is not, not even afraid of them. When they jostle her or crash against her, there is no pain. And when they pass right through her, there is only a little shudder.

It is a wonder she can sleep so long without eating or relieving herself. It is a wonder she can sleep at all with the air so bad and the bunks so very hard and those on the bottom stinking and those on the top leaking, and all around and in between people praying and making sex and arguing but in the dark doing it all in whispers.

There are moments of light when the hatch is raised and the food is lowered in from way-above and a sewage bucket or somebody sick or maybe worse is lifted out, but then once more there is the hot wet darkness and the whispers and here and there a candle that can barely hold its flame and of course the noise from just-above and the sounds from deep-below. And so she sleeps and she dreams. What else is there to do?

Ordinarily she would be plucked out each morning and brought to just-above to break her fast with Father Seddon's girl orphans even though she really is not one of them, an orphan certainly but non-Catholic, perhaps even un-gentile if the smudged card pinned beneath her shirts has been read correctly. No matter. "It's broadening to break one's bread with the lowly and the godless" ... the nuns say someone called The Cardinal said that.

But, since the incident of the convulsion, she has not been called back to the breakfast table just-above because it is better to wait and to see, to let Jesus rather than The Cardinal be the guardian who decides what is safe in the circumstances, because against the ship fever even baptism is no prophylactic. Just look at the seven thousand dead at that damned Grosse Île and the five thousand dead at Montréal, all of them Irish, some of them Protestant! And thank God this is not that damned '47 when they failed even to lift out the buckets! It is The Sainted Father Seddon not The Cardinal who says all that, and his personal novice nods and sniffs and swallows and once again gets called "adenoidal little bum-wipe with a leaking sinus" by one of the nuns under her breath. And so she is left to sleep. And the others to wait and to see. And the SS Laurentian of the Allen Line to sail on into this blessed 1897.

And now there is a change in her dream. Now she is dreaming about how she got here, though she is unaware that is what her dream is about. She only knows that hers is a story told backwards, and she wants to know how it turns out which is where it begins. "If this is the ship fever," she says to herself in her sleep, "it's very interesting."

The first thing in this new dream is the last thing that happened which is the breakfast convulsion. But she has dreamed that before and she does not want to again, so she pushes away the probing fingers and moves on further back toward the place where the being here begins.

Taking on the ballast has to do with it. That is what the men way-above sing out to one another ... "taking on the ballast!" and there is a rolling across the ceiling of just-above which is the floor of way-above. Then a man from way-above comes down and opens a hole in her floor. Then he goes just-above and opens a hole in the floor that is her ceiling. Then, she guesses, he goes further way-above and opens a hole in the floor that is called "the deck." Then he lowers a plank through all the holes, and he leans down and he sings out: "From the deck, taking on the ballast! 'Ware below!"

Then there is another rolling of barrels. It turns out they are barrels. Everyone says so. That is what rolls through the holes in the ceilings down the plank through the holes in the floors ... barrels after barrels into the deep-below she had not known was there until now. She had thought this place was the bottom. It turns out there is a bottom below this one, somewhere even further under the sea with walls that leak like tears, a bottom below this bottom and now it is filling up with barrels called "ballast" with a heaviness inside them called "cement."

That is what she hears later about the barrels when, just-above, one of them catches a boy in tweed who leans too close to the edge to see what is below what is below, and gets carried down the plank along with other barrels that come and come. Had she known that was going to happen, she would have left the table of Father Seddon's girls and walked across the room to the other table and warned the boy during breakfast. But she did not, and it did.

For hours the barrels come. Nothing can stop the barrels. Until they stop. Then the man from way-above pulls up the plank and comes down and closes the hole in her floor. When someone asks him about the boy in tweed who fell, he shrugs and explains what's in the barrels. He explains in a loud voice so that everyone in this bloody place and just-above and everyone else in every bloody part of the steerage of this bloody rolling hulk can hear and can shut up about the boy. Then he goes to just-above and he closes the hole in her ceiling and probably the one above that as well.

Then everywhere begins to move and to roll. And deep-below the barrels lean from side to side and scrape and bump each other, and they make a noise like grunts and mumbles with every so often a moan as if barrels could lament which they cannot. And neither, she says to herself to stop the shivering and to carry on with her dream, can the boy in tweed. And taking on the ballast, a nun says later, that was Liverpool.

And before Liverpool there is the platform that is as far as her train ticket will take her. "Maybe even," says the man with the cap with the badge of a train on the brim, "a little bit further but who's counting." But then she has to get off her bench and get off his train because it is more than his job is worth. So that is where she gets off, and she sits on the platform on her cloth bag and watches the steam push the wheels and the wheels push the cars and the cars push her lovely bench further and further away until it is gone. And then the stars come out, and then the cold comes down, and both the shirts in her bag and then the bag itself cannot keep it out. Even there on the platform she can sleep, though not enough to dream. Every time she tries, she shivers herself awake and has to try again. Finally she gives it up and sleeps without a dream which is when the lady comes.

About the lady she cannot see much because of the light. She can hear her though because the lady calls her "Berthe" and she thinks others called her that so it must be her name. She will think about the others later. And then the lady tells her another thing she already knows and that she will think about later too. Shivering on the platform was no time to think about her name or any other things like those. Right then she only wanted to think about the lady.

Right now she only wants to think about the lady. When she does, the ship's bunk is not so very hard, and there is no praying and arguing and making sex in the dark, and the boy and the barrels do not moan. When she thinks about the lady, even the air is sweet and it smells of morning. The lady's hands are along her cheeks and she hopes they do not let go. Right then she does not want to be let go of because the lady tells her things she already knows. Right then she does not want the lady to leave because the light she brings is warm and the smell of her is sweet. But in the end the lady goes, which is when the nuns begin.

Which is when the nuns begin. "I saw her," says one of the nuns, "because of the light she was in." "What light?" says another, "there weren't even any stars." "Anyway," says another, "how did she get on this platform? There hasn't been a train for days." No one knows how, and Berthe is unable to say, not because she is mute because she is not mute yet, but because she is not in her dream just then and has no way to know.

So the nuns take her along with the forty others like her on the night train when it finally comes, and she sleeps very well on that bench, though her dream this time is in bits. Oh yes, and the nuns say the name of the platform was "Antwerp." And after that they say the name of the bloody rolling hulk waiting for them after the platform called "Liverpool" is the "SS Laurentian" of the Allan Line.

Billy wishes the girl in the bunk above his – the bunk above hers has been vacated in case she really has ship fever – would lie still. He knows she is trying to lie still because he has asked her to, but when she is asleep she cannot. So, while she sleeps, he cannot. So he goes on deck.

He knows a way because he has tried it before, a way that is not the hatch nor the hole in the ceiling or the floor but down a gangway no one would use because it is down, and through a steaming room where half-dressed men lean on their shovels and whistle as he passes, and up a gangway at the end, and up another and one more to the deck where the air is clear and the sailors are on lookout "forward" and "aft" and "port" and "starboard" and "amidships." He knows those ship-words because he may only be lower-steerage-assisted-passage but this is his second ocean.

While he is passing down and along and up and up and up, Billy has to hold on to the rail where there is a rail and on to the wall where there is no rail because, before the "SS Polynesia" got called "The SS Laurentian" to change her luck after the ship fever in '47, she was called "The Old Rolly Polly" because she would roll on wet grass. The sailors on lookout tell him that. Because they are sailors it is more than the truth but, because everyone in steerage has been seasick even in harbour, it is also less.

The rolling is the reason for most of the stink below and the reason hardly anyone is strong enough to be able to find the way to climb out of it. Billy is able to because this is his second ocean. When he tells the sailors that, they smile at one another, and they tell him the story of the ice-lock that is also lies and less than lies and more.

Just about this season of the year, the sailors say, just about this day of the month just about this time of the night, the Old Rolly Polly two days out of Liverpool stops rolling because she gets trapped in the ice floating south of Greenland. Forward and aft and starboard and port and amidships there is nothing but ice. The lookouts should have noticed by the smell of the ice that always comes well before it but, through lack of vigilance and one thing and another and talking to passengers like Billy, they failed to. And now she is stuck in the ice eight days short of Montréal and a day less to that damned Grosse Île.

Running the screws full ahead and reverse does not do a thing to break her free. So the Captain orders everyone up on deck, even the assisted-passage, those as can stand, especially the assisted-passage because there are so many of them, they are called "The Paying Ballast." When he blows the horn, the Captain says, they are all to run from one rail to the other as fast as they can and back, those as can run, and over and over until he blows the horn again. So they do it all that night, and sometime around dawn the Old Rolly Polly begins to sway from side to side, and then she begins to roll in her usual manner, and then the screws turn and she goes forward and the horn blows and The Paying Ballast can drop where they ran.

And that is the story of how the Old Rolly Polly broke the ice-lock and got free to carry on across the Atlantic into the Gulf and up the Saint Lawrence to join the hundreds of ships waiting to be inspected for that damned ship fever at that damned Grosse Île in that damned '47. As for Billy, the moral of the story should be this: beware the smell of the ice though, given the stink of himself and maybe of the ship fever, he probably would not notice! Which conclusion to their story all the sailors find hilarious and so, out of politeness, does he.

Even on deck the stink does not entirely go away because the sailors are right and some of the stink is him. He knows that anyone walking on the deck has a real ticket and is permitted to be there and will know by his stink that he has not and is not, so he avoids them. At this time of the night there are not many to avoid ... the usual knot of sailors who are supposed to be looking out but are playing cards instead and nod as he passes and hold their noses in a friendly way ... the forty boys in tweed who have permission to use the deck chairs when the air even in the upper steerage gets too bad for sleeping, until the little gentleman with a barking manner comes to rouse them and to collect them before dawn so as to clear the chairs for passengers with real tickets. There is a pair of lovers holding hands behind the smokestack, though Billy catches a whiff on the wind and thinks maybe they too are lower-steerage-assisted-passage who have managed to find the gangways down and up. The girl in the couple looks like Clara, which is no surprise. There is not a day that passes without a girl who looks like Clara, though by now Billy hardly remembers what that looks like, and after all this time he is not sure he could guess. In any case, they have seen him looking and are gone.

But now that he is thinking about Clara, Billy cannot stop. So he leans over the rail and watches the foam go past and Canada approach. He cannot recall whether he told Clara he has a living brother in Canada. No, he could not have told her, could he, because he only found out later at the applications office where you have to fill in the details, and your assisted-passage ticket gets written out and stamped. Where in the application form it says "History," he leaves out the part about BILU because pioneers are wanted by Canada and saying that you already have been one and quit might not be what Canada wants to hear. For "Previous Occupation" he puts down "Farmer" because it probably is what the Baron wants to hear, and for "Future Occupation" he does not put down "Haberdashery" because it probably is not. And he puts down his own original two names because he has lied about so much already.

It is only then that the official looks at what Billy has written and looks at a list on the wall and says, "Abraham Vintner? Brother of Chaim? Oh good, a sponsor! He's been looking for you!" and he writes out Billy's ticket and stamps it "Montréal." So he could not have told Clara about a brother he did not know he still had, could he? And even then he did not know he knew, not in the sense of really knowing. So after the applications office while he is waiting for the Baron to find him a ship to Canada, Billy and Chaim correspond because who is willing to take the chance on a stranger unless he is sure it is a brother?

The corresponding begins soon after Billy's visit to Grodno-Gubernya-Succ'va-Dn'ster only to find out that there is no longer a Grodno-Gubernya-Succ'va-Dn'ster, and Clara is gone and where she was is only mud. Billy remembers that the corresponding with his brother begins soon after that failed visit because it is then that he tells Chaim he is engaged to be married, so he must still be hoping to catch up with Clara to make her his, no? He bothers to tell that lie because it turns out that Chaim is married, and Billy thinks that maybe his saying he is planning to have a wife will make it easier for Chaim to be willing to continue to correspond.

Of course it is not so easy to correspond about Clara who, wherever she is, still is just Clara with nothing new to add on. Chaim, on the other hand, is married to a certain Tauba, "a queen among Jews," who, Chaim adds on, is descended from the famous Rabbi Moshe Zentner. "Another one," Billy sighs to himself. "Such a big family from such a little rabbi! Well, let it pass." But now he knows that the corresponding with Chaim began soon after the time of Grodno-Gubernya-Succ'va-Dn'ster when he still had his hope.

And he keeps some of his hope for the months it takes the Baron to find him a ship. Meanwhile during the waiting he learns the haberdashery trade because he only needs to be a farmer while crossing the Atlantic. Once he gets to Canada he can quit the farming and go into the haberdashery, though he does not think it will be in Montréal because why give Chaim the competition? And, besides, corresponding with Chaim he finds out everything about Montréal. At first he thinks: a city with the name of a mountain in the middle with steps to the top like Odessa only colder, so what can be bad? Then he finds out.

In the east end of Montréal where Chaim has his haberdashery, there are Jews, lots of Jews, only Jews. According to Chaim, even the streets there have been named to mark it out. "Jean Mance, Esplanade, Waverley, Saint Urbain," Chaim writes, "take the first letters and what does it spell? French names spelling JEWS, only Mance and Urbain not, but who do they think they're fooling?" It is a ghetto and from a ghetto there is no escape.

Anyway, where would a Jew escape to in Montréal? A Montréal Jew cannot become a Montréal Frenchman, can he? Besides, Chaim writes, all the Frenchmen hate not only every Jew but also every Italian and every Greek and everyone who is not one of them and they even hate those of themselves who hate the Pope and the Archbishop, so in Montréal who would want to be even a Frenchman? They may as well be Poles! And it is not as if a ghetto makes you safe. Even a haberdashery gets burned to the ground, as happened four times to Chaim, only once for the insurance. And in Montréal who is there to arrest a certain rival haberdasher from outside the ghetto when all the policemen are French? Even if he was seen carrying a torch?

According to Chaim, the mountain in Montréal isn't a mountain. It's a wall, on the one side the French, on the other side everyone else, the Italians, the Greeks, the Germans, the Poles, with little mountains in between called Other Mountain or West Mountain or East End of The Mountain which is where they keep their Jews. So Montréal is not Odessa. It is not even Bucharest or Brody or, G-d help us, Warsaw from all of which a Jew can escape. It is another Pale of Settlement with walls all around from which a Jew cannot escape. Worse than that! Every ghetto in Montréal is a ghetto in a ghetto because Montréal may be French but Canada is not. So in Montréal even to be a Frenchman is to be a kind of a Jew, a foreigner in your own country but not an Arab, a lemon in an orchard of oranges but not a Pole. Such a big place, Canada, surely there must be a part that is not like the Holy Land? Perhaps not. So who needs Montréal?

So Billy goes back to the applications office and he says he saw a sign that says the Baron really prefers you to go "Out West" where there is more of everything a farmer needs and more of everything that needs a farmer. So can the Baron please find him a boat to go there instead of to Montréal? And the official says, "From Montréal it's a train not a boat, but why not. Where to? How about Regina? Or Moose Jaw that's one stop further?" And he writes out Billy's new ticket and he picks up his stamper.

Of course it is not possible to ask the applications officer whether there already is a haberdasher thereabouts but, even if there is, Out West probably is big enough for another. Billie does not know much about a moose let alone its jaw but Regina is the name of a queen so what can be bad? So Billy says, "Regina please." And on second thought he asks whether he can delay his train voyage an hour at Montréal to make a visit to his living brother who also is named Vintner so that he can leave a note for Clara just in case?

"Why not," says the official. "In Canada the railroads go everywhere every day and always on time or just about." And he scribbles and he stamps. It is only when he leaves the desk that Billy sees the name on his new ticket has become "Winter" not "Vintner" because that is the season it happens to be outside the applications office. So his life gets decided by a ticket. So what was he expecting?

Leaning over the rail staring into the foam Billy finds himself thinking of the Holy Wall in the Holy Land. One stone on another stone as high as a man can look but no higher. Yes, yes, a piece of the Temple, so? Yes, yes, the only piece of it remaining, so? You touch it, it is stone. You look at it, it is a wall. Maybe to the men who put one stone on another and two stones on the one it was something more than a way of clearing their fields. To them it was maybe a tower to the stars or at least a beginning, though even they must have realized that was unlikely. But while they were building, they still had their hope. So maybe building it was the reason they built it? For them a reason, not for him. Of course he leaves a note for Clara in a chink between the stones of the Holy Wall just in case, as all the others do for their own Claras or sometimes for G-d or Karl Marx. But of course without a result or, as Yankel would say, "so far." Yankel, Yankel, at what point does so far become all there is?

And meanwhile somewhere out beyond the ship's rail and the path of foam is Montréal and Chaim and Chaim's queen of a wife, and after them a city with the name of a queen, and who knows what else and who else and where. It is that point that is approaching. It is there he can give up his hope of Clara. Also approaching is the little gentleman from the upper steerage who barks at the boys in the deck chairs, so it must be almost dawn. Besides, there is a wind coming up and a chill coming down and maybe even, G-d forbid, what is the smell of ice.

So Billy goes below where the girl in the bunk above with maybe ship fever has wakened enough to lie still. He sits on his bunk and he reaches up and takes her hand which usually has the effect of keeping her still until breakfast. And together in the darkness they listen to the noises from just-above.

Somewhere else among the nine hundred and twenty in the lower steerage, Clara is staring into the candle Morris has provided to hold back the darkness beyond their bunks. The noise from just-above makes it impossible to sleep. To go on deck once again so soon is too much effort, and besides from the other side of the smokestack they were looked at by two people with maybe a real ticket who might complain. But how can only eighty above make such a noise? It sounds like a war, but they are only children. Why cannot their adults keep them quiet?

"Discipline," says Morris, "is what's needed." If he had them in his cheder do you think for one minute he would tolerate –

"Shah," says Clara. "Listen."

It is the adults who are making the noise above not the children. Three of them are shouting back and forth across a chamber. From the one side there is the sound of a hungry dog, but no dogs are allowed, only cats for the rodents, so it must be the voice of a man who barks. From the other side there is the hum and the splutter of a roast on a spit and from that same side a whine like a kettle and a hiss like a seltzer, but it is still a long time until breakfast so Clara cannot trust her imagery. Ordinarily she would take one of the pills Morris has saved up to make you sleep until the next mealtime, but this morning the noise is such that even the pill might not work and it is a shame, Morris always says, to waste what could be sold.

When she yawns, Morris once again takes her hand and once again she lets him take it.

"Why can't we," he wants to know, "sleep together in one bunk?"

"The question is the answer," she says.

"We're married," he says.

"We're not married," she says.

"As good as," he says.

"Engaged," she says, "isn't married."

"Years," he says, "is a long engagement."

"Wait until Regina," she says.

"Who knows how far is Regina," he says. "We should wait only until Canada."

"This isn't Canada," she says.

"As good as," he says.

"You'll be glad," she says, "we waited."

They have had this discussion before. Sometimes Clara wonders whether they have ever had any other. Usually she can divert Morris with a question of her own about something he has told her to read so that they can discuss it to make a lesson plan for his cheder, or about something he has told her to cook so that his best student can be invited for dinner, or about something he has told her to put on for the occasion instead of that old thing. But here in the lower steerage there is nowhere to change your day-and-night dress even if your trunk were not somewhere under everyone else's, and dinner is what is left in the lowered basket by the time it reaches you and before it is snatched away by another, and who cares what anyone is wearing when the darkness swallows the light before it leaves the candle let alone reaches the dress. So down here there is not anything to distract Morris from what is uppermost in his mind and nowhere at all in hers. Only this time he says something new. "You're not," he says, "getting any younger."

"Twenty-two," she says, "isn't old." He has surprised her and she said it before thinking. It is the wrong thing to say.

Morris has a plan, and saying what she just said has given him the opportunity to explain it to her once again. In detail. Leaving out the details, the sum of Morris's plan is this: six babies with a year of rest between each ... to make the Yampol Rapids worthwhile, double what he lost. The years of rest in between also are important because it was the lack of them that killed off her father's six wives before they were twenty, leaving that Rabbi's seed like Clara blowing in the wind all over Europe and the world, not to mention the Rabbi's born-a-miracle grandchild, the sister and soon to be sister-in-law who G-d alone could find if there were a G-d. Up to now Clara has been lucky to make an engagement with him and to look forward to a new life in a new land. But six babies in twelve years? At her age the sooner she gets started the better for the both of them.

"And what about," she says, "your age?"

Which is what she should have said in the first place because, Morris decides, if she will not talk serious it is better that they do not talk at all. So they are silent, and they hold hands and stare into the candle. And the noises from just-above become louder.

The discord in the upper steerage has been going on since dawn, in fact since Liverpool, in fact for eighteen hundred and ninety-seven years especially the last three hundred and sixty-three since the Reformation, and facts have not got much to do with it. "One believes," Father Seddon says this time and every time, "or one doesn't believe." His novice who has been shaving him in preparation for the morning Mass, sniffs, swallows and nods.

"Let's see how far believing gets you in Canada," barks Doctor Barnardo from his side of the chamber. He is moving among his boys, checking their tweeds for lice.

"The last time one looked," says Father Seddon, "Canada was still a Christian country." His novice nods, sniffs, swallows, executes a particularly elegant cheek-stroke with his razor and steps back to appraise the effect.

Doctor Barnardo finds a louse, extracts it with his tweezers, drops it into his camphor bottle and replaces the stopper. "Look again," he says.

"After Mass."

"Bells and smells."

"One is reminded," says Father Seddon as his novice whips up fresh foam for the other jowl, "of Transubstantiation, the mystery of which I and my little true believers are about to celebrate in our Divine Eucharist."

Turning to his tousled female charges who are still struggling out of their bunks and through the protocols of their hygiene into the unpliable imperviosity of their clothing without, under the surveillance of the nuns, displaying an unclad limb even to one another, Father Seddon smiles his sweet smile and takes advantage of the hiatus in his own toilette to stroke their little True Beliefs. He increases his volume to broadcast level.

"Transubstantiation, a concept to which I have previously introduced you," he says to his wards in a tone that manages to be both conversational and recriminating, "occupies the very heart of our Holy Mass and enables us to understand how wafers become flesh and wine becomes blood: divine mysteries that continue to exceed the comprehension of one particular little gentleman in our neighborhood, and will never even approach the minds of those little gentlemen littler than he."

The nuns take a moment to aim a fusillade of anti-Anglican catcalls across the expanse of the chamber. These include such high-pitched perennial whizzers as "martyr-less misfits!" "saint-less sinners!" "trinity transgressors!" "disorderly disordinancers!" and, least explicable in the circumstances but most vociferous and many times repeated, "Jew lovers!" Then the nuns resume their supervision of their wards' demure sanitations and intricate modesties, and Father Seddon leans back and signals his novice to shave on.

"Bells," repeats the Doctor, "and smells." Then, up a decibel, "Smokers and strokers."

Father Seddon is not unduly annoyed. He is annoyed but not unduly. He turns the other cheek and receives its lather. "You and your little," he clears his throat and finds the word, "Anglicans are invited to hear our bells and to smell our smells though, regrettably, neither to join in their performance nor, apparently, to appreciate their meaning." Father Seddon's personal novice strops his instrument, emits a sectarian sniff, nods, swallows and resumes barbering.

"Iconic bunkum," barks Doctor Barnardo. "Priestly clap-trap," he spits. "Sanctimonious pederasty," he snarls. Then, permitting himself the indulgence of a shout, "Sacerdotal whoremaster! Holy whores!"

The nuns accept the insults as a few more scourges in the welcome process of worldly mortification. The barber, however, stops in mid-stroke. "Shut up!" he screams. "Shut up! Shut up! Shut up! Shut up!"

The girls and the boys who have been silent throughout the discussion, indeed throughout the crossing, redouble their silence though it is hardly possible.

"This man!" screams Father Seddon's novice. "This man!" brandishing his razor near his superior's throat. "This man is a saint!"

Doctor Barnardo looks up from his current tweed. "Not," he says with a little smile, "until he's dead."

And so it goes morning after morning day after day and, sometimes, late into the night. The devout attention of the children to these instructive disputations is required at all hours, its lapse corrected by an open palm or, administered by the adenoidal novice, with an intimate pinch.

For their part, whether they are foundlings of Catholic persuasion destined for Montréal or Anglican unfortunates aimed at Toronto, all the children of each gender become adept at simulating alertness, their eyes and ears open with the senses shut, their mouths ajar with utterance stilled. Like the breath of the sea against the hull, the roar of their adults recedes into habituation. Like dead men awash in the currents of the deep, the music of their own voices is lost in desuetude.

And so it goes until the morning of the storm.

To be dreaming of a dream, it seems to Berthe, is not unusual though in her experience it is dangerous. Along a corridor down a maze that itself is a corridor through a maze of corridors with, at the end, a door to a street you almost recognize ... such a dream might prove inescapable with no way back. Given the reassuring pressure of Billy's hand in hers, she is prepared to risk it. And so, in her new dream, she visits a time before the train departing from Antwerp platform, a time before the platform itself.

Here there is confusion. Someone must have placed her on that train. She knows she was too little to have done it herself. Someone must have bought her the ticket for as far as it will take her and no further. No face presents itself. She is on the train on her lovely bench, that is all. No one is there but the man in the cap with the badge of a train on the brim, and he is only there off and on, sliding her door open a crack and poking in his cap with the badge and asking if she is still all right or needs him to smuggle in more biscuits. Besides the biscuits, it is the cap she is most interested in, so he removes it and leaves it with her. She cuddles it like a dolly and falls asleep with it under her cheek. When he next appears, he is wearing another just like it so this one must be hers to keep. Where is it now? What does it matter? It was only a cap.

In her dream another cap appears, a cap of cloth, and along with it the sound of a violin. No one is wearing this cap. There is not a fiddler in sight. In fact, except for the cap there is pretty much nothing at all, and no sound beyond the music. No, she is wrong, something is there, something lying under the cloth cap, a dark mound moving and then not moving but still there and, beside it, something else, something just like it but worse. Otherwise there is blackness, a blackness with thick walls, and from somewhere very near there is the mewing of a distressed kitten.

This is not a place she would wish to be, not a place she would choose to be until perhaps ship fever puts her there. None of it is a thing she wishes to see so she chooses not to. Instead she passes through the blackness like a wall, and the moving mounds and the voices of the violin and the kitten fade, and she is in another place.

This is not the place she expected. She does not know what she expected but this is not it. She knows this place, mainly by the smell. She remembers it, though it almost seems the place remembers her. She can see it now as if she is watching from a nook in the wall.

This is a place rather like the SS Laurentian of the Allen Line when you are not in a dream ... damp like way-below, though cold. Here too the air is filled with the smells of things that cannot stop how they smell. And its people are hardly people ... little bundles stored in the crannies and the cavities and the nooks along the walls on bad mattresses or on none. They are wrapped in upholstery sacking ... noisy little squirming lumps, one of which she knows to be her.

There is a lady moving among them searching for that one lump among the many and, with a click of joy, finding it. With the softest of smiles she relieves the nook of its almost-person, replaces the sacking with her own shawl, arranges the cocoon in the cradle of her arms drops her blouse and plunges a nipple into the toothless gap. As much to herself as to the bundle which sucks in her arms and begins to snore she whispers melodically, "Yes, yes, yes, yes, that's what my husband the Rabbi would say I must do."

At first Berthe thinks it is the lady in the light. There is a glow about her too. Perhaps it is only her candle. But after she is gone and her candle is gone too, something of the glow remains to help you to sleep. And she has left you in her shawl, her shawl that smells of milk and makes of your bundle a bigger bundle. It was not the lady. It was only someone who might also have seen the lady and had kept some of the glow. The lady does not come. Not until she is needed. Not until the blackness comes and it is nearly too late.

The blackness is coming and it is nearly too late. The next place in the dream is more than damp. This next place is running with water like a river, a river like a sewer that sometimes comes to visit and, when it does, you had better climb out of it or else. In this place when the river comes, the higher you climb the more you are out of it. In all the time she has been in this place she has climbed very high up the stairs and up the ladder, dragging her mattress, her good mattress, the mattress she received so she could leave the bad one behind. Now she and her good mattress are near the top. Now there is nowhere to go higher than this. Higher than this is only the roof, so no one will think to come up here. Up here she and her things, especially her mattress and her shawl and not much else, are safe. Nevertheless the blackness is coming.

This is a place she knows. She can remember it. She can say its name: "Old Textile Factory." She can say that by now. There are other children here. On the days the river visits, there are more children here than she can count because by now she can do that too. She has been here a long while. She has been here almost forever. How she got here she cannot say. It might have had to do with the lady from the place before this place because Berthe still has that ladies' shawl, the shawl that smells of milk, though by now it smells of everything else as well.

In this place the milky shawl and the good mattress are the things she has. Everything else, the food, the clothes that fit, she must go out and get. She must pass down the corridors and through the door to the street she thinks she remembers. To do that she must leave the good mattress hidden in her hidden place under the roof and hope it is there when she gets back. She takes the shawl with her as a market basket.

Everything she needs is at the market after the market is done. The food is in piles where the stalls once held food not spoiled. The clothes that fit are somewhere in the piles where there once were other stalls with clothes not torn. There is more food and there are better clothes at the Synagogue, but that is the place she cannot go. She is not welcome. Other children from the Old Textile Factory can go there and they do, but she is forbidden. The old old man of the Synagogue forbad her. She does not know why he did, but it is so. She tried once and she found out. The old old man looked at her and spat three times and turned his back, though he let her keep the milky shawl because, he muttered to someone who followed him about and was called "The Shamas," when she was carried away as a bundle, she had no shawl, only a baby blanket that has gone with The Shamas who must have been the one who carried her away first to the Synagogue storeroom and then, when she was big enough, to the Old Textile Factory.

So that is how she got here! She was carried! She is glad it was not the milky lady who carried her. She would not have liked to have known that it was her. It was not even the old old man of the Synagogue. It was The Shamas who got paid to do it, and then got paid again when he said he had not got paid and the old old man was too old to remember whether it had been done. And somehow she knows it is the old old man of the Synagogue who sent to the Old Textile Factory the good mattress that now is hers to keep forever. Perhaps it was the milky lady who sang of her husband who told him to do it. Perhaps he did not need to be told.

She does not know how she knows all that, but she does. Perhaps she learns it later from the lady in the light who tells her what she already knows, perhaps not. But spitting three times in the Synagogue and turning his back, that, she knows, means she is "forbidden." Forbidden is the first long word she learns to say. And the signs in the market teach her to count.

Then one day before the dawn, she comes back from the market with nothing in her shawl because of the rain and the rain and the rain, and she cannot get in. The Old Textile Factory is full. Because of the rain.

But the Old Textile Factory is always full, and there is always room up a corridor and up some others and up the stairs and up the ladder until she is under the roof in her hidden place where no one comes. There is probably room up there today but she cannot get in to see. The door is no longer where there used to be a door or, if it is still there, it cannot be seen because of the children in the doorway. The children in the doorway are packed together like a door, a door that cannot be opened, a squirming door that is turning blue. The windows are just the same, children in every one trying to get in or hanging on to a sill having got pushed out.

This has happened before in her experience, but only once when it rained and rained and rained like this but she was lucky enough already to be inside. This time she is not lucky enough. This time she is not lucky at all. This time there is only the street and it is running with water because, like the time before and probably like the times before that one, the river has come to visit. Anyone left in the street will not be there by dawn. But she is tired today. Today she is tired. Too tired to climb even were the stairs available. So she sits on the kerb where there used to be a kerb, and she wraps herself in her cold wet shawl that smells like nothing much and everything as well, and she waits for the blackness of the river to visit her. Which is when the lady in the light comes.

Which is when the lady in the light comes. So it is the lady who lifts her from the kerb and away from the river. So it is the lady who wraps her in a new dry shawl that smells like morning, and carries her to the platform where the river cannot visit. And just before she is alone again and the dreaming begins, it is the lady who tells her something else she already knows: the name of this platform is "Brody." She is glad she knows that. She is glad she knows it again.

And the ticket? Who buys her the ticket for as far from the platform of Brody as it will take her? It cannot have been the lady because no one else can see her. Perhaps there is no ticket, just the man with his cap with the badge of a train on it who takes her from the platform and makes sure her bench is a lovely one and gives her biscuits and puts her off on the platform called Antwerp where the nuns can find her.

And then she knows something that no one has told her! The ticket was bought by the old old man of the Synagogue! Somehow she knows it but she does not know it, only thinks it because she wants it to be so. Which does not really matter, does it? She wants to tell somebody what she now knows she knows and what she thinks. When she wakes, she will tell the man in the bunk below who kindly holds her hand, though by now he has let go.

Billy has gone on deck to watch the approach of the storm. The sailors on lookout say she is blowing up some weather and he ought to go back below, but he says he has seen weather before and he thinks he should again. They say she is already blowing up something rough and he ought to go back below, but he says this is what he came up to see and it may be his last chance to see it. They say she will blow up something rougher before she gets done and he ought to go back below, but he says that rougher is what he has come up to see and it is not as if this is his first ocean though it is his first with fog and snow. When he says that to the sailors, they smile at one another, and they tell him stories of wrecks they swear they have known and some they have only heard tell about from sailors who have never been known to lie. And, by the way, this is not the ocean anymore. It is the Gulf of Saint Lawrence, which is worse, and the Captain is hugging the south shore which is the worst. "And it's summer, isn't it, so of course there's fog and snow!" Which the sailor who says it finds hilarious.

The Portside Lookout who is scanning the near shoreline to port says it reminds him of the barque named "The Old Millicent" out of Prince Edward Island as went aground and broke up and was lost with all hands in June of '73 just about here off Montmagny opposite that damned Grosse Île on a fine summer's night with only some sleet and a gale no worse than this, and she should have laid by till the full storm struck her and rode it out midstream but on account of his cargo Captain McGoughan thought he would risk hugging the south shore that he knew man and boy like the back of his beyond but what he had not reckoned with was the wreck of The Old Ralph Ramsey as had run aground the night before and broke up and gone down with no one left alive to call it in and so was lying in the shallows ready to snag the next boat by that, as bad luck would have it, was The Old Millicent that, as worse luck would have it, was carrying a cargo of a hundred-and-ten-proof fresh-up from Jamaica, which was the Captain's fee for signalling the importers how to evade the Canada Customs and Excise, and all that rum got lost along with all the rest. And the Lookouts on watch have a drop to the awful luck of Captain McGoughan of The Old Millicent.

If that is what you do in such weather, Billy wants to know, why is their Captain not lying by right now waiting for the full storm to strike and riding it out midstream when it does?

The Portside Lookout shrugs and looks out to port.

The Starboard Lookout squints across his rail into the fog that is making the rest of the Gulf invisible to starboard. "Mid's too close to that damned Grosse Île," he growls.

"Too close for what?" asks Billy.

"Being spotted."

"Being spotted by who?"

"Not who. What."

"What, then?"

"That damned lookout station up their Telegraph Hill as has the semaphore to the Heights of St. François at Montmagny as have the overland relays to the Citadel at Quebec."

Which reminds the Starboard Lookout of the sailing ship named "The Sweet Atlantic" as foundered off Meagher's Rock in the May gale of '36 with her bottom ripped out when young Patrick Leahy as got named ever after "Lucky Patrick" beheld a mass of something dark drifting by the hull whilst he was clinging on to the rigging and, as it passed young Patrick, a low moan surged up out of the floating mass that he reckoned was a collected shriek as got dulled by the tempest, and that dark floating mass was the women swept out of the steerage along with their children to the number of three hundred and ten and got drifted thus to eternity. And all the Lookouts have a drop to the good luck of Patrick Leahy.

"So," Billy shouts against the wind, "what's our Captain hiding from?"

The Starboard Lookout shrugs and looks out to starboard.

"Not what," says the Aft Lookout, watching the path of foam close up behind them. "Who."

"Who, then?"

"Them tending that damned signal cannon up their Telegraph Hill as could well decide to send a shot across the Captain's bow or, if they were so minded, into it."

"Why would they be minded to do that?"

"They would be minded soon enough if they caught the Captain sneaking past them in the fog."

Which reminds the Aft Lookout of the sad sad wrecking of Mr. McKay's pleasure craft named "The Jessie M." out of the Magdalene Islands in April of '07 or thereabouts, no, 'twas '07, as ran ashore in a snowstorm off the northeast tip of Cape Breton Island onto the cruel cruel rocks of Saint Paul's Island as is called "The Graveyard of the Gulf," and the master and the mate and a crewman scrambled over the rocks onto the island and lay there three months till mid-summer, unreachable because of the floating ice though their signal fires must surely have been seen from the mainland where the farmers there were accustomed to such events and powerless to assist or too busy about their farming to try, so that all three castaways starved to death but were thought to have been lost at sea until the day on the main street of Grindstone Village the grieving widow Jessie McKay saw a Frenchman wearing a fine rich coat that was the mate of the one she had given her husband before his last voyage out and she got the Frenchman apprehended and she pulled open his coat and she discovered the initials of her husband as she had worked them there herself, so the Frenchman confessed he was the mate of the barque Jessie M. and he told of its unhappy fate and that of its owner and one of his shipmates, whereupon to recover the bodies an expedition was sent out in the summer that determined by certain unmistakeable marks upon the bones and within them in the case of the marrowy ones that the Frenchman who had survived had done it by making use of those as hadn't, and so it got said of the widow Jessie McKay that by virtue of the coat she had found some of her husband but by virtue of its wearer she had found the sum of him.   And all the Lookouts have a drop to the hungry Frenchman of Saint Paul's Island.

"Why would the Captain sneak past that damned Grosse Île in the fog?" Billy asks.

The Aft Lookout shrugs and looks aft.

"To skip the quarantine inspection," says the For'ard Lookout, looking out into nothing.

"Just exactly like – " says the Amidships Lookout.

"Why would the Captain want to skip the quarantine inspection?"

"The ship's fever."

"Just exactly like – " says the Amidships Lookout.

"What ship's fever?"

"The ship's fever what's aboard us."

"The ship's fever is aboard?"

"A'course it's aboard."

"Just exactly like – " says the Amidships Lookout.

"Where's it aboard?"

"Bunk above yours."

"Blow it," shrugs the Amidships Lookout, and returns to looking out amidships.

"That's not the ship's fever. That's ... that's ... who says it's the ship's fever?"

"Ship's doctor."

"Ship's doctor? What ship's doctor? She's not been seen by any ship's doctor."

"Won't be."

"Why not?"

"Won't risk catching the ship's fever."

"So how do you know it's the ship's fever?"

"A'course it's the ship's fever."

"How can you be sure?"

Five Lookouts look out at Billy and hold their noses in unison and explode with hilarity.

"Even," giggles the Portside Lookout, "on a contrary breeze!"

"Even," guffaws the Starboard Lookout, "in a strong nor'wester!"

"Even," whoops the Aft Lookout, "upwind in a gale!"

"Even – " gasps the For'ard Lookout but cannot manage any more than that.

"Just exactly like," says the Amidships Lookout, rejoining the festivities, "the Old Suzie Q. as got burst apart by her own foul bilge. Which reminds me of – " But Billy has had enough of other shipwrecks, so he excuses himself and goes below to hold the hand of the girl in the bunk above, and to await this one.

Once Billy has gone, the sailors on lookout recall what they know or what they have heard of that damned Grosse Île in '47, which they had not recalled before for fear of frightening the passenger. They recall it now but they do not speak of it for fear of frightening themselves. Only the Amidships Lookout was there himself, and this is a little of what he silently recalls. Being maiden Mess Boy on the Old Rolly Polly as was, three-masted then not yet fitted out for steam, well down the line of a hundred or more waiting at anchor to be boarded and inspected for ship's fever in a sea like a soup and an air thick with stink, it was he who got sent ashore to drop off that night's sum of the Old Rolly Polly's dead stacked like cordwood and to fetch back fresh water, rowing the ship's skiff through a log-jam of corpses dumped without weights, only to find that the burial ground was six-stacked and full, and his cargo of dead should have been dumped with the rest to float till they rotted, to rot till they sank, and there is no water left on the whole of Grosse Île that is fresh not tainted ....

There is more to recall but that is enough. And all the Lookouts have a commemorative drop to themselves and to the floating dead of that damned Grosse Île. And the remainder of the watch is a silent affair.

Chapter Eleven

Grosse Île to Montréal

Meanwhile Morris is hunched over his candle as close as he dares without igniting the page. The pamphlet he is holding is entitled THE FATHER OF CANADA WELCOMES HEBREWS. During the crossing he has read it aloud to Clara so many times he can almost recite the text from memory, which soon is what he may have to do because this is their last candle.

Now only hours from Montréal harbour, he is reading out the pamphlet to Clara in the bunk above for what probably is the last time, and his whisper is hoarse with reverence. He frequently has to pause to raise his spectacles and to mop his eyes.

"… and for those exploiters who intend to treat Canada as a stepping-stone toward or a secret passage into the United States and for those ignoramuses about to discover that Canada is not the United States, we say this: we want keepers not swappers, stayers not passers-through! Hereabouts there shall be no beginning in Lamentations that ends in Exodus! Canada is a land of second chance not a land of second choice! The United States is a great country. But its open-door policy of immigration has brought about unforeseen repercussions to our great North American neighbour. Look at that mass of foreign ignorance and vice that has flooded its eastern seaboard with socialism and atheism and all the other isms corrosive to good government and tolerable society! Canada's door is not closed to worthy guests, but neither is it open to every passing mongrel. Canada especially seeks those vigorous northern races who are culturally sound and spiritually healthy, and quickly will conform to the norms of Anglo-Canadian life: preferably white migrants of British stock, especially Scots.

As well, however, the recent events in Russia and elsewhere on the tired old continent whence we descend offer us an opportunity to place a few energetic optimistic Hebrews into our least populated areas. Not just Russian Hebrews, admittedly a superior type, but even a smattering of their middle-European brethren as yet unexhausted by persecution and untainted by bitterness. They might even do us some good! Yes, yes, a sprinkling of happy Hebrews into the far North West or even upon the more barren stretches of the prairie ... what has Canada to lose by admitting and collecting and dispersing them? Characteristically, they would at once go in for peddling and usury in localities without those facilities, and the others would be of some employment as cheap-jacks and chap-men.

Urban-bound Semites, however, are not to be encouraged. As anyone can witness in the horrors of the lower east side of Manhattan Island, it does not take much cultural marginality, disruptive competition and social clannishness to reduce a once proud district to a cauldron of hawkers, peddlers and mountebanks. No Canadian city needs a Petticoat Lane!

But a few right-minded Hebrews, pliant to Canadian folkways and compliant in Canadian mores, grateful for our largesse and discrete in our society, sit well in the eye of God. And our act of selfless generosity in welcoming them and their benighted brethren might pay us some immediate dividends in attracting investment capital from grateful west-European Semitic financiers, as well as in cultivating useful future influence with their leading co-religionists in London and Paris such as the Rothschilds, the Montagues, the Cassells, the Lazards, the Montefiores, the Ephrussis and even the debased de Hirshes. A few leaden compromises for the sake of a golden future, is that not the Canadian way?

Therefore and thus, my administration that was and any that is or shall become the government of this blessed dominion is pledged to resist attempts to make of Canada's hospitable vastness a sort of anthropological garden in which to plant and to cultivate the waifs and the strays of Europe, the lost tribes of mankind and the freaks of creation. Nor shall we indulge that uncontrolled alien immigration that strikes at the foundation of every labour organization in our land by garnering from the industrial slums of the Old World and throwing into direct competition with the manufactory precincts of the New World Semitic immigrants who have been brought up under conditions that no Canadian worker would accept, and have become accustomed to performing work for wages upon which no Canadian worker could subsist. Nor shall we tolerate the social deviance common among immigrants who, once lodged among us, deliberately set up for themselves ethnic enclosures that are the breeding grounds for filth, immorality and crime.

As Canadians, as Christians, as good plain ordinary folk, of course we understand and have compassion for those poor fragments of humankind who indulge in such unwholesomeness. Emigration transforms the entire world within which such peasants as these formerly lived. From surface forms to inmost functioning, the change is complete. In the process, such miserable specimens become, even in their own eyes and without assistance from us, less worthy as men. They feel a sense of degradation that makes them naturally inclined to promulgate greater and greater depredations and depravities corrosive to the society they have invaded and weakened and, unless prevented, in due course utterly will consume and destroy.

It is not their fault that they are thus invidious and injurious. But they shall be prevented from infesting the web and the warp, the weft and the woof, altogether constituting the admirable tapestry of Canada. Those few who manage somehow to burrow-in to breed shall be plucked from our social fabric and encamphorated."

Morris closes the pamphlet. Its cover displays a portrait of its author above a simulacrum of his signature. It is a good plain ordinary face, eyes set too close together for furrows of doubt to intervene, ears too large to miss a plea for clemency, a recessive chin signalling a willingness to compromise, the narrow brow of no intellectual snob, a mottled nose editorially elongated for the comfort of a Hebrew readership. Reverently Morris passes his finger across the name ... Scots in derivation, firm and fair, displaying its knighthood with the pride of any other immigrant thus honoured. A face too homely to lie, a name too common to enhance, a vanity too transparent to resent, a man of the people accustomed to simple truth in common utterance.

Morris lays the pamphlet on a shelf where the next couple undergoing the passage also will find it and will take heart from it as he and his Clara have done. "You see," he says, "as I always told you, my dear, a clean country, strong and free, where a Jew of knowledge and culture ready to commit and to comply may hope someday to become – "

He has peeped over the side of the bunk above to discover that, despite the snores and the coughs and the embarrassing intimacies from the bunks on all sides, and despite from far-below the screams of the ballast that seem to have got louder though the St. Laurence, everyone says, is a river with currents and ripples not a sea with waves like cliffs and troughs like chasms, Clara has managed to fall asleep unaided and has saved them the expense of a pill.

By the tenth morning of the passage, the discord in the upper steerage has escalated to an unprecedented pitch of volume and vituperation. The precipitating factor – other than this being the tenth of such mornings – is the irresponsible behaviour of Doctor Barnardo and, with his encouragement, that of his forty boys in tweed. Perhaps because of the dearth of available entertainment, perhaps because at journey's end a special diversion is justified, this morning he has directed his wards to accept Father Seddon's ironic invitation to witness the enactment of the Holy Mass.

Previously Doctor Barnardo's early-day instructions have concerned such matters as hygiene, posture, self-abuse and table manners. Choric recitations of the most inspirational passages in the Book of Common Prayer have been followed by a full-voiced *a capella* rendering of every one of the thirty-seven verses of God Save The Queen that also happens to serve as the national anthem of the brave new land which the children are about to exchange for the harsh old one.

Post-breakfast rituals are specifically designed to distract the more impressionable among the boys from the religious vaudeville matins transpiring daily across the chamber. This morning, however, Doctor Barnardo instructs them all to concentrate on every moment of the Popish travesty, to scrutinize with an objective and an unbiased eye its hypocritical, superstitious, vulgar mummery, and to feel free to query its idolatrous procedure and to comment upon its bizarre performance, and to do it during its very ceremony as loudly as possible.

The boys respond to the occasion with an enthusiasm quite unlike their cowed submission to their guardian's previous directives. They flock to the forbidden side of the chamber as close to Father Seddon's holy service as permitted, and they obey Doctor Barnardo's incitement with a muscularity that drowns out the obedient antiphons of the female Catholic congregants. The vigour of the boys' intrusions is amplified by this opportunity to impress forty girls in shapeless sackcloth with the aptness of their wit and the extent of their daring.

Due to conditions in the upper steerage, the ritual of the

Holy Mass has had to be modified in choreography and content. Instead of presiding behind the altar – in this case the communal dining table with the crockery and the shaving implements shoved to either end – Father Seddon stands upon it to provide a better sightline. Thus deprived of a surface upon which to rest them, the sacred vessels of the Mass have been reduced from eight to two, which is just as well because there are only two hands available to carry them: those of the proxy deacon who is, of course, the adenoidal drudge. The Paten for the sacred Host is a tin from the officers' mess containing residual fragments of ship's biscuits. The Chalice is a pewter tankard borrowed from the Captain's cabin and refilled when required from an adjacent cask likewise obtained. The consecrated wine is a cheeky young malmsey the Captain had found disappointing.

Because of the lack of vestry facilities, Father Seddon's investiture takes place in open view. Preliminary to the main event, the boys in tweed find this stage of the spectacle especially diverting. Their rhythmic clapping and provocative asides threaten to terminate the proceeding before it properly has begun. Of particular note is the long linen garment symbolizing a priest's purity of soul – Father Seddon eschews the cord used as a belt representing chastity and continence – which reaches to his feet. Several of the boys evidently mistake it for a version of the sleeping costume they are required to wear. "Oi," they shout, "night night, Granddad!" The ornamental kerchief thrown over Father Seddon's left arm to signify the labor and the hardship a priest is prepared to undergo is similarly misread. "Dirty bugger!" shouts one of the boys. "Look what he's gone and done with his snot rag!" The long scarf worn as a sign that the priest is occupied on an official mission with judicial and magisterial overtones also is misconstrued. "He's not going to bed!" shouts another of Doctor Bernardo's lads. "He's out for a stroll! Oi, Dads, take us along!"

The liturgical colours of Father Seddon's vestments – white for innocence and triumph, red for blood and martyrdom, green for hope and generation, purple for shame and penance, gold (whenever available) for glory – have decayed in steerage to a kind of mouldy beige. In full regalia he resembles an elderly matron in a soiled raincoat and is beyond barracking. By the time the bell-shaped knee-length outer vestment signifying the virtue of universal charity is dropped over the cleric's head, the boys have pretty much abandoned comment, instinctively understanding that one cannot satirize a satire. They are reduced to mincing mime and explosive snorts.

The other high point is the performance of the adenoidal deacon's diffusing of incense. With both hands occupied, he has been obliged to hang the censer from the belt of his trousers. In order to persuade it to distribute its cargo of purifying vapours, he gyrates his hips vigorously from side to side and, when it becomes necessary to cense the congregation, back and forth with explosive finales. The boys are delighted. Their simulated drum-roll accompanies the grinds, their crescendo of groans marks every bump.

Father Seddon does his best to ignore the running commentary. The bum-wipe also does his best, which is not nearly as good. When amid a barrage of heckling he tends to the enrobing of his superior, the back of his neck approaches the purple of the outer tunic of office he himself has donned, the sacred Dalmatic intended to symbolize the joy of selfless service to a minister of God. The audience response to his provocative censing deepens the hue of his neck and spreads it to the front of his face where, from time to time, he glares in the direction of his juvenile tormentors and sniffs and snarls.

On this particular morning, the Eucharistic centre of the ceremony – the communal imbibing of the blood of Christ and the ingestion of His body – has had to be abandoned. The current pitching and rolling of the SS Laurentian, increasing with every moment that passes, already has reduced Father Seddon's congregation by the half who have retired into the recesses of the chamber to return the contents of their breakfast. The remainder retch steadfastly in their places but probably not for long. Malmsey and biscuits are not possible.

Some of these curtailments, particularly those related to the dimensions of his own role, the acting deacon appears to have taken personally. From time to time he transfers his glare from the boys in tweed and focuses it upon Father Seddon with a resentment bordering on the homicidal, though perhaps the narrowing of the eyes and the baring of the teeth are reflex responses to the acridity of his own incense. Even his frequent audible "humphs" might be a simple clearing of the bronchial tubes rather than an overt suggestion that, given the opportunity, he would restore the ceremony to its entirety and could excel his superior's performance of it.

In his sermon Father Seddon makes no concession to the age of his parishioners, the narrowness of their intellect, the shallowness of their spirit and the tumult in their guts. It is, he believes, in their own best interest fully to experience being treated as his equal, no matter how far they fall short of the equation. To accompany the oration and to underline the prose, his deacon unbuckles the censer from his belt and uses both hands to swing it metrically. The augmented fumes also are useful in masking the breath of the sermonizer who has been availing himself of that portion of the Captain's malmsey that remains pre-sanctified and quaffable, though a little short on bouquet with an excess of tannin in the follow-through.

This morning Father Seddon's delivery also is impaired by the sound of the wind beyond the hull and the rolling of the ship, both of which are increasing incrementally. "One is reminded," he yells, lurching as his novice/deacon scrambles to stabilize the crockery at the other end of the table/sideboard/altar/podium and the shaving implements at this end while attempting to maintain the rhythm of his censing, "is reminded of the distinction between fortune and fortuity, and passivity and activity, and accepting one's lot and enforcing it. In the transubstantiation of the classical gods into the Christian Virtues, the fathers of the early militant church, our beloved Paul and Peter, were vividly aware of the divided will: the *bellum intestinum* that inflicts itself upon us even today."

There is a hiatus while Father Seddon settles his own intestinal battleground with a visit to the cask. Charged tankard in hand, he weaves back across the tabletop and returns to his task. "For example," he hiccups, "it's the pagan goddess Fortuna who sits at her wheel and spins out the destiny of humankind and snips her thread with no regard for mortal benefit or individual will or intimate desire. And it's she, precisely she, she and only she, who miraculously is transformed by the masters of the church into that most Christlike of the seven blessed sisters: the saintly virtue they and we name Patience."

Here the ship lurches and the good Father struggles to minimize the spillage from his tankard, choking back an expletive. The temporary deacon, over-employed between tableware and incense, fails to choke back several.

The ordained shepherd stumbles forward and raises his tankard to the good health of those of his flock who seem still to possess it. "You would do well," he cautions them, "to embrace our dear daughter Patience and to clasp her to your budding bosoms."

The implied licentiousness does not escape the deacon. Having attended many such deteriorations in his superior's eloquence, however, he shrugs and continues to pump his censer into the faces before him, more and more of which are turning green.

"You will all," Father Seddon continues, "confront trials and tribulations in the New World no less severe than those you confronted in the Old." Father Seddon chokes with compassion and clears his throat with malmsey. Kicking aside some stray shaving implements, he moves to the forward lip of the table to be closest to his wards. His arms curve outward in a virtual embrace. His manner and his tone achieve a new level of intimate guidance and unguarded confidentiality. "This, then is my pastoral advice. Once we've deposited you in your new land and provided you with available fosterers and abandoned you to their fostering kindly or otherwise, I advise you thus: don't lose touch with one another. Be prepared to reach out to fellows of your lowly kind should you encounter cruelty, exploitation and enslavement. Be prepared to defend another of your miserable sisters should you be called upon to rescue her. Rely upon one another. Defend one another as every moment in your lowly former existence has taught you to confront every personal adversity: swiftly, mercilessly, in the spirit of the pre-Christian virtue who is the militant Patience. Respond to every abuse with direct consequence, your shivvie in your hand, your street companion at your side.

"In dealing with guttersnipes," here Father Seddon's wobbly gesture expands to include his deacon, "it's well to employ a guttersnipe of one's own." Father Seddon is exhausted. He staggers, rights himself, leans against the rolling of the ship and drains the tankard. "That," he concludes with a wave, "is the prescription this old doctor of souls offers you. Go, it's the dismissal."

There are, however, few of his parish left to dismiss. And, observing that their wit-play has been ignored by their nauseous little sisters, the boys in tweed have long since relapsed into an impenetrable sullenness. Doctor Barnardo finds the opportunity to offer a second opinion irresistible. "This old doctor of bodies," he smirks audibly, "prescribes that old doctor of souls a dose of salts. Perhaps he should find a seasoned seaman willing to oblige him."

The incense bearer clutches his censer with a convulsive spasm. "What are you implying, you little son of a – "

Father Seddon calms his deacon with a cruciform gesture, a gentle blurred smile and an affectionate burp. "It seems irresponsible," he slurs, "to remove an able-bodied sailor from his post in such perilous weather. I'm sure that the so-called doctor yonder can recommend one of his own little men for a transfer to my ward. One he's not already himself overdosed."

"This doctor," counters Doctor Barnardo, "doesn't administer to drunken hypocrites, to the chronically depraved or to ordained harlots."

"How dare you – " splutters the deacon, his censer rotating at great speed.

The gentle smile of Father Seddon has hardened and, for the moment, his brain has cleared. Abandoning repartee, he falls back upon research. Addressing the heavens beyond the heaving deck he asks rhetorically: "Thirty-five years after dropping out of medical school? Completing a bogus degree to defend against the allegations of Lord Shaftesbury? Waving it about to attract donations? How much of a doctor is that?"

"Yes!" shouts the deacon at this perceptible hit. "Yes, yes, yes, oh yes!"

Father Seddon lowers his gaze and tries to focus it upon the source of this particular earthly travail. He smiles as the Christ upon the Antichrist with an exquisite combination of charity and contempt. "Doctor?" he slurs. "What doctor?" He points across the chamber. "That little gentleman is no doctor!"

The little gentleman forgets he is a gentleman. "More a doctor than a bum-wipe is a doctor," he yelps.

The deacon forgets his holy office. "Who the hell are you calling – "

"Besides," Doctor Barnardo clenches his fist and takes a step toward the table, "I am a doctor."

"As of ten minutes ago," screams the bum-wipe dropping his censer and reaching for his razor.

Which is when disaster or fortuity intervenes.

This is what Captain Hugh ("Wily") Wylie, recent successor to Captain Robert ("Brownie") Brown, writes in the log that he will update and complete and, in a day or so, submits to the Montréal office of the Allan Line Shipping Company as an account of the most recent Atlantic crossing of the SS Laurentian.

"Mid-voyage two days out of Liverpool south of Greenland a storm struck us: an unpredictable hurricane accompanied by a deluge of rain. The ballast shifted, and our vessel began to list to one side. By certain signs apparent to a weathered eye, I had anticipated the inclemency and had instructed my seamen to herd everyone below deck, and to close and to seal the hatches. The blow lasted three days without a break and, due to our diligence and labour, was survived without great loss. Only two persons died: an old priest and a child, one encumbered by age, the other by curiosity. They were buried at sea. The disorder and disrepair below decks, in particular to the sleeping provisions in the upper cabins of the officers' quarters, was consequent to the listing of the ship before the prompt action of my crew corrected it. The damage to our hull was occasioned by collisions with those barrels of our own ballast that had been jettisoned but temporarily remained afloat. Other than the fatalities, there was no injury among my crew or my passengers.

As there was no illness on board, I did not anticipate a need further to delay our arrival by reporting for inspection at the quarantine facility on Grosse Île, but pressed on at good speed for home."

Captain Wylie writes thus to dispel any suspicion of poor seamanship in the Gulf of Saint Lawrence that might be used to jeopardize his bonus for almost maintaining the company schedule. The report fails to concur with the experience of his crew and his passengers, but there is no reason they will be consulted. Were the damage to the hull to require repair rather than repainting, were the havoc below decks to necessitate greater renovation than a straightening up and a hosing down, were the advertised Allan Line schedule of arrival and departure to experience a more catastrophic breach than a day and a half, there might have been the need for other, perhaps conflicting, testimony. "Not," Captain Wylie chuckles into his brandy, "bloody likely." With Montréal half a day ahead and Grosse Île invisible in his wake, he closes his logbook, removes his jacket, mops its lapels and goes to bed.

It is earlier that day that the incident described in Captain Wylie's logbook as a storm at sea actually occurs. It is not a storm. It is not at sea. It is a grounding, and it takes place in the twenty-one island Île-aux-Grues archipelago thirty miles downstream of Quebec City on the south bank of the Saint Lawrence River off Saint François de Montmagny, the snow goose capital of Canada, just opposite Grosse Île in the fog in the dark. There is no warning. Just a terrible screech of the hull at the abrupt arrest of its forward progress and a universal concussion followed by a series of thuds from below.

That internal cannonade must signify that the barrels of the ballast are rolling across and piling up against one side of the hold. That is the side the SS Laurentian is listing toward and not straightening out and, every time there is a plunge into the valley of a wave or even a jostle against the current of a contrary wash, listing to that same side a little more, and then and then and then a little more, with ominous creaks from each of the mainmasts and preliminary waggles of the smokestack, all holding fast but with every further list creaking and waggling a little more.

The effect below decks is that of a slow catastrophe, though for the first time on the voyage events favour the steerage. According to the logic of verticality, those levels closest to the deck suffer the greatest degree of tilt and, consequently, the greater quantity of pendulating fixtures, smashing glass, colliding furniture and spontaneous precipitations from bed to floor. As the levels descend, the degree of inclination lessens. As well, of course, the further below, the sparser are the furnishings and the less fragile. At the lowest inhabited stratum everything is secured to the floor to prevent pilfering of valuable ship's property such as the triple tiers of worthless metal bunks. Even there, however, the tilt is noticeable, and the thunder from deep-below leaves no denizen of the lower steerage in doubt about the gravity of the situation and its likely outcome. From just-above, there is the sound of eighty children sliding and shrieking, though it filters through the floorboards as a low unbroken moan.

Who knows how the dancing in the lower steerage begins and with whom? On a sloping floor, after all, to dance is not so easy. It takes a concentration, a purpose and an energy that make it difficult to abandon oneself to the flow of the dance, to lose oneself in it and, for a moment, not to fear. Nevertheless, many decide to try.

From somewhere a fiddler has materialized. Except for his cloth cap he is invisible amid the throng, but the sound of his instrument rises above even the thunder of the barrels. In a curious way his music begins to accommodate the thunder, to incorporate it into the voice of his violin as a remote percussive rhythm, even – and the music must grow very animated and the dance must become very inclusive to support this illusion – seeming to dominate the thunder, to lead it from one side of the melody to the other as, indeed, it does the dancers until probably, possibly, plausibly the weight of their numbers and the impact of their stamping shiver the very timbers of the SS Laurentian herself and, as a part of the illusion, she seems to forget in which direction she is listing, and she begins to seem to right herself or at least to resume her habitual harmless vertical roll.

"We're sinking," says Morris. "What are they doing?"

Clara is standing on the upper bunk to improve her view. "Dancing," she says.

"We're going to die," says Morris. "Is this a time to dance?"

"Can you think," says Clara, "of a better time?"

Morris has to agree that Clara has a point. "My dear betrothed," he says, "in what might very well be our last hour together in bodily form, don't you agree that this is the very moment for us to – "

"My dear Morris," says Clara, clambering down, "the engagement is off." It is then that he notices she has put on a headscarf he did not know she owned. It is creased from being kept under her mattress. She makes her way up the incline of the floor to its peak where Billy is revolving at the epicentre. She joins his revolution. When she is certain, she reaches up and kisses him. He returns the compliment. They both do. And again.

"Clara?" he says and touches the headscarf.

"Of course," she replies.

As the dance floor regains the horizontal, a shriek rises above the sound of the violin and brings about the termination of the dancing and the evaporation of the fiddler. Berthe is sitting upright in her middle bunk and has cast off her shawl and is staring at her hands. They are covered with blood. So is her bunk. So is the dripping underside of the bunk above hers. She shrieks again and shows her hands and mews like a kitten.

Billy rushes to her side. As does Clara to his. As does Morris, who has not entirely given up his hope, to hers.

Billy holds one of Berthe's bloody hands. Morris, who does not know why he is doing it, holds the other.

Clara uses her headscarf to wipe Berthe's face and inspects her for wounds and finds none. She sniffs the blood and then she tastes it. Mostly it is wine. Clara offers Berthe a lick to prove it. Berthe licks and licks again, and giggles. Clara smiles.

"What's her name?" Morris asks Billy.

"Berthe," says Berthe.

"Blessed," says Billy automatically.

"What?" says Morris.

"Berthe from Brokhe or Brucha or Bracha or Brecha (ברכה breck-hah)," says Billy. "It means blessed. Or something."

So Berthe remembers what the lady also told her that she already knows. "Born-a-miracle," she adds. It is pretty much the last thing she gets to say. It is Clara's turn to shriek.

Meanwhile, above the empty bunk above Berthe's above the ceiling of the lower steerage, the dining table has cleared itself of the paraphernalia of the Holy Mass. The biscuit tin is overturned and the cask is smashed. The floor is abrasive with crumbs and awash with sacramental wine. In a rare tribute Captain Wylie has left his bunk to attend the scene. He is standing by the table staring down. Sprawled on his back on the floor, Father Seddon is staring back, unfortunately sightless. His head is twisted at an odd angle and he lies in a carmine pool that has stopped spreading but is continuing to leak through the floorboards. Some of it already has congealed.

"His neck," says the Captain, in response to an opinion offered by a nun, "may very well be broken, but his throat is – "

Father Seddon's personal novice is distraught. "The ship!" he manages. "The ship just suddenly ... and he was on the table and he just suddenly ... I was reaching out to him ... I tried to catch him but I ... I was holding ... in my hand ... this hand ... this bloody hand ..." He drops the razor. It grazes the face of his recumbent employer, inflicting little damage. Or quite a lot. It really does not matter. Sobbing convulsively, the sometime barber and recent deacon and erstwhile ship's doctor collapses against the Captain's jacket, his sinuses threatening to engulf them both.

The Captain awaits developments.

Doctor Barnardo is gathering the little Eves of the late Father Seddon into his side of the chamber and permitting them to mingle with his little Adams in what is now destined to become an ecumenical arrangement at his soon-to-be-expanded non-denominational governmentally subsidized and charitably maintained cross-gender orphans' refuge in Toronto. The nuns already are preparing to wrap the body of their saint in the sail-cloth the Captain kindly has had delivered for the purpose. It is a large sailcloth, large enough, one of the nuns observes, for a double burial at sea were all the parts of the boy in tweed to be gathered from the hold. Everyone looks inquiringly at Doctor Barnardo. He shrugs, sighs, separates one little girl and one little boy who are not respecting the occasion and nods his accord.

Indeed there can be immediate burials at sea, Captain Wylie assures them all, though technically it is a river. They do not have to wait for the fog to clear. "Less fuss," he says, "than all that paperwork at Montréal. Properly weighted, just as effective and, since 1847, a Grosse Île tradition." He dispatches a strong-stomached sailor with a shovel and a several buckets into the hold.

And now he wishes to propose a compassionate improvisation. Instead of him performing the final rites, why not let Father Seddon's personal novice officiate? That worthy snuffles, swallows, smirks and nods his acceptance, which saves the Captain's jacket from further damage and frees him to return to his cabin to compose his duplicitous log.

For their hour and a half in Montréal before the departure of the train to Out West, Billy and Clara have gone to the east end to visit Chaim. It has not been a complete waste of time.

Billy gives his brother a decorative head scarf as a memento of the Holy Land and his sister-in-law another that Clara gets the impression will be used as a kitchen towel once it has been washed.

Observing that the family name of his brother's haberdashery already has been made to accord with what was the snowy season of the year when its proprietor's mortgage was arranged, Billy teasingly tries to persuade Chaim to change his other name to Charlie. Chaim's queenly wife insists on nothing less than "Charles" and calls Billy "Baruch" and does not call Clara anything at all.

On the train Out West, Clara and Billy decide after all to carry on one stop past Regina to Moose Jaw. Forty-five miles away from Morris, she reckons, is just about right. It is the jaw of a moose, Billy reckons, so what can be bad?

Morris and Berthe are asleep on the bench opposite, her head in his armpit, a slight glow emanating from her brow although her fever has departed with the ship. She already has had a dream of a prairie metropolis even bigger than Brody, so perhaps she is having it again. She is certain the city in the dream bears the innuendo of a queen. She is only not certain of where it is or when. From what Morris has read to her about Regina recently acquiring its first tar-paper shack with the possibility of a grain silo in due course, she thinks she may be out by many miles and half a century. But Morris is so in love with the idea of implementing his plan with a fifteen-year-old that he probably would not bother correcting her conjecture, and in a few days and nights they both will know the truth so why mention?

Berthe readjusts to Morris's armpit and pulls her shawl about herself. It smells of morning or perhaps mid-day. For the moment she has no dream at all, and the glow recedes from her brow. Then she dreams of the silo at Regina rising out of the flatland like a standing stone, like one in a circle of standing stones, like the remains of a windbreak, of a rampart, of a battlement emblazoned in the great wall of a city with, in the middle, a tower to the stars or at least a beginning. And she dreams that there, beside the aspiring silo and the man in the cloth cap who built it, the lady in the light is smiling and beckoning and, to the music of the wind through the fiddlehead ferns, is dancing on the prairie like the dawn. And a little of the glow returns.

Morris sleeps. In view of the occasion he has taken the pill.

Clara stares at her niece. Then she stares at Billy and shakes her head. "What a business!" she says.

"Business?" he replies.

"Dozens in steerage, what were the odds?"

"Well," says Billy, "it was a dark and stormy night."

"But mostly," says Clara, "it was an accident."

Chapter Twelve

The Tie Rack

I could tell it was handmade because the sides were not symmetrical and the rail between them designed to hold the ties I did not own because this birthday was only my seventh ran slightly off the horizontal. Even then I knew that, when I was old enough for ties, they would slide sideways and machines do not make mistakes like that. My mother insisted on displaying it because her father had made it by hand and he could barely afford the stamps to mail it to me from Regina to Montréal. So I persuaded her to hang my tie rack on the inside of my bedroom cupboard door where none of my friends with perfect birthday bicycles would see the humiliating hole in its plywood frame formed from the template of a heart.

Before the tie rack I was five and I kept a ladybird alive in a matchbox for three days and three nights, sitting up with my mother in a day coach from Vancouver to Montréal because sleeper berths cost extra and my father who had gone on ahead months before us still had not found a job because as yet The War had failed entirely to heal The Depression. We broke that trip at Regina for a few hours with my mother's parents. Decades later, going through my parents' correspondence unearthed from a green plastic garbage bag after they died, I discovered that my father had written from Montréal to Vancouver to remind my mother on the Regina stop-over not to allow her father to touch me nor me to touch my Grandpa Morris or any single thing he recently had touched, which prohibition must have included my Grandma Berthe since I remember nothing of her except that she never was given the chance to say anything and that her shawl smelt like sleep. The ladybird, however, was round and red and speckled and preferred sesame seeds to breadcrumbs and liked being touched and had never had TB.

After the tie rack I was nine and my mother's five brothers and sisters bought their father a return ticket from Regina to Montréal because he needed to explain to us how he had wakened in the morning to realize that his Berthe had died beside him in the night and he had lain there weeping beside her for hours and had seemed a little down ever since.

His visit coincided with the time God instructed me not to eat because my food was poisoned and not to sleep because I would not wake. Later it was discovered that my father's youngest brother, just returned from The War, had been taking me into his bed to describe the smell of burning bodies covered in machine oil and to explain to me why, after The War, for a homeland the Jews should be given Germany. But that discovery came after my Grandpa Morris had returned to Regina to die in the same bed as his wife and before my mother could explain to him why his grandson had failed to cheer him up or to speak to him at all. Oh, and for his visit she had forgotten to move the tie rack temporarily to the front.

I guess the tie rack hung crookedly in the shadows throughout the years my bedroom cupboard door came to bear slogans of cynical irony and posters of the impossibly fit and a full-length mirror that never quite gave back the tough symmetrical image behind my eyes. By the time I finally acquired some adult ties that required hanging, the tie rack had vanished entirely to the back of my memory where it limps to the front on occasions such as this. Of course all that happened before I understood that lopsided does not mean imperfect. It means made by hand.

The Oliphants and the Jews

Of those despatched to Brody by the Mansion House Committee, Laurence Oliphant was the most famous and the least Jewish. In fact he was a little famous and not Jewish at all, but adept at amplifying the first when required and simulating the second when beneficial.

His renown was based upon the identity of the men he had served and the words he had written about them. The men had been great and his words recorded the greatness of his service. His sponsors and intimates – generally aristocratic eminences and political grandees, the lords Russell, Stratford, Elgin, and Ashley, the prime ministers Palmerston, Russell, Salisbury, Disraeli, and Gladstone among them – were internationally consequential and, in their service and sometimes on a service more secret than theirs, so was he. An unlikely choice for the Mansion House mission to refloat Jews beached in Brody by distributing a little cash among them, there was evidence – albeit gossip – that Albert "Bertie" Edward, the Prince of Wales, had nominated him.

In an age when imperial diplomacy was abetted by the undercover operation of globe-touring amateurs, Oliphant had journeyed as far and as perilously as any Livingstone, Burton, Stanley or Mrs. Trollope, and he wrote about it better. A participating sycophant in that system of secrets among the British elite that was known – then and now – as "honour," he was present at and actively involved in the repression of French Canada and the savage dispossession of its aboriginals, the siege of Sevastopol, the filibuster of Nicaragua, the annexation of Nice, the ceding of Venetia, the rescue of Calcutta, the capture of Canton, the penetration of China, the rape of Schleswig-Holstein and the birth of modern Japan.

He was instrumental in designing the Crimean Campaign, in determining the route of the Panama Canal, in laying the transatlantic submarine telegraph cable, in strategizing the Indian Mutiny, in provoking the unification of Italy and abetting that of Germany, in collaborating with the partisans of the Polish Revolution and in causing (inadvertently) the Second War of Schleswig.

He cavorted with Jung Bhadur Ranam, bantered with Ahmet Pasha and dined with Count Cavour. He manoeuvred (naively) with Jay Gould, conspired (obediently) with General Garibaldi, cautioned (vainly) the Emperor Maximilian, negotiated (absurdly) with Chancellor Bismarck and lobbied (disastrously) for Prince Frederick of Augustenburg. He survived poisoning along the Volga, depression in Circassia, migraines at Primkenau and Gotha, assassination (barely) at Edo.

As gentleman adventurer, man of letters, sometime diplomat and spy, he was endlessly enthusiastic, recklessly intrusive, disarmingly perceptive, politically pliant, indefatigably opinionated, permanently newsworthy and occasionally dependable. He spoke eleven languages and wrote in five. He was glib in prose and conversation, mother-fixated, guru-inclined, probably bisexual, possibly syphilitic, reputedly hermaphrodite (or castrate), repressed, explosive, bald, plain and stylish. He was flirtatiously charming and intermittently insane. In the word of his Queen and Empress who knew him as well as she cared to, he was "interesting."

Oliphant's intricate role in the loss of Schleswig-Holstein – a loss to Denmark and its ally England, a gain to Austria and

Prussia until their war over its ownership two years later – along with his outrageously indiscreet published criticism of his own party's Prime Minister and Foreign Secretary, buoyed by his cheerful self-confidence that he was expressing the (unattributable) pro-German opinion of Victoria and her late dear Albert – combined to terminate his career as a freelance diplomat and a secret agent.

Faced with this dead-end, he decided on a more settled existence in an England he barely knew after ten years spent mostly abroad. Almost as an afterthought he ran for Parliament and won a seat in the very ruling party the leadership of which he previously had alienated and now continued to offend with a first novel satirizing the veniality of the high society that they and he represented.

In his maiden speech (charitably curtailed by the Speaker) he was condescending to his seniors and flippant about Ireland. In his debut motion for debate (embarrassingly withdrawn by his Whip) he managed to undermine his own party's keynote bill. For two years he bedevilled his government with politically inexpert and bizarre uninvited interventions into foreign affairs, and he served his constituents with his entire absence from his constituency. Then he resigned his seat due to, he said, "headaches and all the symptoms in my head of softening of the brain." There was another reason, or perhaps another version of the same one. Laurence Oliphant had entered the early stages of a two-decade thraldom to an American charismatic and charlatan: Thomas Lake Harris, founder, leader and deity of "The Brotherhood of the New Life."

Wooing of Oliphant to the messianic sect had been unnecessary. Within days of meeting Harris whom he feared and admired, within weeks of the death of his father whom he admired and feared, he abandoned his country, his career, his reputation and most of his friends (he took his mother with him), and he sailed off to share the "Great Awakening" and to live "The Life" and to join "The Use" of the "Worldly Holies" (vs. the "Wholly Worldlies") and the "Hero Martyrs" at "Father Faithful's" socialist / spiritualist / utopian / totalitarian commune in the backwoods of upper New York State on the border with Connecticut.

Through nearly a decade of "purification and humbling," Oliphant (renamed "Woodbine," a creeper) lived in squalor and performed demeaning tasks, hand-gathering manure and embroidering petticoats the least of them. He was then dispatched back to England, partly as a further spiritually cleansing exercise in personal humiliation – England obliged by cutting him when he appeared in society and ignoring him when he did not – but mainly to earn money for the Brotherhood by a resumption of what threadbare political leverage and rusty journalistic skills remained accessible to him.

From the beginning of their association Thomas Lake Harris had spotted Laurence Oliphant's true and original talent: the ability to see a business opportunity where others – Harris proudly counted himself among these – could see only the will of God, though with Father Faithful that perception amounted to looking in a mirror. The first test of Oliphant's perceived vocation had occurred when Harris sent him into the gold-rush atmosphere of desolate coastal Newfoundland – the famous transatlantic submarine cable was scheduled to surface there – to sweep up for the benefit of the Brotherhood what commercial windfalls might become available.

On that mission the student exceeded his mentor's mandate by single-handedly manipulating the Canadian and the British governments into breaking the monopoly of the Anglo-Canadian Telegraph Company. His instrument was the Marine Telegraph Bill of 1874 which he personally devised and, by a combination of influential acquaintance and outright lies, lobbied through the Canadian and the British parliaments, convincing each government that it was in danger of exploitation by the other, thereby promoting for himself a lucrative position at the New York headquarters of Anglo-Canadian's principal rival, the U.S. Cable Company. Gathering the bulk of Oliphant's salary with U.S. Cable into the coffers of the Brotherhood, Father Faithful advised the disciple that his guru forgave him the degradation of these worldly accomplishments and assured him that he was protected from the loss of his humility by the contempt of the rest of the Brethren who had remained at home in the commune to pray.

On his subsequent European money-raising quest, Oliphant was given similar covenants and blessings in advance, with the added instruction that the funds he would earn abroad and send home should be derived from British or French sources which, at the moment, yielded the more stable of the international currencies.

Popularly remembered as a potentially great man ruined by an unfortunate but modish peccadillo rather than as a middling man stretched beyond mediocrity by great acquaintance and a talent for impersonation, upon his return to the continent of his birth Laurence Oliphant found *pro tem* employment in Paris as a foreign correspondent to THE TIMES. Almost immediately this marginal post became magnified by the surprising outbreak of the Franco-Prussian War. Alert as always to fortune amid misfortune, he managed to play both sides for the duration, narrowly avoiding arrest in Frankfurt and lynching in Lyon. For a year and a half he turned in copy regarding his first-hand witness of France under invasion and occupation: the destruction of Châteaudun, the taking / relinquishing / retaking of Orléans, the battle of Beaugency, the bombardment of Paris, the surrender of Rouen and, finally, the negotiated armistice and the short violent life of the Commune.

Midway through these horrors, in an emotional seizure that not even Thomas Lake Harris could have foreseen, Oliphant was alerted by a bullet that missed. He panicked, rushed back to New York State, plucked his mother from the privations of the Brotherhood and returned them both to Paris where, until the cessation of hostilities, her talismanic presence could protect him from bullets yet to be fired.

There, with the calming reassurance of his mother, he was introduced to a fellow religious enthusiast named – despite her being English – Alice le Strange. Then his mother died and, after a spell of suicidal grief, he failed to. Instead he married Alice and transported her to the New World to introduce her to the profundities and the ecstasies of the Brotherhood.

Together they underwent a further decade of humiliation and despair. Alice's humbling included being temporarily buried up to the neck to indicate the transience of her (considerable) earthly beauty, and being exiled to Father's vacation vineyard on the Pacific Coast where she resisted adulterously becoming a part of his summer harem. Laurence's calvary featured a guru-ordained sexual abstinence within marriage, applicable on the rare occasions when he was not separated from the commune and his virgin bride by his continent-wide money-raising enterprises on their behalf.

Then Laurence quarrelled with Father Faithful over a personal matter. Father faithfully responded by banishing both Oliphants to England where they vowed to continue to respect his sexual proscription until it was rescinded (it never was), and to reconsider the extent of an unquarrelsome devotion to The Use.

Such was the history and the condition of Laurence Oliphant when he arrived at Brody to play his part in the charitable Mansion House mission to aid the stranded Russian Jews. Back in England where his war reportage was still remembered by connoisseurs of bloodshed, he had been nominated for the jaunt by an unnamed royal in a nudge toward rehabilitation via association with philanthropic endeavour and, probably, because he was known to have been an intimate of Count Adam Potocki whose Polish family were the hereditary governors of the region.

As well, Oliphant alone among the Mansion House delegates actually had been to Brody ... once, accidentally, twenty years earlier during the Polish insurrection against Russia when, in the midst of a covert operation, his map case was stolen and he got lost. On that inadvertent visit he had noted Brody's native Jews – a miniscule population of them in comparison to the later surge – in their long black coats, long black beards, curled black side locks and stiff black hats "buzzing and swarming the arcaded market square like iridescent dung beetles going about their loathsome business." Thereafter, wherever he encountered "the nation of Jewry," it always claimed his attention, especially those aboriginals at its ecstatic extremities.

These were the sum of Laurence Oliphant's complicated credentials for his assignment to the Mansion House delegation. His last-minute inclusion increased the contingent by a half, not a third. At his non-negotiable insistence, he was accompanied by his wife.

In her youth no single feature of limb or lineament accounted for the beauty of Alice le Strange. Every nuance of her manner contained it, every flicker of her deportment displayed it, making instruction in decorum unnecessary and advice on demeanour redundant. Cosmetic enhancement, haberdashery complement and decorative embellishment scarcely found a place to begin.

An inclination to tubercular bronchitis left Alice's figure slim and her complexion transparent and her posture and perambulation cautious, a combination fashionably perceived as elegant. Had she the misfortune of falling from a great height and a bystander the capacity of analysing her descent in a series of tableaux, he would be unable to isolate a single frame in which the distribution and the line of her plummeting body contained other than a graceful harmony sufficient to make him wonder how such a compendium of poise and balance ever came to fall.

In male society young Alice's modesty was calculated. Her voice was limpid, her stare unchallenging, the composition of her facial features tranquil and only slightly bovine. Her accomplishments were uncompetitive – hemming and horticultural husbandry among them – if a little rural. Her talents were discreetly concealed. Her devotion to chapel, charity and chastity was reassuringly conventional, and her personal fortune was unspectacular but adequately greater than the needs of a lifetime.

However, among similar daughters of Norfolk gentry whose families also contained noble residue – the full name of Alice's late father, a conventional but lucrative religious watercolourist, was Henri l'Estrange-Styleman Le Strange – such attributes were not unprecedented, and they required an additional ingredient to distinguish the bearer from her peers. Alice found hers in a spiritual enthusiasm that exceeded Protestantism. As youth gave way to womanhood, she practised it in private, imparting to her cheek a febrile flush and to her conversation a hectic unpredictability.

Doubtless it was the sum of these singularities that attracted young bachelors to Alice and the singularity of the sum that restrained them from curtailing her independence which, as she neared the end of her twenties, was threatening to amount to a conspicuous state of spinsterhood. Latterly she sported as well an intimidating Continental manner brought about by her mother's developing taste for salon life in literary

Paris where her daughter's maturing beauty might be displayed luminously amid the luminaries.

It was in Paris that Alice's mother met the mother of Laurence Oliphant basking in the reflected glow of her son's distant scintillation as disgraced spy, notorious author, failed MP and, more recently, as war-observer for the ("incroyablement!" "impardonnablement!") neutral THE TIMES.

The ambitious widows struck it off at once, each initially overestimating the other's cultural endowment, both eventually content to secure the companionship of a kindred ineptitude amid the bookish babble of over-rapid French. They also discovered a mutual interest in arranging a brilliant match for the matchless brilliance of their respective shining lights.

The meeting between those two eligibilities was artfully arranged and skilfully managed. The venue was a travel lecture instructively illustrated with hyalotype slides of Egypt. The means was a pair of adjoining chairs. The strategy was several prolonged withdrawals to the powder room by both parental chaperones.

In the limelight flicker of the magic lantern, the radiance of Alice's person proved almost as compelling to Laurence as his mother's approval of their better acquaintance. It did not lessen Alice's enthusiasm for him that, when excited by the impassive projected image of the Sphinx, he whispered that his real mission amid the godless barbarians of Fleet Street had been the subsidizing of a sect of transcendental illuminati ... a saintly American community he and his mother intended to rejoin now that, with the conclusion of the Franco-Prussian *divertissement*, his usefulness to it as a cash resource in Europe seemed to have run out. It was at that instant that she offered her burning cheek to the coolness of his lips.

Their formal betrothal was something of a respectable travel arrangement complemented by the prophylactic presence of Alice's future mother-in-law who continued to mistake her son's foreign employment to be an heroic rather than a fiscal crusade, and to persist in believing that his return to upper New York State was a progress toward spiritualist coronation, and to foresee that her own destiny would be that of a queen mother well-placed to wreak vengeance upon those colonials responsible for the sickening indignities of her earlier time among them.

Thus, in a surfeit of anticipation, Laurence's mother grew over-excited and died and, after a decent interval for his self-recrimination, her son and Alice married. Then at last they embarked for Thomas Lake Harris's theocracy to secure his pontifical permission sexually to consummate their union. Her duty to her daughter satisfied, Alice's mother receded into the indifference of a second marriage.

Alice Oliphant's travail at The Brotherhood of the New Life paralleled that of her husband's first decade there, but it contained episodes specific to her nature and peculiar to her gender. The particular barbarity of it was related to Father Faithful's reaction to her pulchritude and, despite his sacramental assurances of his own unageing eternality, to his senile prurience that especially flourished in the throbbing vineyards of his summer retreat under the California sun.

The cruelty of Alice's induction and the humiliations of her daily persecution – required to dwell apart from her fellow communards, her service to them was invariably scullion and frequently excremental – were also associated with the fact that it was Laurence, the trusted financial mainstay of the commune, who had caused her to be there. Initially christened "Lily Queen," she was demoted to "Devil Incarnate" when it became known that, without Father's permission, in the fertile soil of postwar Paris she had matrimonially wreathed with Woodbine. The deity's permission to carnalize their entwinement was indefinitely withheld.

The fortitude with which Alice bore "The Life in The Use" was her own, the enforced abandonment of her by her itinerant husband during that terrible decade being virtually total. The permanent target of Father's obscene fantasies and pursuance, she was on the verge of suicide or, worse, capitulation. Her escape was timely and to a large extent accidental. On one of his rare visits home to the commune Laurence happened upon a draft contract in Father's distinctive hand that consigned Alice's personal property and the property of her person to the exclusive proprietorship of one Thomas Lake Harris. The couple's reaction to the discovery was instantaneous and, in the circumstances, rather brave. Bearing only the property of their persons, they fled.

To the former acquaintances who encountered her upon her return to England none of these vicissitudes seemed to have had any visible effect on the enduring comeliness of Alice except, perhaps, around her eyes that had narrowed in their sockets to produce an expression that in another plainer countenance might have been described as sly, and in her lips that had thinned and become set in a fine dry line with, at a single corner, the hint of a bitter smile. At Brody, ripe for an epiphany to release herself and her husband into their next transcendental servitude, she displayed an eagerness at the verge of ecstasy.

Post-biblically the restoration of Jews to the Holy Land was not a new idea. Laurence Oliphant did not feel comfortable with an idea that had not been stretched and suppled before he wore it as his own. He did, however, prefer one unlikely to be reclaimed by its former owners after he had become comfortable in its use, so he never named them, hoping they would not be alerted by the wearing or offended by the alterations or notice the omission of a label.

For some time before Brody, Laurence had his eye on a doctrinal vestment newly fashionable in Evangelical circles.

The recent re-popularized prophecy that the second coming of Christ would occur and the souls of the righteous be saved only when the Jews were restored to Zion was a kinder use of those necessary enemies of Christendom than Cardinal Manning's earlier one that made them the enablers of the Antichrist, and it was a gentler forecast of their future than conversion or assimilation or the more forthright third ("final") solution. For Laurence and Alice the prophecy was an attractive alternative to the threadbare theology of Thomas Lake Harris who lately had taken to announcing himself as the embodiment of the "Come-Again" and wherever he stood as the "Land-of-Holies."

In classic Evangelistic interpretation, once the Jews were returned to Palestine they would be inspired to accept Jesus as their Messiah and would rebuild the Temple. That architectural signal would usher in the thousand-year reign of mankind's True Savior who obligingly would return to take up residence there. Originating in pre-Christian debates among Jewish eschatologists who were preoccupied with "the messianic kingdom to come" and were obsessed with the prediction of its date, duration and postal zone, there was no Biblical reference which specifically recorded this prophecy; for those fanatics and for the Gentile pedants who followed them there were only extrapolations of text – in particular of tangled passages in Daniel and Revelations – which tended toward it. Eighteen hundred years after Christ's brief first visit, entire sects and movements at the mystical extremities of Protestantism had come to be based upon these "readings."

One of the premillennial schisms postulated that the lost tribes of Israel actually were the genetic forebears of the Angles and the Saxons and the Danes, and that Britons therefore actually are Jews and the Holy Land is an entitled dominion of the Empire, a sort of Canada where sand replaced snow. In her teens Alice Oliphant had flirted with the concept largely because of her father's commissioned watercolour of its "Revealed Prince and Prophet," a swashbuckling Canada-born healer, teacher, necromancer and officer in the Royal Navy. She lost interest when she learned that the beautiful man had spent the last thirty years of his life in an Islington asylum for the criminally insane designing flags, uniforms and palaces for his "New Jerusalem."

A slightly less bizarre spin-off a generation later had provoked a feasibility study by four Church of Scotland ministers. On a "Mission of Inquiry to The Jews" they travelled through France, Greece, Egypt and Gaza, seeking out Jewish communities and cheerfully inquiring their readiness to accept Christ and their preparedness to ship out to Zion: "a land without a people," in the current sloganeering of Protestant restorationists, "for a people without a land." On their return trip they made the mistake of calling in at Brody where they observed "a complete air of Judaism over the whole town" but "tolerable cleanliness with a hospital and several wooden sidewalks" amid a demographic of "forty rich to several thousand poor with some learning among them, the Jew-men argumentative and aggressively mercantile, every daughter of Zion possessing a fondness for a fine headdress."

That brisk appraisal was based upon one overnight stay, and it featured the souvenir purchase of a prayer book, a prayer shawl, phylacteries and a door-post talisman, the acquisition of which "superstitious mementoes" they were called upon to explain to the local constabulary who had been observing, and suspected them to be agents of Austrian espionage or, at the least, proselytizers on a mission to convert. Their arrest, interrogation and release served to make the gentle Presbyterians painfully aware of "the system of jealous espionage maintained in this kingdom of Popish darkness," and sped them on their way back to Scotland in an ungenerous spirit of relief.

In his youth the published report of the Scots' mission was among Laurence Oliphant's favourite reading, and its crusading star performer – a preacher, pastor, poet and prodigy among divines who died heroically of typhus and overwork at twenty-nine – became his earliest paragon. Inspired, a youthful Laurence enthusiastically pressed himself into service among the Jewish poor of the east end of London. His guide on those expeditions was Laura, the elderly Lady Troubridge, an experienced dispenser of a cold and determined Evangelistic charity of the sort that, in her earlier days, had prompted her to ready her children for a party and then, when they were dressed and dancing in anticipation, telling them there was no party and sending them back upstairs in tears: a salutary life experience, she assured them, of disappointment and grief. A similar hard-edged attitude to philanthropic endeavour in Whitechapel, she assured young Oliphant, would prepare the Jews of their soup-kitchen for "enlightenment and return."

Typically, Laurence bore the ferocity of his wizened companion and the squalor of their mission for the sake of making a greater acquaintance. This was accomplished when Lady Troubridge introduced him to her hero – and that of every Evangelist in England – Lord Anthony Ashley Cooper, lately become the seventh Earl of Shaftesbury. It was the example of Shaftesbury, the crusading parliamentarian, pre-eminent social reformer and universal philanthropist, that added political, strategic and commercial dimensions to Laurence's immature premillennialism. Returning Jews to the Holy Land, the Earl recognized, was one thing; returning the use of the Holy Land to the Jews was quite another. Since the entire area enclosing Jerusalem presently was an outlying province of the Turkish Empire, to render it hospitable to a Semitic influx would require an unravelling of the historical fabric and a reweaving of the geographical tapestry, altogether a considerable political undertaking potentially eased by the current happy coincidence of the virtual emptiness of the Turkish treasury and the relative fullness of the British.

Unlike emphatic Lady Troubridge, Shaftesbury developed arguments in support of his cause. Because of the continuing power of the premillennialist prophecy among Evangelists in England and America, an appeal based upon it would release large sums of money on two continents. Settling Jews into that part of the Turkish province of Syria which presently contained the biblical Holy Land could be used to promote a British protectorate over the entire region. And, other than the administrative expense of distributing a little bribery (i.e. "charitable contributions"), none of it would cost the Exchequer a penny!

A perfect Shaftesburian blend of ethereal motivation and terrestrial utility, awaiting only the appropriate religion-political catastrophe to justify its implementation[9] ... who could resist it? Not the Mansion House Committee nor the Royal House of Saxe-Coburg-Gotha. Not the Rothschild plutocracy nor the Zionist crusade. Not the Protestant imperative nor the Catholic pragmatic. Certainly not Laurence and Alice Oliphant. Fair game, then, for a reciprocal exploitation: mine.

Photographer: Mrs. Jackie Winter

Bio-bibliography

Two and a half generations after the stories in this novel, I was born in Moose Jaw. I completed my university education in Montréal and Toronto, and taught English literature, modern theatre and creative writing at several Canadian and British universities including Collège Militaire Royal (St. Jean, Québec), University of Toronto (Toronto), York University (Toronto), University of Prince Edward Island (Charlottetown) and University of Bristol (UK). For twelve years I was the resident playwright and the dramaturge at Toronto Workshop Productions[10] as well as a freelance playwright/producer/director/performer. Then my British wife and I moved to England where I have continued to lecture (occasionally to teach) and to write stage plays, radio and television shows and cinema films, academic and popular journalism (in MODERN LANGUAGE QUARTERLY, TIMES EDUCATIONAL SUPPLEMENT, THE GUARDIAN, THE OBSERVER, THE TELEGRAPH, PRIVATE EYE, COUNTRY LIFE, THE POETRY REVEW, POETRY SCOTLAND, CANADIAN THEATRE REVIEW, THEATRE RESEARCH IN CANADA, etc.), prose fiction and nonfiction, and several poetry collections: SCALES (Montréal: McGill University, 1958), THE ISLAND (Fredericton: Fiddlehead Poetry Books, 1973), MISPLACED PERSONS (Cornwall: Peterloo Poets 1995), THE BALLAD OF BLADUD (Bath: Bath City Books, 1999), NOMAD'S LAND (Bath, Bath City Books, 2000). My most recent books are THE TALLIS BAG (Ottawa: Oberon Press, 2012), MY TWP PLAYS: A COLLECTION INCLUDING "TEN LOST YEARS, (Vancouver: Talonbooks, 2013), and THAT BUSINESS AT BRODY (Winnipeg: At Bay Press, 2024). Recognition for my work includes the Telegram Theatre Award for the Best New Canadian Play (BEFORE COMPIEGNE), the Chalmers Award for the Outstanding Canadian Play (TEN LOST YEARS), the Canadian Film Award ("Etrog") for the Best Documentary Film (SELLING OUT), an Academy Award nomination ("Oscar") for the Best Short Subject (SELLING OUT), the Ontario Arts Council Senior Writer's Award, the Canada Council Senior Arts Fellowship, the C. Day-Lewis Fellowship of the Greater London Arts Association, the Arts Council of Great Britain Creative Writing Fellowship (twice). Or, in the words of a colleague, mentor, friend and fellow subsidy addict and victim: "Chrissake, Jack, will you go out and get a job?"[11]

Notes

1. I can believe it. On September 28, 2018, the mayor of Kyiv, Ukraine, reversed an earlier decision and announced that, after all, a tourist hotel will not be built near the famous ravine at Babi Yar. For fear of visitors being put off by the lingering smell of 33,771 murdered Jews?

2. *Laurence Oliphant 1829–1888* (Oxford: Oxford University Press, 1982).

3. *Moses of the New World, The Work of Baron de Hirsch* (London: Thomas Yoseloff Ltd., 1970).

4. *The Little Immigrants, The Orphans Who Came to Canada.* (Toronto: The Dundurn Group, 2001).

5. *Ship Fever* (London: Flamingo, 2000). It serves up the Grosse Île I do not have the stomach to provide.

6. *Canada's Jews, A Social and Economic Study of Jews in Canada in the 1930s* (Montreal: McGill-Queen's University Press, 1993).

7. *Code of Jewish Law*, Hyman E. Golden, translator (New York: Hebrew Publishing Company, 1961).

8. For further information regarding this sect within a sect the reader is referred to my novel TALES OF THE EMPEROR (Vancouver: Talonbooks, 2015), in particular the chapter entitled "The Gerrhi" (pp. 209-229).

9. In the event, it would take a slow sequence of historic catastrophes and coincidences such as the failed Russian Revolution of 1905, the collapse of the Ottoman Empire during the First World War, the Balfour Declaration of 1917, the 1922 League of Nations authorization of the British mandate over Palestine, the Holocaust and its resultant fugitations, the various acts of Zionist terrorism leading to the 1947 United Nations vote to partition Palestine leading to the British withdrawal of its mandate leading to the proclamation of the state of Israel in 1948 and the series of provocations, expulsions, partitions, encroachments, land grabs, economic strangulations, racist apartheids and less subtle atrocities, lies, betrayals and open warfare

between Jews and Palestinian Arabs beginning in 1929 and continuing in one form or another in Israel and Gaza to the present day and tomorrow.

10. An obedient chronicle of TWP is provided by Neil Carson, HARLEQUIN IN HOGTOWN: GEORGE LUSCOMBE AND TORONTO WORKSHOP PRODUCTIONS (Toronto: University of Toronto Press, 1995). An account of sorts appears in Alan Filewood, COLLECTIVE ENCOUNTERS: DOCUMENTARY THEATRE IN ENGLISH CANADA (Toronto: University of Toronto Press, 1987) and an eloquent, perceptive, and knowledgeable one in Gordon Vogt, CRITICAL STAGES: CANADIAN THEATRE IN CRISIS (Ottawa: Oberon Press, 1998). Unique insights are contained in Steven Bush, CONVERSATIONS WITH GEORGE LUSCOMBE (Oakville: Mosaic Press, 2012). For a personal history of my time with TWP, of that theatre's method of work, of its aspirations, achievements, frustrations and fatalities during those dozen years, the reader is referred to my literary memoir, THE TALLIS BAG, as well as to the "Writer's Notes" in MY TWP PLAYS.

11. CONVERSATIONS WITH GEORGE LUSCOMBE, 130.

OUR AT BAY PRESS
ARTISTIC COMMUNITY

Publisher – Matt Joudrey
Managing Editor – Alana Brooker
Substantive Editor – Doug Whiteway
Copy Editor – Danni Deguire
Proof Editor – Danni Deguire
Graphic Designer – Lucas c Pauls
Layout – Lucas c Pauls and Matt Joudrey
Publicity and Marketing – Sierra Peca

Thanks for purchasing this book and
for supporting authors and artists.
As a token of gratitude, please scan the
QR code for exclusive content from this title.